CROSS MY PATH

CROSS MY PATH

Clea Simon

This first world edition published 2018
in Great Britain and the USA by
SEVERN HOUSE PUBLISHERS LTD of
Eardley House, 4 Uxbridge Street, London W8 7SY
Trade paperback edition first published
in Great Britain and the USA 2018 by
SEVERN HOUSE PUBLISHERS LTD

British Library Cataloguing in Publication Data
A CIP catalogue record for this title is available from the British Library.

ISBN-13: 978-0-7278-8787-0 (cased)
ISBN-13: 978-1-84751-910-8 (trade paper)
ISBN-13: 978-1-78010-965-7 (e-book)

All Severn House titles are printed on acid-free paper.

Severn House Publishers support the Forest Stewardship Council™ [FSC™],
the leading international forest certification organisation.
All our titles that are printed on FSC certified paper carry the FSC logo.

Typeset by Palimpsest Book Production Ltd.,
Falkirk, Stirlingshire, Scotland.
Printed and bound in Great Britain by
TJ International, Padstow, Cornwall.

For Jon

ONE

Something is amiss. I can feel it in my guard hairs. In my whiskers, flared to catch the slightest vibration. Something has gone wrong.

I wake with a start, blinking as I take in the scene before me. A rundown office, its only furnishings a torn sofa, a battered desk, and two bookshelves, nearly bare of books. A girl sits at the desk, scratching away with a pen. A young woman, really, curves beginning to soften her spare frame. No, there is nothing to be feared here. Nothing is out of place. Nothing has changed since I lay down to rest, only moments before. It was a dream that woke me. A recurring nightmare of three shadows – men – who loom, waiting, as I sink into oblivion. Into death. But they are not here. We are alone, the girl and I. My eyes begin to close once more.

Then – a silhouette. A visitor stands in the doorway. It is her arrival, her tentative knock on the door, that must have woken me, but she is no nightmare figure, nothing like the ghouls who haunt my sleep. She is female, frail. A skinny thing in rags who rushes forward, oblivious of me, seated here and watching.

'Thank you.' The woman is sobbing, she's so grateful. She grabs the girl's hand between her two bony ones, as if to press home her words. As if they were in a throne room instead of this spare chamber, two flights up. 'I can't begin to . . .' She breaks off to breathe, her wide eyes more eloquent than her words. 'Thank you so much.'

'It's nothing,' the girl – Care – responds, as my own ears pitch forward at the echo. As if unconsciously aware, she catches herself and corrects, her voice mature for her years. 'You're welcome, I mean. It is what I do. I find things. Do the needful. Locate that which is lost. Right the wrongs, the ones I can.'

I hear her words and relax. This is her creed, inherited from her mentor, which she's reciting now. The words rote, but memorable, explaining her profession to the world in a way that will be understood and repeated. That will be shared with others. For it is her trade that has brought this woman here, and the recognition of a task completed.

'You did! You found him.' The woman's acknowledgment confirms my memory. She wipes her tears with one hand, still holding Care's with her other. 'I had thought that he was lost.'

Releasing the girl at last, she rummages through her garment, locating a pocket hidden in the oversize skirt's ragged folds.

'No, really.' The girl holds up her hands. 'It's not necessary.'

She means what she says, the demurral in her tone as well as gesture. Even my casual appraisal sees the truth. Care has, at this point, more than the poor woman who stands before her, and her concerns, for the moment, do not involve either sustenance or shelter. But her words are to no avail, and when the woman finally fishes out the coin, its edges chipped away, the girl accepts it, as she would a grand prize. The woman's dignity is at stake and is more to be valued than this one degraded coin. Although her senses are not acute as mine, even the girl can see how solemn the woman appears as she hands the penny over. How sincere.

'My boy would have been lost without you,' she says, her voice calmer now. Hushed. 'He would have been taken – shipped to the islands, or worse.'

Care nods. There is nothing left to say. She did rescue the boy, who had been taken, press-ganged into service, and so completed the job for which she was hired, as she has now several times since I have come to join her. But even as the woman turns to go, her departure marked by more tears and pronouncements of gratitude, the girl stays silent. Something weighs on her, I see. Some burden not alleviated by the retrieval of one small child.

I watch her, and I wait.

We cats excel at waiting. Our sense of time is fluid, and less regimented than that dictated by the ticking clock. It is a trait I would share with the girl, if it could be taught. For although she has learned much, the trick of patience still eludes her grasp.

That almost doomed us yesterday, when we were hunting for the boy. The girl had done her due diligence, chatting casually with the vendors in the market. Noting who had seen the child wander off, had witnessed him drawn to the sweet vendor's cart and disappear.

At that point, patience had no place. This is an evil world for those too young or weak for their own defense, and she had acted, cornering the vendor as he turned into an alley. But neither promises nor threats – her knife, though small, is sharp – had moved him from his story. He'd brushed the small child off, he'd said, his wares too dear for charity. More like, he saw the mother hovering, I'd thought, with a disdain I could not express beyond the lashing of my tail. Still, his evasion set us on our path. If the boy had craved a sweet, he'd likely sought a penny, if not some larger coin. And thus he'd been ensnared. Down closer to the docks, full-grown men fight for work, but a child's labor can be cheaply bought. And once obtained, the fee – much like consent itself – may be reclaimed.

Care had pieced his path together, then, between the penny and the place, a block from the high-walled pen just off the wharf. 'They've taken him,' she'd said, under her breath. I've found she likes to speak to me. I have no illusion that she can tell I understand. 'I'd heard they were beginning to gear up,' she said. 'People are talking about a ship.'

My ears pricked up at that, though I could not tell you why. It is possible that in the past, in another life, I traveled. I have not been a cat always, I have learned. In this form, I have no recollection of any ship, nor would I willingly venture forth on water.

Not that fire is my friend either. As much as I may value its warmth, I do not need its light, unlike the girl, whose eyes are woefully insufficient in the manner of her kind. I saw her squint and lean, as daylight faded. We'd staked out a perch across the way from the high-walled pen. Her impatience made her restless, and she rose often to surveil the street. It was on one of those sorties that she saw it – the fire in an adjacent alley. I had smelled it, of course. The smoke and ash disturbed me, but I am no kitten to panic at the first hint of some distant threat.

I had not counted on the girl's impatience, however. A failing aggravated by her discomfort in the night as summer winds to an end. Although she has earned enough to stay starvation, her raiment has grown thin and threadbare. More than need be, it must be said. Pennies that could have been put aside for winter went instead towards a noxious compound, a coloring agent of sorts. My lack of language has rarely stymied me as much as when I would have argued against this purchase. But so it goes. Her hair is pink again – ridiculous color – and though for a night it stank like a befouled nest, she appeared pleased rather than otherwise with the results, eschewing even the ragged wool cap she sometimes dons.

The change of seasons could be felt with the coming of the night. I, with my luxuriant coat so thick despite the scars that mark my hide, do not mind the chill. The damp that rises from the harbor, this close by. I was content to crouch, my limbs compacted beneath my body, and my guard hairs extended ever so slightly, to ward off the mist the dark had brought. Not so the girl. So when she left our vantage point to sidle along the nearest wall, I followed. I would have continued to wait, as I have said. But our interlude appeared to have served its purpose.

'You coming?' I started, I will confess. I had not known that she could see me, a black cat in the night, and found this over-sight disconcerting, as if I were not the beast I believe myself to be. I looked up, into her green eyes, and saw her smile down at me, and that eased my dismay. She is not a random stranger, this girl. And I have encouraged her to be aware of me. Hoped, indeed, that she would learn to read what signs and signals I can give. I blinked back, slowly, as a sign of trust. *Yes*, I would have her know. *Where you go, I will follow.*

I would regret this thought – those words, unspoken but understood. For moments later, I saw where she was headed. Sensed it, unbelieving even before the glow gave it away. By choice and of her own free will, the girl was heading toward the fire. Walking toward it, by all appearances unafraid.

I froze and watched, unsure how to proceed. It was a small thing, in truth. A smoking wreck, more ash than flame, smoldering red around the pieces of a broken plank. Nails, not yet rusty, protruded like metal thorns from the fragments, and yet the girl grabbed one of these and, with it, shoved its fellows. Then she knelt beside the rough pile, blowing, and coaxed a yellow flame to life. I waited, knowing she should run. Should flee. Any healthy animal understands that such a flame cannot be contained. For although I have come to enjoy the comforts of her company – our office home, the sofa – I would no more approach an open fire than I would a rabid dog.

'It's OK, Blackie.' She saw me. Saw how I crouched, head down, preparing for attack. 'Come here. It's good by the fire. Warmer.'

She continued to feed the demon. Sat by it, the light playing on her face. She did appear happier then; the tight, pinched look was gone. But I, who know the face of danger, could only approach so close, and sat, alert, out of range as the fiend before her cracked and burned. We waited, then. She for an opening – an opportunity to free the child. Me, for the danger that I sensed loomed close, under the guise of a friend.

Indeed the fire almost betrayed us, with its bright and gaudy appeal. It drew that guard, as it had the girl, and had he been a shade more conscientious, we would have been discovered. As it was, I was able to alert the girl, my sharper senses notifying me of what she – night blind for all but the blaze – had missed. The man's approach from the gate had me drawing back, retreating into shadow, a move I made right by her side, so close she could not miss it.

'What is it?' She turned and blinked, as if she could clear her sight. I could not answer, nor would I make the attempt – even her hurried whisper had the guard looking up. But even as I backed up, away from that treacherous light, as I would have her do, the girl seized on another path. While I stared, aghast, she pulled a splintered piece of wood from the fire and tossed it, low and far, sending sparks into the air.

'What the—?' His words an echo of her own, the guard stepped forward, toward the brand, which bounced and rolled to a halt, smoking on the damp ground. She darted then, running low and fast. Circling the curious man, she ducked behind him, into the enclosure.

I confess, this move, as reckless as a kitten's, took me by surprise. Even the flame alarmed me, as it must the man, who had reached the charred timber by then. But luck – or other forces – held, and as he kicked at the charred wood, she emerged, pulling the child behind her. Still, her precipitate action could have rebounded on her, catching her up with the child. The guard, no fool, had turned by then. Had seen her start to run.

'Hey!' His voice cut through the night, summoning a second guard. But then her fickle friend proved true.

'Fire!' the second man shouted. His gaze drawn by the illumination of the original blaze. Untended – unleashed by the girl's rash action – it had begun to spread. 'Come on, you laggards! Bring the buckets.' Before they could extinguish it, I was away, behind the girl and the timid boy, scared into silence, even as they ran.

'You coming?' Her voice breaks upon my reverie once more, bringing with it the light of the new day. She smiles at me, her thin face brightening with unmitigated cheer. The job fulfilled, the payment unexpected but still welcome, she celebrates, that much is clear, and does not weigh the element of chance that swung her rash action toward success.

Her query springs more from fondness than any fancy, more than belief in my comprehension of her words. Still, I jump down and precede her to the door. We have a routine, this girl and I. And if she believes herself the leader of our team, I am content to follow, secure in the full certitude of my seniority in this particular game.

It is this certainty that nearly trips me up, once we are out on the street. I had assumed her route known to me, believing she would follow the prompts of hunger to the open place where food and other goods are exchanged. Indeed, trusting her path to be such, I had ventured off on my own, looking to sate my own appetite as she would soon hers. Even in the light of day, a change in the air presages autumn, making the smaller creatures frantic in their search for provisions and for warmth. This city is not kind to its human inhabitants, but in some ways it has become more hospitable to my kind. Water and air are still foul, poisoned by industries long gone, and there is more of waste and decay than I recall, in dim memories of the city at its peak. More of the shadows in which those such as I hunt may hide. I had thought to feast on such, my appetite whetted by a whiff of fresh droppings – a tight clutch of rodents gathered together for warmth.

It was not their cries of alarm that distracted me. The sun was near its zenith, and they slept soundly, unaware of how my claws had begun to dig. It was another sound – or the absence of one – that flipped my ears backward and caused me to pause in my repast. To sit up, and then to turn and run.

The cooler air tamps down many traces that a breathing soul may leave, but I am a hunter. It is the work of moments to correct my path and to find where the girl's route diverged from what I had expected. When I stop on the pavement, one paw raised in readiness, it is not uncertainty that holds me still. It is confusion, as I work to understand not only where she has gone but why. For as clearly as I make out the trails of bugs and beasts and one young, light-footed girl, I now see: she is heading back to the waterfront. To the pen by the wharves from which she had so recently freed the boy.

I move quickly, despite my age, through passages too narrow to allow even her slight frame, and reach the area before she does, an enclosure on a busy harbor street. Despite the silt the tides have brought, the makeshift pier that stretches out to where the deeper water lies, this meeting ground is bustling. Sea and river, city and shore converge here, spurring on what commerce still remains in this benighted land. Broad daylight brings the trucks and barges, too, and so I must be wary. The vehicles are loud. The street rumbles at their approach. The men who labor, loading and unloading, can be less obvious, when they choose, and may vent their rage on a smaller being such as myself.

Hugging the curb, I slink the last block to the enclosure, a large and high-walled structure within shouting distance of the wharf. Within smelling distance, too – I make out fish and rot, and those that feed on both and am intrigued – but there I wait. When the girl arrives, near as silent as I have been, she joins me in the alley opposite, our perch of the night before. The remnants of the fire stink of ash, but this remains a prime vantage point, across the street from the pen's front gate.

'Blackie!' Despite the note of surprise, her voice is muted. She is careful, this girl. Aware as I of the violence in the men around us. 'I thought you'd taken off. I never know what you're thinking.'

I would tell her, if I could. She crouches down beside me,

not far from the sooty pile, and her hand is warm on my back. She is waiting, I can tell from the tension in her body, the careful intake of breath, although I do not know for what.

This place is not safe. The blackened lumps beside her are now cold and still, but other, more dangerous elements have begun to gather: the hook boys who work the ships – or used to, back when vessels regularly plied these waters. Known for the grappling hooks they carry, they hold themselves above the regular laborers, those who fetch and carry for a penny. Their tools have other uses, though, ugly ones. Memories emerge as if from shadow but far more sure, prompted by the sight of these rough men. I do not know if they are why she has come here, if she follows the rumors that they spread of a ship or trade.

For now, the girl is hidden, tucked in the shadow of the alley, her scent covered by old smoke and ash. For myself, I would move on from here, if it would not disrupt her concentration. Other senses are more vital to me than sight, a faculty on which these men rely overmuch. I would take advantage of this weakness – avail myself of shadows, of the glare of this bright day – to approach the enclosure without their notice. Such proximity, coupled with distance from the fire's reek, would enable me to make my own exploration – reviewing odor and sound to fill in what may have happened over the intervening hours. What may yet happen here on this busy street of busy men.

As it is, I am thwarted, my nose constrained by smoke and ash. Anchored by the girl even as she takes her hand from me to rest on the curbstone and shifts, preparing for the wait to last.

But fire does not stop my ears. Regarding her, I can tell she does not hear, as I do, the footsteps inside that high metal wall. The drag and clatter of materials being moved inside. If she could, perhaps she could make sense of the pounding that follows. The shouts and the commands. Perhaps she does sense them, in some vague and unclear fashion, and perhaps these are what weigh upon her thoughts. What bring her back, again, to this strange cage-like structure, so close upon the river wharf, a still, cold place at the heart of the city's commerce.

Or perhaps she has another quest in mind, I think, as the

gate itself moves and two men march out. Together, they survey the street, as if they could sense us here. A prompt of memory, more likely. Then one sets out. A patrol of the perimeter, I suspect. The other stands, though once his mate has gone, he removes a cigarette from some hidden pocket and lights it. Even without that gesture – the distinctive smell of cheap tobacco – I would recognize him. It is the guard who last night left the gate ajar. Whose negligence enabled the boy's release.

Beside me, she nods, with a low wordless sound revealing that she has reached this same conclusion. The gasp that follows causes me alarm. The guard has looked up, his cigarette dangling from his lip. But it is not his colleague who approaches. The rounds of the pen take longer than the few moments that have passed. It is another, scrawnier figure who darts like a rat from a neighboring building. Tall and lean – his ragged clothes separate as he moves to reveal ribs and welts like tiger stripes along his back. To reveal, as well, a long wooden handle, like that of a tool, tucked into the waistband of his pants. He scans the street even as he runs, and when he comes close to the guard, they both move back, as if to shelter by the wall.

Care is frozen. I can feel how tight she holds herself, studying the two. Their exchange is brief – less than two breaths' worth – and then the scrawny man retreats, crouching low before he runs back across the street and disappears into an alley not far from where we shelter. There was something familiar about the man, about his gait and build. But as I lift my nose to catch his aroma, to capture something other than cold ash and smoke, I find myself disappointed. I had expected something else – a bitter, biting odor – and not the funk of sweat and fear. Still, I know this man. Or knew him . . .

'AD,' says the girl beside me, her voice aghast.

Of course! My tail lashes in frustration. Sight is an imperfect sense, but in this case one that has proved more reliable than those my feline self enjoys. The wet leather of my nose finds his scent and I scrutinize it for confirmation. The man, AD as he was once known, no longer stinks as he once did, infused with the acrid smoke of the drug that he produced.

Nor does he move with the swagger and pride that were his wont. For the sorry creature who has slunk away was a leader once, the alpha male of a small pack of feral children. Care was one of these, when I first met her, a waif who took his dubious protection in exchange for acting as a courier. For helping to distribute the noisome substance, and although she did not, like some, fall under its addictive spell, the web of threat and violence with which he maintained control is not one I would wish on any living thing, much less a child.

This memory – this man – recalls me to a different time. I was of another form when first I met this girl, this Care, and became aware of that man. Even then, I recognized her superior intelligence and strength of character. It was my wish then to free her from this man and from his mode of life. That I have succeeded, even as my own fortunes have changed so absolutely, amazes me. Not that I alone take credit. The girl herself has shown a wit and fortitude beyond what I had hoped. Through her efforts, this man has been foiled – removed by the authorities for penal service or for worse.

Or so I had thought, as his reappearance throws into question his apprehension and sentencing both. His condition – starved and bruised – speaks of some punishment, and his furtive manner suggests that he may have escaped rather than been freed. Both these factors may have weakened him. May lessen whatever power he has over this world, over the girl. But I cannot dismiss his guile, nor whatever object he has secreted beneath his shirt. The man is a danger, still, and one I had not anticipated. My fur bristles at the thought of him, even as his all too human odour fades.

So, too, should his memory pass away. Across the street, the second guard has made his round, and the two now wait for the gate to readmit them to the pen. It is a very different scenario than what we saw last night, more disciplined by far, and my ear twitches back as the girl beside me shifts. She, too, must note the difference. Must wonder what it means.

But, no, I have read her wrong, if I thought she meant to examine this pen again. To seek out the source of the sounds of pounding and of laboring within. As the gates close behind the two, she rises. And to my dismay, she turns from the street to tread softly toward the alley that led the scrawny man away.

I hesitate, full of foreboding. I have dreaded her return to this area, her investigation of whatever had engaged her so. But to follow, instead, her old gang leader? That is foolishness, an errand as likely to deliver trouble as any useful intelligence. She is free of this man, and he is clearly hunted and unwell.

And yet, she has a look about her with which I am intimately acquainted. A way of holding herself in readiness, her body near to quivering with curiosity barely kept at bay. I smell no fear on her, brave girl, nor any of the lesser trepidation that might serve to caution her. But she is wise for her age, and she has learned. As she turns into the alley, she crouches low, keeping to the shelter of the near wall.

I do not know what she hopes to gain, or why. But I love this girl, whose life is intermingled with my own. And so, unable to communicate my concern, I make the only choice that's left. I glance around the street for signs of pursuit. I sniff the air for signs more fresh than one old fire, and then I follow, quick and low.

TWO

She is not a cat, this girl, but she has learned some of my skills. As she tracks her prey – that scarred and scrawny man – she stays low, hugging the side of the alley and then the street beyond. In this way, she can follow without being seen.

I am grateful for her caution. This city is no safe place for a lone creature, especially not a female of her tender years. It has not escaped my notice that those who come to her for help are primarily female, too. A network of advice and whispers refers them to her, as, like the apple vendor, they solicit help to find the lost or redress for petty theft. These tasks she has fulfilled, and thus a reputation grows.

As I follow the girl down a deserted street, I am reminded of her innate ability. Not only how she follows, holding herself back and avoiding any sudden moves. But that she retains an awareness of her environs – and of the danger that a cornered man may offer, even one as starved and ragged as she now follows. It is daylight, and yet she remains unseen. Although she is larger and of a different hue than I, she shelters, as I do, in shadow, darting from stoop to doorway, from the rusted out hulk of a vehicle to a pile of bricks, the remains of the building that once filled a vacant lot.

She moves quietly, as well, although I could tell her that the man is too far ahead to hear any sound her slight form might make. I observe as she steps charily, mindful of the loose slabs of concrete that could tip and throw her or dislodge stones that might draw attention.

But she is not a cat. She lacks my acuity of smell and of hearing, and thus she does not know what I do: that this man she follows has abstained from the drug that once gave him both wealth and a kind of power. The substance on which he built his trade, and which, in turn, caused his capture. Instead – as we pause at a corner, I raise my nose and open my mouth to take in the air, fresher now – I catch pheromones of another sort. Not sexual, but close. The man exudes eagerness and a kind of glee. Nor does her inferior hearing pick up that his steps are becoming lighter as he races down the city street. For all that he appears to be on the run, he is heading toward something – or someone – that promises happiness of a sort.

When he pauses before a large brick building, I hear her gasp. She throws herself back against a wall and blinks, as if to clear her eyes. In truth, I did not know where the man was headed, but I am not surprised. This warehouse, a looming structure both larger and better maintained than many in this district, is known to me – to us. Unlike many in this ruined city, it retains its original use – a place where goods are stored while readied for transit, either out onto the water or back into the city. Care and I know this well. We have been inside its high black doors, have gone up the wide, worn stairs, to meet with the men who do business here. We have also seen authorities encircle it. Witnessed some – such as this man – taken into custody, while others met more permanent ends.

If the girl thought that it would no longer be in use, she is more naïve than I would choose. But perhaps it is simply the surprise of seeing her onetime protector return to the site of his most heinous crimes that has, for the moment, stolen her breath. The realization that some things in this crumbling ruin of a city will never change.

I, for one, am not taken aback. Although the reappearance of this ruffian is unexpected, his destination causes me no shock. For although this girl, this Care, may have thought she snuffed out an evil when she turned him in – when she brought about the raid that swept up AD and so many of her former colleagues – I have long known better. Indeed, it is with a sinking feeling that I see her crouch and lower her brow, the better to examine the building that lies across the way.

She came here on the heels of that man AD, a fugitive by all apparent signs. That he may seek his preferred poison is a likely possibility. That he may be searching out the few criminal associates who remain another. Whatever his motive, he has led her to a place of evil, and, I fear, back into the realm of one more toxic to us both. As she settles in to wait, crouching in the shadow of the neighboring building, I make my presence known, leaning my body into hers. The hand that settles on my back is warm and dry, the pressure comforting in ways I do not fully understand. And as she sits down at last, back against a pitted wall, I too relax, wrapping my tail around my forepaws as my eyes begin to close.

The afternoon sun passes, the shadows growing longer. One in particular extends, a finger reaching out across the empty street. Through slitted eyes, I see it creep, and I remember another time and another shadow.

Three, tall against the sun, the central one approaches, looming larger. Menacing. 'What have we here?' His voice is cold, his colleagues do not answer. Nor do I. Held against my will before – beneath – them I can only stare back. I try to memorize the face . . .

'Blackie!' I wake with a start. The girl beside me looks on with alarm. I have lashed out, I can tell, from the way she holds her hand up to her open mouth. From the tension in my claws. I am ashamed, a mere beast incapable of holding still. And yet, that dream – if dream it was – must not be lightly discarded. The threat in it, if not its timing – here and now – is real.

For all her wits, this girl is woefully ignorant of one important fact. And I, in this feline form, cannot share what I know. To wit: the shadowed figure, the one who haunts me, is very real. And unlike the evildoer who once controlled this building, he is still at large. The very fact that Care's old gang leader has returned here sends a shiver through my luxurious fur and, perhaps, sent that vision as well. It has certainly raised another option, one that I would I could share. He has many minions, this foe, and AD's arrival here leaves me wondering if something more than mere appetite has drawn him here. This place, this warehouse, was where Care helped bring him down. If he or one who controls him sought to understand how that was done, this would be a place to begin.

Would that I could warn her. He is not one of the great men, the ones who broke the world, this hidden man, this shadow. But he is of their ilk, a man of power. A big man, and although I do not believe he would consider smaller entities such as we are under other circumstances, this girl Care has come to his notice. Though unintended, the girl did him a service recently, exposing through her work a minor perfidy – a man whose laziness, or whose eye for a greater gain, had him holding out

on his superior. Until the end, that is, when the girl's investigation, although otherwise directed, brought on that foolish man's
head a terrible vengeance, one that still causes her to cry out
at night and disturb her sleep.

This could be, perhaps, what has brought her to his attention,
through some vestigial sense of honor. Why it is that he regards
a girl of no apparent worth and has even, I suspect, made
gestures to ease her path as she attempts to ply her trade.
Perhaps. A prickle along my spine suggests otherwise, and if I
do not always understand the clues that make my fur bristle so,
I have learned to respect them. Is it the scent of a larger predator
– whether man or feral dog – that has raised my hackles, or
another sense, one honed in a previous existence, that makes
me ever heedful? Such questions serve no purpose. Better I be
on my guard for whatever may yet come.

But not today. The sun has sunk behind the building where
we shelter, stretching the shadows almost to that towering hulk,
and still we wait. If that starved man, that AD, has left, he has
done so by another egress, and while I would wish it so – would
wish him gone – I understand the girl as she mutters to herself.

'He came to the front door,' she says now, as if weighing
the words. 'No reason he'd sneak away.'

Plenty of reasons, I would tell her. Many of which depend
on what he found inside. Perhaps he retrieved some relic, some
token, that would explain his fate. Perhaps he was directed on.
This place was routed, after all, and may no longer be a seat
of power. Still, she has a point. And more relevant still, she
could not keep her guard on all entrances at once, even with
my aid. I gaze up at her, my green eyes seeking hers, and believe
myself recompensed when she smiles down at me.

'I guess we've wasted enough time here,' she says lightly,
as if I were a child. 'How about some dinner, Blackie? Tomorrow
is another day.'

It is with tail up that I trot alongside her, back to the office
we call home. I have my suspicions, and there are leads I would
investigate. This girl is better off away from here, however.
Away from that broken man and the shadow I fear he has
returned to serve.

I muse on the possibilities as we make our way to the open

square that serves as a market these days. With coin in hand, the girl is able to purchase fruit as well as bread, and a small block of cheese brought in from the provinces. I see her glance over at me, and I turn away. She is generous and would share her provisions, but I can fend for myself. Indeed, I have fed on fresher fare than any on offer here.

She must sense this, I believe, because she avoids the corner where the butcher displays his wares. The meat he proffers is overpriced for either its quality or its freshness. I cannot tell what her nose discerns, but surely she must smell the rancid sweetness that hangs over the bloody cuts, even if she cannot quite make out the animal source of those smaller, darker steaks.

'I got some cheese,' she tells me. Her marketing done, I have trotted to her side. 'We'll have a feast.'

I am warmed by her generosity, but I do not respond. It concerns me that she did not notice me, watching her. That she has settled in to celebrating this bounty so easily. However, the day has been long, and we have covered much ground. Although I may appear as glossy as a younger beast, I feel my age. The scars on my hide bind and catch as I walk; the badly knit bones of my left hind leg begin to ache.

'You're limping!' Her voice catches me up, and I stop just as she bends to scoop me in her arms. 'Poor Blackie,' she says. 'It's your bad leg, isn't it?'

I can no more sensibly answer her question than could that block of cheese. But the kindness meant, as well as the warmth of her arms, wring their own response out of me. My eyes close and I begin to purr, and when she settles me into her carryall, atop that fragrant cheese, I am content.

Perhaps I doze, the rocking motion of her stride as lulling as a mother's tongue. Perhaps that marvelous aroma serves to confuse my senses. Perhaps I am simply old. All I know is that I wake with a start when the girl halts, frozen outside her door. She has crossed the city and climbed the stairs, all without my knowledge. Now, every hair alert, I poke my head up, the better to take in the sounds and smells around me. The hall is dark, the building quiet. But it should not have taken the girl's sudden stop to alert me to the truth: the door to our office is ever so slightly ajar. Someone waits inside.

THREE

'Who's there?' Before I can scramble down, the girl has made her move. I wince as I hit the floor, less from my sore leg than from her voice. Better to find out what one can before announcing one's presence, I would tell her. But she is no longer my pupil, not in any way that matters. And she has not my natural aptitude for analyzing the world around us.

'I know you're in there.' I sniff, mouth open, sampling the air. And as she readies to kick the door, I slink past her, tail held high. 'Blackie?' I hear her whisper, confused but not – I am glad to see – for long. Following my lead, she pushes the door gently. It has been broken, like so much of this building, and does not latch securely. Still, it swings open quietly enough. Quietly enough to not wake the ragged figure sleeping on the couch.

'Tick?' She barely breathes the name.

The figure on the sofa stirs and mutters, still caught up in a dream. But that suffices, and all caution gone, the girl rushes forward to embrace the slight figure.

'What?' He jerks awake, flipping as he does to face us. His face is white beneath its grime, his eyes wide with horror and with fright. 'Care.' He sees her, and relaxes, collapsing back into repose.

'Tick, where have you been?' She squeezes in beside him, as he pulls his feet up, staring as if she would feast upon his face. 'It's been – a while.'

Days, she could have said. Weeks, perhaps, as these two measure time. Only I can hear the tension in her voice. She is holding back, restraining herself as one does with a wild creature, so as not to scare it off.

'Don't, Care.' He sits up and rubs his eyes. He does not see how she bites her lip, as if such an act could contain her words. 'You know I'm working now. It's easier if I stay near the plant – with the other guys.'

She nods in sad acknowledgment. She would not have him labor at the factory, so young and slight. Still, she knows he does so willingly, which is more than many in this world can say. And that he is paid, though little enough, and takes some pride in earning.

'I'm just – something's brewing, Tick. I don't know what, but I'm not easy.'

'Care—' he starts to interrupt.

'No, listen, Tick. I had a job.' She tells him, then, the rough outline of the night before. I study him as he listens. He's not surprised, this boy, though his face lights up as she describes the burning plank.

'Must have been something,' he says, the sound of wonder in his voice. He has missed – or ignored – the concerns she has outlined about the doings on the waterfront. About the activity she has seen. She looks deflated at his response, though I do not understand why she would have hoped for more.

'Have you eaten?' She shakes off her disappointment, and her mood lifts as his face lights up. Before he can respond, she is already rummaging through her sack, pulling out the foodstuffs.

'I can pay you back,' he says. She smiles, keeping her mouth closed. Again, a point of pride. She is learning, this girl, how in this straitened city, the spirit may be sustained by self-esteem. And as he tucks his feet beneath him, I leap to my accustomed post on the sofa's high back. From here I watch as they eat in what becomes a companionable silence, the shared refreshment salving the wounds of desertion and distrust.

'So, can you stay?' She has begun to clean up, the question tendered only as she looks away and begins to wrap the remainder of the cheese.

'Just for tonight.' He knows that he has hurt her. That she worries. There is shame in his voice, which sinks low. 'I wanted to see you, Care.'

She turns, partly. She can hear in his voice as well as I that he has left this sentence hanging. I do not believe she perceives the other signs of his recent activity. Or if she does notice the change in wear of his threadbare pants, the nature of the dirt on his feet and beneath his nails, she refrains from comment.

This boy's condition has evolved since last she saw him. If he labors still in the factory, the garment workshop where cheap goods are made for export, then his duties have altered. It is a riddle I do not know how to read, and so I wait too to hear what this boy will say.

'To let you know.' He's waiting, and she can sense that. Putting the cheese high up in the cabinet – unaware, as she does, that it is not her caution that keeps our stores safe from gnawing teeth – she returns to sit beside him, her eyes on the eager face turned up towards her. 'I've been promoted,' he says, the pride apparent in his voice. And something more, as well. 'I'm not a runner. I mean, I'm off the floor. No more switching bobbins and spools anymore.'

She nods and smiles, acknowledging his growth.

'They trust me. Now.' His voice fails, but no further words are needed. It was Care, in truth, who exposed his former boss. Revealed his treachery and brought him down. But the boy was instrumental as well, and also kept his quiet – held his tongue – in the flurry of investigation that followed. The fact that he remained, a willing worker, says a lot and speaks, I believe, more to the values taught by the girl than to any ingrained character of his own. Still, it has paid off, apparently, in a position of increased responsibility.

'I go on errands,' he explains. 'I'm fast and I know my way around. You're right that there's things going on now. They need to keep in touch.' That he'll come back is the unspoken trait they likely prize most. 'And, Care, I see things for myself. Hear them, too.'

She bites her lip again, and I can smell the blood. She is waiting, as am I, for the substance of his message. For confirmation . . .

'AD is back,' he says, at last, the words tumbling forth. 'I saw him. I didn't believe it, but it's true. He got away, and he's asking questions. He's looking for you, Care. AD is looking for you, and I'm scared.'

On the last words, his voice falls away. The eyes that look up, dark and large, blink back tears. And finally, he is once again the boy Care knows and loves. Too young for such problems and to survive such a life.

'Oh, Tick.' She says no more, whether out of circumspection or circumstance, I cannot tell. For with those simple syllables, she opens up her arms, and he goes to her. One sob is all he lets loose, the habit of fear and silence quieting him as much as the comfort of her embrace. Still, she holds him, until his breathing slows and lengthens and once more he sleeps, reclining in her arms. Only then does she release him, to lay him gently back on the sofa. Only then does she cover him with the old coat that serves as her blanket. She pauses then to take in his face, grown soft in slumber, before returning to the desk – her desk, *my* desk – and to the papers that she studies to explain her fate.

She has been trained, this girl, in what to notice. With discretion unusual in one so young, she marks down what she sees and what she hears, noting not only what is told her, for her consumption, but also what she perceives of other, hidden motives. Of such elements is her tradecraft built, a discipline she carries on despite the loss of her onetime mentor, of her friend, for though he – *I* – watches over her still, she knows it not. It was that mentor who taught her the value of information, which mayhap explains her reticence with the boy. It was this mentor who taught her the importance of what is missing – the words not said, the questions not asked – in the search for accuracy. That is, I believe, what she does now, although I, in this feline form, can only imagine what she sees.

'They're building.' Her voice is soft, her words meant for no other's ears. But they wake me, and suddenly, all is clear. It is not AD who concerns her now, not even with the boy's warning. No, it was the raw board, broken and discarded, that fed the fire which has occupied her mind. The steady pounding in the enclosure. I, for all my acuity, missed the obvious, this city having fallen into such decrepitude as to make any such construction rare. Or no, I catch myself. The fault is mine, having been too long removed from the ways of men, I did not piece together the lumber and the noise with any sight the girl may have spied in her brief glimpse inside the enclosure walls.

Building. I mull the term, so foreign to me now. And if the word is not as unfamiliar to these children, the concept must be. Shelter being what we find. Beside me, on the sofa, the boy sleeps, his side rises and falls beneath the wool of the long coat. We need no more. But it is not only the denotation of these words, but the pressure beneath them. The question. Jumping lightly to the floor, I approach the desk, the girl, and brush my silky fur against her leg.

She is intelligent, this girl. Bright, if not yet wise, and I would encourage her in her deliberations. Would will her to pursue any query that would lead her to forget her former leader. If what the boy has said has any merit, the scrawny man may yet be a danger, and I would have her evade him and the shadowy one he once worked for, at least until he reveals himself – or I can uncover his latest machinations.

But can I? I lean in, deep in thought, musing on methods and memories. Without looking, she lifts me up, and in my distraction I let her. My cogitation continues, as she holds me in her arms, even as her fingers begin a familiar motion. Soon she is rubbing the base of one ear, absently, as she reads. I feel the purr once more growing in me, a sense of contentment at odds with the reality I grapple with and that I would have her understand.

'Curious,' she says, her voice soft and low. It relaxes me, even as her hand continues its gentle pressure, and my eyes begin to close. I should not let them, I remind myself, not while such strange occurrences demand deliberation. I should ponder, at least, how to communicate my concerns to her. Her hand is warm upon my fur, my back. The motion soft and soothing.

I should not rest, not yet. I should resist this kind caress. I should . . . No matter. Such thoughts are futile, for tonight we are safe. We have fed and we are warm. When the girl pushes her chair back with a sigh, I leap again to the floor and wait, while she makes her ablutions. And when she has tucked herself into the other end of the sofa, her feet lying alongside those of the boy, I join them. I will be up before dawn to hunt again and to surveil. For now, I add my warmth to theirs, and closing my eyes once again, I sleep.

FOUR

I nstinct, perhaps, is recompense enough for what is lost. For when I wake from evil dreams to hunt under the fading moon, I find the city as I left it: cold, certainly, and hard, but no more threatening than in nights prior. I do not smell that ragged man, AD, nearby. And as I proceed to sate my hunger, I tell myself that he has done the same – though our appetites surely differ in their substance. No matter. There is no trace of him or of that bitter drug nearby. My nightmare is just that.

Dismissing the remnants of my fear as unbecoming to a beast, I bathe. Dawn is breaking as I return, refreshed, to the building where the girl and her sometime charge slumber still. I can hear their breathing, even and untroubled, as I pass through the alley, a bolster to my uneasy calm. The window from which I descended is still open to the waning night, and I pause to take in their scent in the damp air, as warm and peaceful as their sound. Even as I peer up at my egress, I know I have to avail myself of a more conventional approach. Despite my glossy coat, my bright green eyes, I am not young. For me, this morning, a door and stairway, such as lesser creatures use.

The front entry is ajar, the door held open by a slab of brick. I can still recall when this breach would have worried me; back in my reckless days when I put my trust in locks and catches. Despite my own facility with manipulating such works, I valued them. I chose this building, the office where the girl now sleeps, for other reasons. At one point, this was a busy street, full of commerce of the sort to draw both high and low. I established my practice here, the trade the girl now carries on, offering my services in finding and unraveling. I did not think I would be so undone, though as the world declined and the city fell to ruin, I had inklings of what might come. Trade, I knew, would continue, and so in my pride I thought I too would persevere and for a time I did, as new powers took up the reins of business and of rule. That my arrogance would lead me too close to these dangerous men, I did not foresee. Now, in this form, I have learned a belated caution. I sniff the air before I enter. I tilt my ears. I wait.

The drunk beneath the stairs snorts and turns, his sleep made restless by the rotgut he imbibes. His funk befouls the air, covering over other, less obvious leavings. I slip inside the opened door and cross the foyer, alert to every movement.

That's when I hear it, the sound that makes me freeze in place and every hair along my spine rise instantly alert. I have been a fool. A heedless animal. Another, not asleep, is above me on the stairs. Light footsteps creep carefully along the edge, where the treads are not yet worn through. I hear the deliberate footstep, the cautious breathing. But animal still, I possess strengths that I once lacked. In the growing dark, I will seem invisible, even as my pupils widen, taking in the unlit stairwell to view who ascends before me.

A bulky figure, clad in grey, is leaning on the banister. She moves slowly and with caution. But not, I revise my initial supposition, for purposes of secrecy. No, the dim light breaking outside has not reached this far into the building, and the figure steps with care for other reasons, watchful for the broken places, for the smooth spots in the treads. I realize as I watch the measured steps, this one – a woman – is aged or unwell. Despite her size, she is not strong and hoards her energy for another purpose. She is making for the girl.

I have no such issues. For although I am aged, too, for my kind, I am more vigorous than she. More stealthy, as well, and it is the work of moments for me to dash up the far side of the stairwell to the landing. From here I can better judge this intruder, this woman, and plan my next move.

She pauses, as I do, and turns her face toward me. She cannot see me in this shadow, but she must have spied some motion in the murk and thus holds back. Not from fear, I think, but caution, the reasonable hesitation of one who would muster her resources, weighing present need against those upcoming. There is something in her eyes . . .

'Hello?' she calls into the dark. Her voice, though tentative, is firm and low. 'Is someone there?'

I step forward, and sit in a patch of scuffed linoleum that

now glows faintly, with the rising sun. The beam that has
breached some begrimed window gives little of warmth or
brightness but should serve to illumine me, at the top of the
stairs, and so let her take in the sight of a domestic animal,
glossy and still.

'Well, well.' Her face is old, older even than I'd thought,
lined and craggy beneath the softening halo of grey-white hair.
Despite the pain, the wear I spy, a slight smile begins. Her eyes
recede into the crags even as her face lights up, but I can feel
her gaze upon me, upon my own green eyes. My one torn ear,
the blue light reflecting off my fur.

'Hello there, sir.'

My ears prick up. This is not the usual appellation for one of
my kind. And although I once would have expected such courtesy,
I find myself caught off guard. Surprised and curious, both. She
has stopped, a mere three steps from the landing, and reaches
out. Her hand does not quite extend as far as where I sit, and so
I rise and stretch torward her, the better to read her scent, to
gauge her past and thus to judge what she intends.

A chuckle, low and throaty. Almost, it comes to me, as if it
were a purr. But enough – I close my eyes and let my jaws part
slightly. The smells of earth and sweat, the common odors of
those who live and eat and labor. And something more – spicy,
rather than sweet. A deep perfume that brings me back to another
time. I am clad not in this scarred hide, but in wool and linen.
I do not sniff the hand extended toward me, I make to grasp it,
and—

'Whoa!' I jerk back, as does she, holding to the banister for
balance. It is my paw that has provoked her. Claws bared, I
have reached for her, for her hand, if only to draw it closer, to
read it more thoroughly. And yet . . .

'Perhaps I can do without the introduction,' she says,
righting herself. She does not offer me her hand again, but
smiles, her mouth closed and not without warmth, as she
attains the landing and then, with a deep breath, approaches
the office door.

'Find what is lost, right the wrongs.' Care is reciting her litany
of services for the woman, who eases herself onto the aged

couch. 'When a child has gone missing, I will find him. When a friend is taken, I endeavor to discover where. I will ask the questions, until I find the truth.'

It's a good patter, personalized as the cases add to her expertise, and she delivers it well, speaking softly but with gravity from her seat at the scarred wood desk. She was seated there when the woman knocked. I heard her steps as she walked to the door and ushered her visitor in. As she did, the boy took off, ducking out as the big woman entered and wearing, I was quick to note, the girl's knit cap against the chill. They eyed each other with curiosity, but I saw no recognition in either face, and the boy did not linger, sidestepping me in his rush down the stairs.

I hesitate, for I would know more of what he knows. But by then the woman has settled back, and so I slip inside the door. Care has resumed her seat, behind her desk, her face a mask of calm acceptance. Only I, who know her well, picked up the girl's surprise and, yes, dismay at the sight of the new arrival. No, I correct myself, as I slink through the door before it closes. Dismay at the interruption. For although I catch the girl's glance, her quick smile, as I dart past on my way to the sill, she is not pleased, even with the promise of new custom. The papers on her desk – her notes – enthrall her still, and she would return to them, if she could.

Still, she is courteous. Her patter done, she waits. In the quiet, I hear the visitor shuffle on the sofa. She is settling herself. Readying to speak.

'I want to hire you,' she says at last. Her voice is calm and sad. Her case is not immediate, not pressing. 'A man – a person I knew well – went missing sometime last year, and he had something of mine. Something I had loaned to him.'

'I can attempt to find him.' Care's voice ends on an upward lilt: a question. Even she hears that the woman has left something unsaid.

'I don't think you will,' the woman says. 'I think – I'm pretty sure that he's gone. But I would like to recover his effects, and such.'

Sitting on the windowsill gives me a particular vantage. The sun has topped the buildings now. It streams in behind me to

brighten the room before me. It warms the face of the girl at
her desk, playing up the shadows as her eyebrows bunch in a
question. She is confused. Saddened too, but she knows to wait.
The woman is not done.

'I don't have much for you to go on,' the visitor says. 'We
weren't close. Not anymore. But this matters to me.'

Care nods. In these times, families are strained, even beyond
the norm. The slight catch of her breath prefaces the question
that I know must follow.

'His effects.' She uses the woman's words, repeating them
for surety. 'You have reason to believe he has died?'

She leaves it open, an invitation for the woman to continue.

She nods, once. From where I sit, I cannot see her face. No
matter, to one such as I, the posture, the way a body is held,
breath taken or released, provides as much information as a
frown or pursed lips.

'Yes, he's dead.' Her voice is flat, the words clipped. 'I'm
sure. We had a bond.'

She raises a hand, although I do not believe the girl was going
to interrupt. 'Please, I know what that sounds like,' the woman
says. 'He dismissed the idea himself. And yet, when we were
younger – he was younger than I – I would always know. If he
were hurt, if he were hungry. We came up in better times, days
you wouldn't remember, but we were close, once upon a time.'

Care nods slowly, taking this in. She is thinking of the boy
Tick, I believe. She worries about him, and this concern is
keeping her from the most obvious question. The one I would
have her ask.

'So you're now out of touch. You *were*, that is,' she says,
correcting her mistake. The woman nods, and Care reaches for
a sheet of paper. Her contract, such as it is. I can see it in her
movement, as surely the visitor can as well. She has decided
to take the case, and her diligence has been faulty.

She begins to write. Her pen scratches at the paper, as I jump
to the floor and saunter forward, making my way between the
couch and desk. Care is distracted, caught up in her work, and
does not notice, but the woman cocks her head. Regards me as
I pass on my way to the girl. I would have her notice me. Notice
my preoccupation.

'Is this your cat?' It is the woman who draws her attention, speaking up even as Care writes. 'I met him on the stairs.'

'Blackie?' Care responds. Despite our current situation, she was gently raised and answers from force of habit. 'Yes, he – we found each other.' She smiles at the thought, although our meeting was anything but genial. 'He looks out for me.'

'I thought as much.' Care looks up at those strange words. Sees me at last, the way I stare, and then, finally, follows my line of sight to the woman on the couch.

'You did?' She keeps her voice light, but I hear the strain in it. She's reevaluating her potential client. Her sanity, perhaps. And finally, I hope, her motivation. 'Maybe you can give me some more information, then, Miss—'

'Call me Augusta,' the visitor says. 'I was a summer baby.' She smiles at something far away, and I relax. This is the posture of the storyteller. The visitor readies herself to explain. 'But, of course, you'd want to know his name as well, I'm sure.'

Care nods. Holds her pen ready.

'Well, that's the question.' The woman sighs and nods her head. 'When we were growing up, I called him Panther. I was Blaze, then, my hair the brightest red. That was here, in the city, back before things got bad.'

I remain in place, seated halfway between the sofa and the desk. To walk away would draw attention to myself. Disrupt the flow of words. Her words compel me, but I do not want to appear conspicuous. I reach around with an agility that belies my years, and I begin to groom my lean left flank.

'His name, originally? That's long gone. Nobody knows it now. He went by many names. But he kept in touch. I'd get notes – letters and little gifts – all with a mark. A seal, of sorts, that he would make using a small carving he kept on his watch chain. They stopped about six months ago, and it has taken me this long to get back here. To try to trace where he – and where that seal – had gone.'

My flank shines where I have licked it, each guard hair lies flat against its neighbor. I lift one foot and stretch to separate the pads.

'I'm sorry.' Care speaks again. 'Without his name, I don't see how—'

'He was a singular individual,' the woman interrupts. Even as I work, biting at a claw that has grown too long, I prick up my ears. The visitor's voice is rising slightly; her breathing tightens. She is working up to the crux of her story.

'An extremely private man.' She swallows. 'His only confidante, when I knew him, was one of these so-called keepers, some kind of scribe. I went to see this man immediately upon arrival. It was from him that I received your name. He told me what you do.'

She pauses and shifts. From the corner of one eye, I see her looking at me, almost as if she can tell that I am listening. Almost as if she knows. With feigned disinterest, I begin work on my other paw. I bite another claw, the act allowing me to conceal the emotions roiling inside me. This woman – who is she? Why has she come here? But before I can find a way to voice these questions, Care begins again.

'And did he tell you that I could find what you seek?' Her voice is low, as if she would not break the spell. 'A watch fob from a man without a name?'

'Not exactly, no.' The woman sighs again. 'But the scribe – the keeper – said you're good at finding things. And maybe, if you spoke to him . . .'

She stops. We all do. The girl, at her desk, holds her breath. I sit, one paw raised to dry.

'His last missive was a warning,' she says at last, and I sense her eyes on me. Running over my midnight fur and my outstretched paw as if feeling for a gap, a break where the fur, the black leather, will give way to something other. I find the scrutiny disconcerting, and I turn to walk away.

It is enough to make her pause again, but as I pass by the sofa where the old woman sits, she begins to speak again.

'He wanted to take care of me, and he did,' she says. 'He sent me funds for me to make my escape. So I can pay, if that's your other question. Only I can't leave without knowing what has happened, and for that I need his seal. It's more than just a watch fob or an heirloom. It's – it's who he was, you see. The last remnant of my baby brother, whom I loved.'

FIVE

Her words catch me up and I freeze, the hairs along my neck bristling.

'Brother,' she has said. This woman who has seen me. Who seems to recognize in me some semblance of consciousness. Some kind of kinship. *Brother?*

I am a cat. A predator, though one of diminutive stature. Both roles require me to be alert to my surroundings, a state I had considered mastered. And yet this – this woman, this *human* – has taken me by surprise. A thought, suggested by her words and yet – no, it cannot be.

Does she refer to me? Do I – *did* I – have a sister? I have no recollection of such, but neither do I recall any of a prior feline life. My head reels with the possibilities, with all I do not know, as I try to make sense of what I have heard.

Above my head, the women talk – one young and dear to me. The other – what? A sister? Despite the keenness of my velvet ears, I hear nothing, I am so lost in thought.

Confused, I wash, frenetically wiping away at my face, my whiskers. I am not some human, prone to sentiment. Ties of blood do not bind creatures like the one I have become. Nor, I suspect, as my grooming slows into a reassuring rhythm, did such connections matter much to me in my previous incarnation. The hunt – the tracking – this is what drew me on. The case, as I would have termed it then. And this . . .

I blink as my mind clears. Resume the calming ritual of bathing once again. But more slowly now, the strokes of paw and tongue on fur a slow self-soothing. My mind, as much as my fur, begins to settle and smooth out. I have been jarred, but I remain myself. I require information to make sense of what I've heard.

My ears are up now, listening to more than mere conversation. I take in the woman's breathing and the girl's, inhale their distinctive aromas. Both are sad, weighted down by grief and trouble, and, now that she has unburdened herself, the woman's sighs, a long susurration of relief. Perhaps Care can hear this too, the release of tension after a long trial. For she appears to believe this woman and speaks to her of process and of timing.

She accepts her story of a brother dead and gone, at any rate, if not of funds left that will finance an investigation – or of some keepsake long sought after. I know her well enough to spot the clues – a sympathy, if not hope of an accounting. In truth, the larger loss fits more with the kind of employment she has been getting. In these days, people are more likely to be sought than items, or perhaps it is simply that clientele such as the girl attracts do not have much in the way of possessions to lose. The bauble sounds a poor thing, anyway, serving no useful function that I can ascertain.

My fur now sleek and shining, I feel myself restored. I turn to take in the old woman, apparently our newest client, and see that she regards me as well. Perhaps she is admiring my glossy coat. Her eyes are cool, though not as cool as mine, and with the morning sun behind her, I cannot make out their color. Beside us, the girl is scribbling. The contract, I assume. Or more notes, pursuant to the start of a case, as she asks the woman about the keeper who referred her – about this object that she seeks.

I am a cat, and as such I know myself to be beautiful, perhaps especially to an aged, heavy creature like this woman is. My fur, once ragged, has grown full. My eyes must be reflecting emerald in the early light. Still, I find this woman's gaze disconcerting as she speaks, and with a shiver that runs over my hide, I realize why this is so. Without intending to, I have crossed directly in front of this woman, and yet she, of an age to recall a different time and different mores, does not flinch. Does not mutter nor make the sign to ward off evil. So accustomed to such gestures am I even among those that would befriend my kind that I am left ill at ease. At odds, and wondering if, indeed, our paths have crossed before.

'Here.' Care stands to pass a page to the woman on the sofa. A contract, then. The case has been accepted. We both study the woman as she reads. Even I can see how her eyes scan the paper. Her mouth tightens slightly as she weighs some word or legal point, a nod as she finishes another. She is educated, then, her story not some fable in this particular at least.

'I agree,' she says at last. 'Shall I sign?'

Care's brows go up, but she covers, turning quickly for the pen. We have come to this, in this city of ours. Literacy is a rarity, with most of the populace as dumb as beasts in such matters. As dumb, but lacking the acuity of senses that such as I enjoy.

The woman rises, passing in front of me, to take the pen and, leaning on the desk, scratches out a name.

'Huh.' The girl accepts the page back. 'It's funny . . .'

'Yes?' The visitor waits.

'When you said your name, I thought—'

'I told you what I am called – what he called me,' the woman says. 'But for a contract, I've signed my legal name.'

'That explains it.' The girl adds her own name to the page and shakes her head. 'I think I may have seen your name once. Long ago, or maybe something like it. Now, to get me started . . .'

Coins change hands, and more information. At the name of the keeper, the scribe who passed along the last message, I look up. We know this man, and that is good. A reference surpasses currency for putting my mind to ease. The woman has little else to offer, though she has talked of funding, and as they talk of meetings and reports, I confess I stop listening. Although my ears are set as wide as an owl's – fit for hearing the slightest scrabble of tiny claws – my mind is elsewhere. I have garnered what information I can. I have ascertained the honesty of this woman's claim to come from afar. The mud on her shoes does not stink of the river, or not entirely; a drier, older soil clings deep, beneath the oily ooze that seeps from these city streets. That she has lived in cleaner air is apparent from her body. Simply to reach such an age, she must be strong, though time now drags her down. Her skin wears the ravages of time, but not of smog and stress.

No, her body confirms what she has said, but what preoccupies me is not her person. It is her words – her words and that strange moment on the stairs – that perturb me. Did this woman see in me more than an animal? More than a former feral, who age and some atavistic memory have driven into partnership with a girl? Did this woman *know* me? Am I, in fact, the brother she has lost? And if that is so, what has brought her here? To me and to the girl.

The girl. I turn to face this young, thin female, for whom I would give much. They are still discussing terms. The woman has no fixed abode as yet, she is explaining. Not in this city at this time. She will come back in a few days' time, and if more is needed they will talk. She offers Care her hand. I envy that contact, knowing I could make more of it than the girl, and reach to sniff her skirts, her leg. She moves to leave before I can fully take her measure, although as I pass once more before her I am able to gauge her reaction to my presence – to me.

'Excuse me,' she says, as I stare up at her worn face. It is not familiar to me, although age and distance, the changes I have undergone, have made more than one memory fade.

'What?' Care looks up – looks over at us.

'It's nothing,' the woman responds. She shakes her head, ever so slightly. 'It's only . . . your cat. I almost thought . . .' She shakes her head once more and then is gone.

'Blackie, what is it?' The girl is staring. Time has passed. A bemused smile is playing on her lips, making me realize how ridiculous I must appear with my mouth slightly open, tail lashing. I have been thinking, deep in private reverie, but I must seem absurd. I still my tail, that traitor to my privacy, and stifle the low growl that would protect my dignity. I am not some clown – a pet made to amuse. My concerns are serious. Profound. And yet, the girl has little enough of levity in her life. If I can incite her to laugh, even at my own expense, I should not begrudge it.

My ears, which I confess had begun to lever flat, spring up and I approach, rubbing my cheek against her leg. 'Mew,' I say. For all that I cannot.

No matter. We have no time. Word must be spreading. The girl's competence gives her a minor kind of fame. For before she can start out on her investigation, a soft knock interrupts her preparations.

'Come in,' she calls without looking up. Distracted, she cannot hear the difference in the rap against the door. Does not hear the heaviness of the tread, and believes that her client has returned.

I am not so deaf to these unspoken signals, but I am also not alarmed. Something in the way the newcomer hesitated, a slight shuffle in his step, assures me that he is a supplicant rather than a threat. Still, it does no harm to be alert.

'May I help you?' The girl is good. She hides her surprise rather well, though I can hear the tightening of her voice, the added warmth that comes as her pulse quickens. The man who has come in, pushing the door open just enough to slip by, is small for his kind, but larger than she. Although he sways as he steps in, his muscular arms must more than compensate for his bowed legs. Only the worn cap he holds in both his hands, working it like a kitten kneads her dam, discloses his assumption of the subordinate position. His understanding that he is the petitioner, come here to ask for aid.

'Miss Care?' His voice reveals his station. Harsh, a little cracked, it has been weathered by outdoor work on the docks or in a field. His words speak of another time, when certain norms still held. 'You are Miss Care?'

'I am.' She stands to greet him and to usher him to the sofa. She lost her family young, this girl, and yet some innate sense of dignity or poise directs her into hostess mode. He sits gingerly, perched on the sofa's edge, and looks down as if newly aware of the coarse dungarees he wears. For a change, she sits beside him. This does not make him more at ease, but it is a kind gesture, and for that I love her more.

'My name is Peter,' he says. I note, again, the formality of his speech, uncommon in these difficult times. 'I hear that you – that you find people.'

'I can try,' she says, her voice soft. She begins her patter: 'I find that which is lost, I right the wrongs . . .' He nods as she does, as if in recognition. Or, no, it is a test.

'That's right,' he says, when she has finished. 'That's what I heard.'

She looks at him, the question in the tilt of her head.

'I asked around,' he says. 'When he went missing. I asked for who could help.'

She waits, as do I, my ears pricked up to catch whatever he

does not say aloud. But the man only looks down at his knees again, where his cap rests, and at his hands, which now clasp and wrestle each other like kittens in a litter. I watch those hands, as does the girl, but when I hear the intake of her breath, I glance up. She is readying to speak.

'You are looking for someone?'

I lash my tail and wait. In part, the movement is involuntary – like my ears and whiskers, my tail projects my thoughts unless I consciously still it. Right now, I am grateful for the movement, the wide sweep its midnight fur makes across the floor. The girl is missing the point, and I would have her notice my agitation. Perhaps, like me, she remains troubled by our previous visitor. It matters not. She is not asking the right question. But the man has begun to speak again.

'It's Rafe.' He looks up, his eyes wide with unshed tears. 'He's my – he's like a son to me.' His head ducks again, although I do not think he sees much now.

'This Rafe, what can you tell me about him?'

She is speaking calmly, in a voice designed to elicit as much information as she can. But as he starts to talk – to tell her about a young colleague, new to the city, whom he had taken under his wing – my mind races. They have worked together for some years now, the man is saying. As common laborers on the docks, where the river still functions as a connection to the outside world. But the youth was restless, says the man.

'You fear misadventure?' Her words, well chosen, make him wince.

He nods, and I wait, but still it does not come. Yes, she needs clients, and it is a good thing that her reputation is spreading. That does not mean she should be careless. If anything, she has more liberty now, and should use it. Following an issue that sprang up some months before, she has been cautious. Diligent about tracing the provenance of each client who arrives, as one trusted person refers another. That woman, now, she came from the keeper. But if her custom serves to upset the girl's routine, her worth will have been mitigated. I lash my tail again and strive to catch her eye. This man has not said how he came here. He has not said who it was who told him about Care and about her expertise.

'I can pay.' The hands unclasp as he digs into the pocket of his dirty canvas coat. 'I have money.'

He draws forth a small bundle of bills, and Care gasps. Paper money is not much used these days. And certainly not by the likes of a laborer, as this man claims to be. I glance from her face to his, curious to see if her reaction provokes a response.

'I'm – I'm sorry,' he says, his voice heavy with sorrow. 'This is what I have. My friends . . .' He pauses to wipe his nose with the back of his hand. He blinks back tears.

'That's fine.' She takes the bills and counts them out. Two she keeps, the others she presses back into his hand. 'This will get me started.'

Now's my moment, and I stretch to sniff the edges of the notes that extend from her hand. Sweat, of course, like onions left too long in damp. Dirt and clay, I think, moist with the casings of beetles and worms. No surprise, as these suffuse his clothing, even to his skin. This man has slept rough, I think, and spends time out of doors. But beneath these, beneath even the foul warmth of his grimy hand, I catch it. Something – bitter. Biting. Strong enough that I pull back my head, and in that moment lose my chance. The notes move out of range.

There was none of that iron tang of blood at least. For that I must be grateful. Despite his adoption of a subservient position, I am hesitant to take this man at his word, but I believe him in this one particular. This money has been held by a variety of hands, which may explain that particular scent – the assaultive chemical bite – but it does not carry the most obvious taint of crime.

'You last saw him when?' Care is listening, making mental notes. But also, I can see, observing the man. Good. She is not as gullible as I have feared.

'Three – no, four days ago.' The man's eyes roll up, as if he would count the stars. 'We'd worked a full shift at the warehouse. We were flush.' The ghost of a smile plays around his mouth. 'I was tired, though. I went back to our shack to sleep. When Rafe didn't show up, I thought, maybe, he'd met someone.'

He looks away at that. As if the girl wasn't a denizen of this city, wouldn't know what money can buy.

'And then?' she prompts him gently, undeterred.

'I slept late,' he says. Intoxicated, I interpret. Not that I judge; the lives of such men are harsh and consolations few. From the girl's slight nod, I see that she thinks so too. 'And then when he didn't show, I thought, well, good for him. Only the next day, a rumor went around. There was work again. A ship was coming – something big – and they were signing men. Not just hook boys, either.' He pauses, then, remembering. 'Him and me,' he says, when he sees her looking. 'We're a team.'

Care tilts her head.

'The bosses,' the man explains, anticipating her question. 'They like to hire teams. Two men to lift and carry. And Rafe and I – he's tall, but I'm still strong – we work well together.'

Care nods. She must see what I do, that our visitor must rely on his younger colleague to get hired. To get work and to keep it, despite his muscular shoulders, those big arms. 'You must have asked around,' is all she says.

A nod. One hand disentangles to rub a bristly chin. 'Nothing. And that was four days ago.' He shakes his head, as if he cannot believe his own words.

'A fight, perhaps?' The girl has a natural delicacy, but her visitor gets the point.

'No.' He shakes his head. 'The hook boys brag, and Rafe's not the type to pick a fight. Besides, there's work coming. Everybody says.'

'Well then.' The girl returns to her desk, extracts a sheet of paper and begins to take down notes. This missing man – this Rafe – is tall, we learn, his coloring light, with reddish hair and freckles. When Care asks about his age, the other man sighs. 'Sixteen, maybe? Eighteen? Still growing, anyway.'

I watch as the girl writes. Sixteen is young for such work, hauling bundles on the docks. But Care isn't even that – is barely fifteen, I believe – and yet she has assumed a grown man's job. His office and his career. This work she does she was being trained for, not eight months before. Apprentice to a master of detecting, of 'finding that which is lost', as her second-hand cant brags. An aged man, who schooled her in deciphering both clues and language. That skill betrayed him, ultimately, as he followed a path set to trap him, as his hubris overcame his intelligence and that trap brought about his end.

Finally, she is done, having asked all the questions except for that one all-important query that I would have her give precedence, the matter of who sent him to her. She looks up, weighing, I believe, how best to seal the contract. A thumbprint or an X, I suspect.

'In all fairness,' she begins, 'I should let you know—' I turn toward her in surprise '—I have taken another client on – another missing person case – and I'll have to give that one priority.'

'Sure, sure,' says the visitor, who, task completed, now looks eager to be gone. 'I mean, there's no rush now. Is there?'

Care must realize, as do I, that despite his earlier demurral he believes the boy is dead.

SIX

I am not happy, and I cannot pretend to be. As the girl gathers up her belongings, I pace and mumble, my tail expressing my unease even as I prowl the room. I have not been easy since that woman – Augusta? Blaze? – climbed the stairs. Her disconcerting gaze, her words unnerve me still. And now, this rough man – this laborer . . . where did he come from? How did he come to solicit the help of a girl not half his age? Yes, I am aware that she is capable, this Care. And that she is building a reputation for her talents, I am glad. That is what the old man trained her for – what *I* trained her for – in a different form, a different life.

But as much as I appreciate her industry, I am discomposed. Forcing myself to sit, to focus, I concentrate on the threat at hand. This man, and worse, her oversight. There's danger here, a risk as clear to me as that faint but stinging trace. And if she cannot sense that contamination, I would have her question its source – the bundle of bills from a poor man's pocket. A laborer from the docks.

Her clients, until now, have been largely small-scale merchants or purveyors of more personal services. Women, mainly, who pass Care's name among themselves as one who can undertake the search for a child or a necessary object. Those most likely to be misused by society are most likely to have need of such services, as with the mother who came by earlier, with such heartfelt gratitude over her son's return and who paid in one poor penny, its edges scraped for use in some earlier exchange. And while those who work the docks may number among the roughly used, it is rare to see such generosity and fellow spirit from among them as those pooled funds would indicate. My tail whips back and forth as I weigh the improbability of such largesse against the emotion clear in the man's eyes. Perhaps it is simply the novelty that unsettles me, and I seek the comfort of more wonted custom. The surety. As much as there can ever be, in this city reverted back to something wild.

She is quick, this girl, and learned well the arts by which to
uncover the lie and to discern the truth through interview and
observation. But she is young yet and susceptible to the sentiment – and the palpable fear – of others. Under its influence,
what she has overlooked, it would seem, is the essential art of
self-protection. She did not insist on a reference from this rough
man, and I am worried. I am concerned, I am . . .

I still my tail. Two factors must be considered. The first is
that I, her mentor, may not have stressed the importance of such
defensive measures. For it was only by my own demise that I
truly learned how vulnerable we are. The other is that she,
unlike me, is human. A child still, and likely more prone to
emotion than I ever was in any form, but while this may seem
a weakness, I cannot utterly discredit it. This girl, this Care,
has saved my life, knowing me as no more than a struggling
creature. Her compassion is not calculable by such a one as I,
but as much as it goes against my nature, I should not discount
it entirely.

'Blackie?' Her voice breaks into my thoughts. She stands at
the door, her old canvas carryall on her shoulder. She has grown
used to my company, but still this summons is a curious one.
'Are you all right?'

Of course, my pose – eyes wide, ears laid flat as if readying
for a fight – make my agitation apparent to such a careful
observer and highlight again the dissimilarities between us. Yet,
if I must now come to terms with such physical manifestations
of my distress, so too must I accept her body's limitations. She
is an observant girl and clever too. It was not pity that drove
me to pick her from the pack in that other time, to select her
from the group of half-feral, half-starving children who ran my
errands back when I had other form. No, she was special. *Is*
special, I correct myself. But the senses of a human, even a
sensitive and intelligent young adult, like this Care is becoming,
are nothing compared to the acuity of even a day-old kitten.

It maddens me that she cannot perceive through scent or
sound what I could scarce avoid, but there it is. She cannot,
and I can no longer teach her, nor even warn her of what she
may have missed. It is all I can do to pad along after her like
the dumb beast she believes me to be, and so I do, slipping out

of the closing door to follow her down the stairs and out, once more, into the street.

I did not have to worry so, not really. Although she is quick enough to understand the value of improvisation, she follows still the system that I taught her. She will begin her work as she has learned, with groundwork and observation, building from the known to the unknown to reveal that which has been hidden. That she gives priority to the woman's case she has made clear; her confession of this to the man was what bothered me, as it derailed the line of inquiry I would have had her following. But it was a courtesy, and in that had some value.

For this reason, as a gesture of my own, I let her see me trailing her as she makes her way down the day-lit street. Although it is not my nature to jog like some dog at her heel, I keep pace in my own way, darting from shadow to shadow alongside her, at times moving forward, at times dropping back. As the heat of day rises, so do the aromas of the street, and I take my time, surveying them as the girl takes in the visual landscape she passes.

The building we are leaving, for example, has withstood much. As we walk along its length, I breathe in the dust of decades. Good brick, once, though it has begun to crumble, water and the poisoned air clawing away as surely as any work of vermin could do. If I pause and close my eyes, I can taste the source of that red clay, as I can the sand of the mortar that still holds, more or less, in place. A riverbank, drenched in sun, its mud redolent of spawn and tadpoles. A remnant of memory – heat, scent – that makes me salivate.

Many springs have passed since then, and I do not know if such a waterway still exists, nor how I would find it again. Still . . . at times the girl has talked of leaving this city. Of heading south. Talk it usually is, something to entertain herself or sooth the boy who comes to visit and to shelter with her at night. I lick my chops and wonder. Could there be a place, still, where such abundance could be found? Surely, if there were, others would be heading there. Would already have gone.

For there is nothing here. Nothing healthful, at any rate. And with that I wake from my reverie, to find the girl is gone. As I have mused, distracted, I have let her pass from sight and hearing. My fur comes to a rise. If I have been wrong . . . But, no, with racing heart, I scramble down past our building and past the one beyond, and find her there. She has turned where I expected, being forced by her human form to take a surface route that I could have shortened for her, if she could squeeze beneath a fence and overtop a trash bin as easily as I.

I race toward her, eager to take in her warmth, her fragrance. To reassure myself that she is not as lost to me as that forgotten spring. She pauses and turns with a smile.

'Blackie.' She makes as if to stroke me, then stops herself. Her caution – or her solicitude for my dignity – overtakes the natural desire of a child to touch my gleaming fur. 'You're panting. Are you OK?'

I sit and stare up at her, willing my heaving sides to be still. It was panic more than that flustered run that has my old heart beating so. I lick my chops to erase the memory of that old scent, and wrap my tail around my forepaws, to illustrate my ease at sitting so.

'You're right at attention.' Her gaze is quizzical. 'I almost think you're waiting for me to give you a treat or something.'

I cannot help myself. My ears flip back. She does not intend derision, and yet her flagrant disregard for my focus, for the offer of my superior senses, irks me. More than it should, I remind myself. She is a child, for all that she has grown in our time together. And unlike me, she is not accustomed to be alone. She had a family once, parents who cared for her as few do these days. A father who was taken from her unlawfully, and a mother who declined as a result before they both were killed. It is natural for her to reach out to others, to try to recreate this clowder she once enjoyed. When her foster home did not provide such nurturing, she left it, but she took the boy Tick with her. And although she never gave all her allegiance to the gang that took them in, she did seek a form of family there, I know.

She is not a cat, this girl. She must be lonely, although she is not, in fact, alone. I recall myself and force my ears to rise. Rising on my hind paws, I push my head into her hand. I feel her fingers around the base of my ears, on the soft fur beneath my jaw. They are tender, teasing out the rough spots where scars hide beneath my fur. If she noticed my flare of anger, she forgives it, as silent in her acceptance of my penance as I am in her gentle grace. For a moment, we are one and we are warm. She pets me, and I purr.

'Care!' The voice butts in, as intrusive as a rock, shattering our peace. I turn with a snarl. The boy, Tick, stands by the avenue that we just left, his arms akimbo, mouth ajar. 'Wait up,' he says, stumbling closer. He has been running. That much is clear from his fresh perspiration, as well as his high color and the ragged breath he draws.

'Tick, are you OK?' Care turns from me without a thought, though if she heard my aggrieved growl, she still would not likely credit it. She knows I have no love for this boy, taken too young from any parent to learn his proper role. She still believes her nurture can relieve the gaping need in him. 'Shouldn't you be at work?'

He nods, not even questioning her statement. Care does not approve of his job at the factory, a hellish place even I would have him flee. In his preoccupation, he barely notices. 'I'm on a job,' he says. 'I'll get back in time, but I had to find you. I've done some asking. You know, like you do?'

She nods, biting the inside of her lip.

'About AD. He's going to work again. To cook.' He pauses, scanning her face to see if she remembers. How could she not? The sting of the drug, the web of addiction that bound their gang to its leader. Care learned quickly enough the price of shelter and protection.

'Scat?' One word, but there's a question in it. I wonder if she too could have sensed the stink – or notes the lack thereof. Perhaps she saw a sign in his ragged attire, or his haste.

The boy just nods. 'He's rounding up the crew, those as got away. Asking everywhere for folks. You know, Rosa and the others.'

'We're not going back.' She kneels to study the boy's face, looking past his words. His mother was a victim of the drug. He, too, nearly fell prey.

'I know.' He nods, his mien serious. 'I can't. Not ever. But, Care, he's talking big this time. About protection, about working for the boss.'

'AD?' The slightest huff of laughter. 'I can't see him answering to anyone.'

'He's just being careful. You know. This time.'

She nods. She was instrumental in the gang leader's downfall. If, this time, he has sponsors . . .

'I'll be careful too,' she says, in answer to the unspoken question. She does not hide her gentle smile.

'You better, Care.' The boy, affronted, stands up straight. 'I won't always be around to tell you things, you know.'

'I know.' The smile grows broader, warming her face as it reveals her affection for the boy. She does not hear the growl that rises once more in my chest, the warning I would give. For she responds, as she always has, to the boy before her, to the affection they have come to share. She does not hear, as I do, the rising note in his warning. A note that speaks of the future, and of the man he may yet become.

'Tick, why are you really here?' I confess, I am surprised by her question. Maybe she is more aware than I credit. Or, maybe she sees more in the boy's troubled face than I can understand.

'Just, to warn you.' He looks down, a poor dissembler.

'Tick?'

'You aren't working with anyone else, are you?' His eyes, wide, plead like a child's.

'Never.' The smile returns, and she reaches for his hand. 'Only Blackie here.' She nods toward me, and I start back. She gives too much of herself, this girl. Shares too openly with the boy. But I know that she is lonely, with a craving for her own kind that I cannot assuage.

'Good.' The boy nods, as if confirming a private thought. 'I'm glad, Care. I'm really glad.'

And with that, the boy turns tail and runs off, leaving the girl behind. She stands and looks after him as he races down the rutted street. While I have mastered the art of reading faces – the human visage being so much more mobile and expressive than my own – I cannot fully explicate the mix of emotions I see in hers. Sadness, for certain; regret, though at the boy's words or the way he runs; anxious to complete his task; I do not know. But there is also longing and something like anger in the grim set of her mouth. Not at the boy's words, I think, for they held no surprise for her. No, I realize, as she watches him race down the deserted street, at his having brought them. She does not approve of the boy serving as a messenger – or believing that he is her caretaker.

Two blocks down, the boy looks up and turns. Checking a marker, perhaps, since street signs are nowhere in evidence in this part of town. His shoes are worn, the mud in the road dried to dust, and he slips slightly. Care gasps as he stumbles, one hand out to catch himself on the rutted road. But the boy is young and agile, and he rights himself before his pale palm can hit the dirt. His course checked, he runs on without stopping, and the girl beside me waits, staring after him as he veers around a grey stone building and disappears.

Her sigh is deep, lifting her narrow shoulders as she resumes her walk, and I press close once more, rubbing my side against her leg.

'Thanks, Blackie.' That is not my name, but I have grown used to it. Grown used to the girl's casual assumption of friend-ship, as if in some small way she recognizes me for who I am. 'I know you don't like Tick much, but he can't help it. He's a boy.'

I twitch one ear in acknowledgment. I do not know what cruelties the boy is capable of, but it is not the casual malice of a child that puts me off. His appearance just now spoke well of him, showing up as he did to warn the girl. Unless . . . my back stiffens. My ears and whiskers stand at full alert. No, I see no sign of any other human. None of the shuffling footsteps or heavy breathing that announces their presence. It may well be that the boy was sent on a mission – sent to identify the girl and mark her for another – but I do not anticipate an immediate attack. Yet, I am not easy about his arrival, and I still my tail only with a mindful effort.

It is with a more vigilant air that I accompany the girl through the narrowing streets and into the area once known more for printer's ink than for blood or water. Leading Row, I recall the name, like an echo from a distant past as we turn into a passageway barely wide enough for two humans to walk abreast. It must be close to midday by now, but the way is in shadow, from the buildings that loom above, and the air here is musty still, as if the rag fiber from a long-lost trade still lingered from days long past. Type Square lay ahead, the open area where once the hawkers gathered up their bushels and plied their trade. Already, ahead, I see the few paving stones that remain, shining silver in the sun.

And a shadow. I freeze, desperate to pick up a motion. A scent. In this thick air, I cannot, but the girl notices my sudden halt and stops herself.

'Blackie?' One word, her voice dropped to near a whisper. She would query me but has the sense to keep silent as she follows the line of my gaze, staring out at the bright opening ahead. Pressing herself against the pitted brick wall of the narrow passage, she inches forward. Her brow furrows as she strains her eyes to see, and I find myself again regretting her human frailty. Only vision truly avails her, and in such a circumstance as this – her field limited, the way ahead wiped clean by the noonday sun – she is as blind as a day-old vole, unearthed and vulnerable.

It is not a choice. I creep ahead of her, toward the alley's end.

'What is it?' I hear alarm in her voice. Concern. She would not have me risk myself, although she knows not what we face. No matter. My senses are not limited by the confining walls of the passage. Sound and smell tell me more of the outside world than even my keen green eyes. I flick one ear backward, hoping she can comprehend this as my acknowledgment, and move on.

The passage is clear, my senses tell me. But as I scan the square, where vendors of another sort have set up their tables and their wares, I hear the girl come up behind me. My advance has emboldened her, I fear. I would that she had stayed behind. And as I hear the rasp of inhaled breath, I descry the reason why. In this open square, there are a plethora of sounds and aromas. But the girl, with eyesight attuned by familiarity, has picked out one face among the others. A moment after that startled breath, I too spy what has provoked it. That man, AD, is standing at the far side of the square. His face is in shadow as he rests against the wall. There is no doubt, however, that he is waiting. I do not know for whom he waits, nor if he is aware of the girl's role in his downfall, but I cannot discount the possibility. Nor have I forgotten the tool he carries with him, not that his own hands, his wiry build, would not be enough to overpower one who is smaller. Who is younger and more gently reared.

We have one advantage. AD is not the kind to welcome a fight. He would want surety of success before he risked a confrontation. A guarantee of pain and of punishment. He is not likely to make a move in the open, even if he hopes to find her here.

He will not catch her unawares. Not now that she has seen him. I hear the effort with which she controls her breathing. I feel her lean back once more against the damp brick of the wall. I would she would talk to me. Share with me her thoughts. Does she suspect the boy of setting her up? Does she wonder why he came to her with his news, his warning? Or does she credit him for it? My ears flatten against my skull as I mull the reasons for such duplicity. The opportunities the boy has had to serve his masters, to better himself without turning on the girl.

A shift. A foot sliding on the dirt, and I turn as the girl does and see the man across the way stand. I see him straighten up, his attempt at concealment abandoned. I brace as he reaches toward his waist. I recall too well the potential weapon he carries there.

But he only hikes his loose pants higher and then brushes empty hands on the thighs, as if he would clean them, before setting off across the square – and away from us. Whether he had counted on the element of surprise or some other factor has played into this change of course, I do not know.

As he walks away, I find myself nearly regretting the missed opportunity – a confrontation here, with warning, would be preferable to other options – and worrying, as well, about when he may next appear. We will have to be on our guard, I know. For whatever else the boy has said, in one respect he spoke truly. That man may have put out an invitation to his former cohort, but it is no more than a ruse. He looks on us with hate. Indeed, I am impressed by the discipline he now demonstrates, leaving without another glance in our direction. He strides quickly, perhaps to avoid the temptation. Or perhaps, I muse, he goes off in search of that substance in which he once dealt. A source of courage, perhaps, to bolster any plans for revenge, at least by the light of day.

It is with only a slight twinge of concern that I follow the girl as she leaves the darkness of the alley in pursuit. I am as eager to follow this strange man as she is, to learn what compels her former leader and tormentor. That he may have been stalking her, I would have her realize, although I lack the means to tell her. No matter, we are the hunters now, and our quarry is in sight.

SEVEN

The man is heading toward the waterfront. I should have known. The riverfront, with its hulking warehouses and shipping traffic, is home to trade of all sorts, and to violence as well. The river brings both here, opening to empty itself into the basin and, beyond that, the sea. Ships are fewer now. The long pier is often empty, even when the tide floods in over the flats, and the air about us stings with salt. This is where I met the girl – and met my end, in some sense – it is where death and life commingle. That is the nature of the waterfront, a place for worlds to cross.

Or was. Men from foreign lands still make their entry to the city from the wharfside docks as well as from that one remaining pier, although fewer come than before. Now more wait than work, as what trade remains avoids our failing harbor with its silt and shoals, and those who labor are as likely to be paid in blows as any coin. Women, too, I know, their strange tongues and tattoos marking them as exotic, a dangerous distinction in what has become a tribal and vicious land. Maybe it was always such. Although I have no recollection, the murmurs keep the memory alive. Of vessels packed to bursting with goods destined for abroad. A commerce underlaid by labor of another sort, a trade whose name is whispered still, its curse upon the land.

But there remains brutality here of a more domestic variety as well. As the man makes his way, and the girl follows by a more circumspect and cautious route, I find myself remembering. A drainage ditch – there, along the side of the road – where the paving has given way, in a steep slope down. I had thought it a channel, at first. A violent flood in torrent, as I struggled to right myself. To pull myself ashore, to breathe. Now I see it for the low, dirty thing it is: a sewer, and no more. An outlet for the effluvia of the city. Only I was caught in it, my sodden fur working against me as the rush of a rainstorm pulled me under. As the girl pauses, crouching in the cover of shadow to mirror the actions of the man ahead, I glance over toward the ditch. I cannot see its depth from here, beside the girl, and I would not leave her to revisit it. But I can discern the foulness of its mud, now drying in the sun. In it the remains of other creatures less fortunate than I.

A shiver comes over me, rustling my fur in waves. Smell brings back the memory, even without the roar and tumult of the water. That mud, that low place. I would have perished there had the girl not saved me, pulling me from the flood by my scruff as if I were a kitten. As I sank for a final time.

The rattle of a pebble, and I start. The girl has moved on, her passage nearly silent but for the loose gravel that fills in for the cobblestone and tarmac now. I recall myself to the present, and watch her, taking in her fledgling stealth. She could be a proficient hunter, this girl, the way she tracks her prey. Almost she seems at home here, as we progress. As the scarred and scrawny man makes his way to the waterfront. To what end, I cannot guess. That he answers some summons is clear from his open and purposeful progress. That he has found some matter to become involved in does not surprise me. Not here, where land and sea mingle, throwing all together.

Long before the rotting wharves come into view, I can smell them. The sweet decay of fish and garbage. The tang of salt in the brackish water and the sweat of those who labor there upon those docks or beneath them, scratching out a living in the silt and mud. One more block, and they are upon us – the buildings giving way to open space. More gravel, to accommodate the transit of trucks that growl and bustle more mindless than any beast. More dangerous, too, to such as we.

The girl stops by the last building. Observes as the man advances toward one group of men. Laughter rises, the sound of bonding based more on shared cruelty than on humor, and then two break off. As we wait, we see them pass along the line of piers to where one small building, grey stone and low, sits alone. Too small for a warehouse, I think. A memory tickles at my conscious thought. But the right size for an office of sorts – a counting house, perhaps, where jobs are levied and accommodations reached.

If this, then, is where AD was headed, it raises questions

about his purpose and his goal. Working for the boss, the boy said. Well, his presence here lends that concept credence, although I question how the brutal small-scale alchemy that AD once practiced fits into such a stolid establishment. Not that it matters much. Stone or straw, this is no place the girl can enter. Not in safety. Nor can she even cross the open ground undetected to peer within the low, small windows set on each side of the door.

If she were other than she is, she could make use of the men here. Of their greed and casual cruelty. The hook boys have no love for the laborers. They call them slaves – reviving that once-forgotten term – and beat them for no reason, while the laborers will do most aught just to survive.

Instead, she hunkers down to wait. It is the wise move, and I am grateful. The building sits smack against the harbor's side, where tar-stained logs make a low barrier, preventing trucks from backing to their hazard. It is isolated, and when the man leaves, she will be able to pick up his trail again, though part of me would wish him gone. If he remains inside, perhaps, she will relent and leave this place. Remember her commission and return to her original quest to seek out the scribe and keeper who held that fateful message for our client.

The sun moves slowly, this near its peak. But here, against the warehouse, none have spied the girl. The brightness of the day only deepens the shadow cloaking her. For myself, I have no such concerns. Beasts such as I are welcome here, one of the few places where this is true. These traders count their losses dear, and vermin like the fat grey rat I see darting across the open cost them profits they cannot risk.

That rat. He pauses, and I believe he catches my scent. I have his, rich and glossy with the oil of fish carcasses and more. He has fed recently, on the unlucky young of one of his own kind, a meal that should repulse the remnant of civilization within me. Perhaps it does, and I desire vengeance. For suddenly, I am overcome by the urge to hunt him down. To feel my still sharp teeth breaking through that lustrous hide.

I peer at the girl. She waits, so quiet she could be sleeping, but for her eyes, intense and focused as mine can be. I follow her gaze. The low building, its door unopened since AD and his companions entered. I lick my chops. I will not leave her. The rat, unaware of his salvation, leaps forward to the tarred barrier. I see him hesitate, sniffing at the wood until he finds a rotted part. The logs give way there to a fall of earth and stone, a gap that grows with use. He could leap the low wall easily but, vermin that he is, slinks through the wreckage. In a moment he is gone.

My eyes follow him and linger, until a gasp recalls me. A truck has pulled up, obscuring our view of the stone building. Beside me, the girl rises, stretching, as if through her height alone she could view over metal and wood. She takes a step, and then another, and I must act.

Crossing in front of her, I dart out into the open. It is a risk, for she may see me and cry out, simply out of a misguided concern for my safety, as a smaller and apparently witless animal. It is a risk I must take, moving too quickly for her to grab me, as she is wont. I trust her not to pursue, once I am in the open square, for she, as well as I, know that I am better able to elude pursuers, even if any in this area would choose to chase a cat.

But she is wise, this girl. She holds her silence as I dash across the open space. Beneath the truck, now still and idling, and onto the pavement on the other side. Men mill in groups, here, by the wharf's side eyeing the two small skiffs at anchor. Hook boys to one side, laborers off on their own. The flatboat making its way to the sagging pier. The door to the low building remains closed, as I approach. I am circumspect: such buildings must have another exit; it is a bolt hole for those seeking anonymity or freedom from pursuit. If only she will wait, I will spy out the ground beyond. I will make my way around the small gathering – six men, no eight – that even now is breaking up. Once this outlier passes, I will—

I stop so short, my leather pads can gain no purchase. I skid off a cobblestone – one of the few remaining – and catch myself at a puddle's edge. Yes, it is he. Our client. I recognize his tread, the waddle that marked his passage up our stairs. Even his smell, this close, is distinctive, despite the area's headier perfumes. He hurries, despite that swinging step, head down, along the wharf front, his passing hidden from the girl. I cannot tell from where

he came, but that he is walking quickly, away from that low
stone house is worrisome, and I would inform the girl.

Then it happens. A growl – a roar that shakes the earth – and
I realize I am trapped once more. Exposed. No cover as even
the broken stones have been pounded flat by usage and by time.
A rumble and that roar again, and I dash, as fast as I am able,
to the wharf's edge. To where that low wall of tar-stained wood
holds back the sea. To where a log has given way. The scent
of one fat rat is only the latest contribution, the damp and
constant attention of a thousand tiny creatures have left their
scent on this pulpy mass, no match for the rain or tide. No
match for the trucks that must maneuver—

I catch myself. I turn. The scent of prey, intoxicating as it
is, gives way to reason once again. The truck, for that is what
made the fiendish noise, is growling still. A grind as of gears
working, and a roar like hell's own cry, as the driver shifts the
giant vehicle once more. He backs up toward the broken wall
but stops, and, managing a turn, drives off.

I sit, abashed. I should be inured to such aural violence by
now, as a denizen of these streets, this city. I should recognize
the difference between a mechanical and a sentient growl. Yes,
I was distracted. By hunger and by fear. Made restive by my
concerns and by my discovery of the man Peter, who so lately
visited our office. But still . . .

I see now that my self-recriminations have had the effect of
compounding my error. For not only have I humiliated myself,
I have lost the man. I stand and stretch, reaching out with mouth
ajar to catch his scent. I seek the pattern of his walk, that slight
off-center limp, among the dockside crowd. I cannot hear him,
for he was not speaking and the truck now on its way drowns
out any lesser sound. I have lost him. He is gone, but before I
can head out in search of him, I hear a familiar voice. The girl.

'Blackie!' She is rushing across the open space, heedless of
the men who turn and stare. 'There you are. I was so worried.'
She catches me up in her arms, pressing me against her warm
body. 'I found you.'

I push back. Now is not the time to be treated as a pet. To
be restrained, even by sentiment. Not when such a suspect
character may yet be tailed and found.

'I was scared.' Her voice is soft, her breath on my neck, as she bends her face into my ruff. And then I feel the tears, the warmth, for their slight dampness does not penetrate my fur, and I relent. That man, the client, is gone, but Care is here, and holding me. If I can give her comfort, with my presence, then I shall. Besides, her embrace is warm. I begin to purr.

It is with some surprise, therefore, that I sense her, moments later, tense and tighten her grip. In response, I push back, pressing my paws against flesh that is no longer so soft or yielding.

'What?' The question is more an intake of breath, barely voiced. Beneath the leather of my pads, I feel her heart accelerate.

I look up, the better to gauge what has provoked such a response. To take in, as well, the waterfront crowd that may have provided such a threat. But no, the men who had been milling about before the truck arrived remain, still unoccupied by anything more than their stories and their dreams. They have even ceased to wonder at the girl, her drab attire hiding her incipient beauty where others broadcast more easily accessible wares. The truck is gone. The stone structure as silent as before. But the girl's breathing has not resumed its deep and steady flow. Her pulse races, and I pick up fear in her scent, as well as a new paleness in her skin.

I would understand, but she does not look at me. Instead, she peers over the low wall at the water's edge. With a twist and one more push, I free myself, dropping to the ground beside the barrier. The girl does not protest. She barely seems to notice and instead falls to her knees and leans forward, to peer over the rotting wood, over the crumbled place where access may be had. And so I join her, disciplining myself to ignore the rich sweetness of the creatures burrowing within, the juicy plumpness of their grubs. The rot that billows forth. This log does not interest her, but something does. The piers, perhaps, or the water below.

Only the tide is out. The rich and ever ripening fetor should have told me that, had I disciplined myself to recall the cycles of water and of sand. The drop below is steep, and access will be difficult, despite the fall of earth and rock that have made their way through this broken area. A path may be made, albeit a precipitous one, down to the strand below. For what lies down there seems solid, if not dry. The tide has gone, revealing a slick grey surface – river silt and sand – that now reflects the noonday sun back at us, wavering and pale. A crab breaks that reflection. It scuttles sideways across the damp, as if it would eclipse the white face with its black body. The trail it leaves is pocked and crooked, even as it makes its way and joins its fellows, converging trails serving to stripe the sun further. Cloud across the surface. Stripes laid on the moon. Only the girl is not looking at the reflection, the brightness that ripples as water overlaps it. She is following the passage of that crab, those crabs, to where they have begun to feast on the body of AD, broken and still, lying on the wet below.

EIGHT

S he doesn't scream. The girl is not so callous as to be inured to violent death, I have felt her start and heard her sudden intake of breath, but that is all. She has grown much over the last few years and has learned to control her responses. To hold herself in check. To be quiet and still.

These are the reflexes of a prey animal. A creature anticipating violence, and in response I flick my ears, surveying the scene for threats. Behind us, the rough conversation continues apace, voices broken only by bursts of loud laughter, which fades as quickly as it erupts. There is a forced quality to their merriment, a strain that undermines the illusion of mirth. But it is only desperation that I hear in that affected cheer, no immediate danger. Not to the girl. These men are scared, and while such may lash out in their fear, may seek power in the oppression of others, their focus is on each other. They bolster themselves with volume, not action, and will not move on until a stronger provocation is presented.

There is activity, still, back along the warehouses that may explain much – that may, in fact, include the man I spied. But that is farther from us, and besides, I am out of time. The girl has straddled the barrier and stares down at the body below – arms akimbo, head at an unnatural angle. One eye stares upward, no longer darting with suspicion or anger, its gloss fading in the sun. With an effort that is obvious to me at least, she turns away. Studies the slippage descending from the rotted place. The harbor wall is less clear cut here, its steep side giving way to crumbled rock fall. For one such as I, sure-footed and small, the path would be manageable, assuming I did not mind the dampness that oozes forth. For the girl, it is treacherous, despite her agility and slim build. I cannot see where her feet may rest or her hands gain purchase, and already the tide has begun to return.

Her visage, however, reveals her determination, her brow knit as she takes in the fall of pebbles and grit that angle their way down. It is a dangerous path, leading to an unstable floor. A floor, I see, as the crabs scatter and gather again, which is rapidly becoming subsumed by the incoming tide.

She points one foot down and digs her toe in the rock fall. A spray of sand streams out, and some of the stones follow. She adjusts, and tries again, finding a more solid perch. I feel my hackles rising in alarm. The dampness of the wall is already darkening the leg of her jeans. But it is not simply the rising waterline, the damp reek of which brings back too many memories of my own near demise. It is that crumble and her reach. Even were she to descend safely to the body below, her return will be more difficult, and she will not have the luxury of time.

She shifts her weight. She seeks another toehold, determined to descend, while still gripping the barrier. I mount the wooden tie beside her as I struggle to communicate my alarm. She will be trapped. She will succumb, and I, who know such death intimately, will be unable to pull her forth, as she once did for me.

'What?' She turns, her concentration broken.

I am unaware of having spoken, although my tail lashes in alarm.

'You don't have to follow me.' She smiles, the girl, despite the dire descent she is about to attempt. No, I realize, the horror growing in me, she smiles because she has mistaken my alarm. She sees in me only the natural abhorrence of a furred beast for water. Of a cat, afraid to get wet.

I hiss. It is instinctive. Immediate and unbidden. And it is, I realize immediately, the wrong move. Hearing the fury, the spit of sibilance, accompanied, I am ashamed to say, by the automatic arching of my back, she draws back in alarm. The part of the barrier to which she clings must have seemed solid, although its breach had allowed her easy access to the fall beyond. It is not, and as she jerks back I can hear and, hard on that, smell its rot give way. A foul sweetness, more profound than even what I have scented before, is released as the wood beneath her crumbles. I see her turn in panic, widening eyes taking in the dark fragments as they fall to the wet sand below, more crumb-like than splinters. And just as quickly, her own weight shifts. She braces, leaning on that toehold in the wall, and I – I would reach for her. I would pull her back to safety. Back to me.

Only I am not as I once was, a man. A mentor. I am a black cat, feral and puffed with fear. And by instinct older than recall, she reacts – recoiling from my outstretched claw. It is too much. The wood gives way, breaking free. And although she grabs for the edge that still remains, she is overset. Her own weight will drag her down.

I cannot breathe. I stare. But she is smart, this girl. Agile, quick – with instincts near as sharp as mine. Nimbly as a possum's, her fingers grasp the wall. Balancing on her one foothold, she feels about and finds another, close below. I see her momentarily close her eyes. She takes a breath, and shifts, her weight carrying her down to the next hold, and the next. It is an awkward descent, precipitous and rough, but she arrives at the bottom intact, except for some scraping on her palms, which she rubs against her thighs.

The sand beneath her changes color, sighs out its moisture and lightens as she steps. It sucks at her shoes as she walks carefully, away from the wall and toward the body that lies close by. The crabs scurry, moving from her as she approaches. They bob in the water that now laps at AD's legs, clamping onto his ragged clothing for purchase. The girl, however, seems indifferent, even as her own shoes grow dark and sodden.

I stare down in alarm. The sand is clearly saturated. The water rising. The man she now kneels by is beyond any saving, even if he merited the risk she has taken on his behalf.

'Hey! You!' A man's voice close at hand. Care looks up and I turn to see her client – Peter – by my side. He cranes over the blackened timbers of the wharfside, his lined face bright with alarm. 'Miss Care!'

She stands, her knees dark from the water. 'Can you help me?' She gestures to the body in the sand.

'Let's get you up.' He calls then turns and stands. More yelling and some gestures, and two men come, a knotted rope coiled over the leader's shoulder. Laborers – the rope is borrowed at a cost. 'It's not safe down there.'

Care doesn't respond. The statement so anodyne as to be meaningless. But when one man – the larger – descends and makes to grasp her around the waist, she draws back, stepping into the shallow water.

'No, I can climb,' she says, and gestures to the body. 'It's him – AD – you've got to take him up.'

'He's past helping, Miss.' The man shakes his head slowly, his voice sad. 'But the tide comes in fast here.'

'I have to see—' She steps toward the body. Kneels again and reaches for his shoulder. She will turn him over. She is looking for a wound. A knife cut or the piercing of a grappling hook, I think. Only the man moves closer to stand by the body's upper torso.

'Miss, please.' More yelling up above. 'Yo!' My fur bristles as others crowd too close. 'Come on, girly!'

'Wait.' She checks his pockets, her hands coming out empty.

'Miss!' A little wave – a boat's wake, perhaps – overtops the body. The man shifts his stance, water puddling when he lifts his feet. 'He's just – this guy, he wasn't in good shape. Please.'

Another wave over the body. AD's outstretched arm begins to float, one hand moving as if to beckon. His head begins to turn. Care stands and stumbles back, and the large man has her. 'Please, Miss.'

She nods and swallows. At last, the danger – or the horror – hitting home. 'I need to see—'

She'd pull away to carry on in her investigation, but one more wave sweeps in, catching her and wetting them both up to their knees.

'Go!' He pushes her to the rope and she begins to climb. She is halfway up when she stops and turns. The water washes over the body; the tide has begun to move it toward the piers. The limbs float free, gesturing.

'Here you go.' Her client, Peter, extends his arm and almost out of courtesy, Care responds, taking his outstretched hand and letting herself be pulled onto the wharf. The men cheer, and cheer again as her would-be rescuer follows, to drag himself over the top. He is soaked, from head to toe. The sand below already obscured by water, deep enough to be dark. Rough, too.

'Could we get a boat?' Care turns toward the water. AD is still visible, the hump of his scarred back breaking the surface as he spins, caught on some outcropping of the pier.

'What do you want to do that for?' a dark-haired man, weathered as those timbers, asks. 'He'll be gone before the rozzers can get here. Let him go. He was just a scat head.' He is dry and scowls in disapproval, though whether at the fuss or the appropriation of the men – or the rope – I cannot tell. The four-pronged hook that hangs at his belt marks him as a master here.

'No,' she says. 'I knew him.'

The man eyes her, suspicion on his face.

'I know he cooked – that he was a scat dealer.' Indeed, that drug, which they so quaintly name, was what kept their small gang together. 'But he didn't use.'

'You seen him lately?' A tilt of the head toward the water below. 'Skinny as a rail.'

'It's true.' The speaker nods, lisping through his missing teeth. 'I heard him, yelling for it. "The scat, the scat," like he was mad.'

'And you saw him fall?'

A shrug. The toothless man looks at his colleague. Despite the hook at his own belt, he chooses not to commit.

'Nothing you can do now, Miss Care.' The client – Peter – has found a rag, which he hands to Care, and she wipes her lower face. Her eyes she keeps on the body as it makes its way to the deep. She doesn't argue anymore, and the men begin to disperse. She has no evidence – no proof to refute what they've said, and in truth, the fall is high enough that a step, badly chosen, could result in a neck as neatly snapped as a rat's, were I to grab and shake it.

I regret now my hesitation, as the opportunity to examine the corpse is swallowed by the tide. My superior faculties could have discerned much about his death, both in terms of timing and the cause. But even before the water took him, I caught no whiff of the acrid smoke that the drug produces. Nor was there any sign of intoxication in the man as he made his way here not long before. No, I am unable to share any of this with the girl, but as I look up into her solemn face, I believe the evidence has taken her to the same conclusion I have reached. This body was not supposed to be discovered, left here as the tide flows in. This man, AD, was murdered.

NINE

see her store these thoughts away, her face as closed as a trap. She wipes it, again. Pushes her damp-darkened hair back from her face and stands.

'Nothing to see!' The man Peter turns to his colleagues, away from Care. 'Girl got spooked and fell, that's all. It's all over.'

Arms upraised, as if he would shoo them off, he stands with his back to her. It's a protective stance, and despite his size – smaller than his colleagues, lame – he acts as if he were guarding her. Or claiming her, I consider, as I slip by to press myself against her leg. Silent, she faces the water still. A dark shape can still be seen, drifting.

'Go on now.' Muttering, the men disperse, and, as if with effort, the girl turns to her aspiring guardian.

'I wasn't spooked,' she tells him. It seems an odd time to explain her motive. A show of frailty may be dangerous, but this man has already displayed a willingness to protect her, not to mention that he requires her services. 'I knew him.'

He glances back and then looks away again, a little too quickly. He cannot have heard what she told the larger man who joined her, down on the harbor floor. His ears are nowhere near as keen as mine. But the rapidity of his response implies something. He knows this – or something like.

'His name was AD.' Care continues, studying his face. She is looking for a reaction, I believe. 'He used to live around here. He's been in prison, or on a work gang. I'm not sure. But he wasn't – he didn't use.'

Peter nods, his mouth set in a tight line. He doesn't ask how the dead man came to this place – came *back*. This is not enough to raise the girl's concern. The inquisitive do not fare well in this world. But as he reaches an arm around her, she starts and pulls away.

'We should leave here,' he says, as his arm falls back by his side. 'He was right about the rozzers, but still . . . if they come asking. It's not a good place.'

She turns to him as if finally seeing him. The body has finally disappeared. 'Peter,' she says. 'Why are you here?'

'Me?' His eyebrows shoot up. It's too much, and I feel her tense. She knows he is hiding something. 'I work down here. I told you – with Rafe.'

She nods, but the way she bites her lower lip lets me know she is considering his words. His truthfulness, and it occurs to me. She has not questioned how AD came to be down on the sand. How he came to die.

She had only moments to examine the body, and she lacks my sense of smell. Still, she must have seen that he lay intact, with none of the bleeding one might expect from the mouth or of the nose had he died of the impact. From the fall. The tide was coming quickly, as if a willing collaborator in the concealment, but it was those men who rushed her from the scene, their charity possibly hiding their complicity with the act. Once again, I reproach myself for not joining her on the silty bar, for in close proximity to the dead man's body, I may have been able to discern much more.

The opportunity is lost, but I would have her question the figure now before her further. He stands waiting, as if expecting such, or, perhaps, a reprimand.

'So you did,' she says. 'But you also said that without Rafe, you couldn't get hired.'

He nods, again a shade too quickly. 'Yes, but I was hoping. I thought maybe I could get picked up as a single hand. An extra.'

She cocks her head. She must hear the same false note as I. 'It's after noon,' she says, her voice reasonable and soft. 'The hiring is done.'

A shrug. 'Not like I have any place else to go,' he says. He's looking away. Past her, but not – I note – at the low stone building. 'No place better. And word is, there's a ship due soon. A big one. With those, sometimes there are extra shifts, and the bosses less picky about hiring.'

'You don't need the money.' Her voice is quiet but clear. 'You have cash.'

'That's—' His glance is furtive. Scared. 'That's not mine. There was a collection.'

'Peter?' She's waiting.

'Look.' He turns to face her, full on. 'It isn't safe for you here, Miss Care. It just isn't. Please—' He gestures toward the warehouses. Away from the wharfside – and the stone structure there. 'Please, I know you're working to find Rafe, but this isn't a good way to start.'

She opens her mouth as if to speak. She has already told him that she has another client – the woman – whose case she must undertake before she begins his. That she did not come here on her prior client's business, that she came here on a quest of her own, is not of his concern. But she stops before she corrects him. Before she gives away information about her own movements and motives.

'Do you want me to abandon your case?' she asks instead. Because of his bowed legs, he stands not much taller than she does, making it easier for her to look into his face. 'Give you your deposit back?'

'No.' He turns away, much as I would do were someone other than the girl to stare straight at me. 'No, I don't want that.'

'Well, then.' She nods. 'We'll talk. And, Peter?'

He turns back toward her, some mix of hope or sadness dragging his face down. 'Yes?'

'Thank you for helping me.' She hands the rag back. 'It was kind.'

He takes the rag then, and as he walks away, he bows his head, almost in obeisance. It is an acknowledgment, much like the title with which he addresses her, of respect. Of the difference in their states. Perhaps of the role he has come to accept, hobbled by his body and by age.

She studies him as he walks off, that peculiar rolling gait taking him slowly across the open cobblestones and toward the shadowed streets beyond. She may be green, this girl, but she has had some training. Perhaps more important, she has sense – an innate intelligence that works to piece together the apparently unconnected events of the day. I know she is curious about what brought her former gang leader here to the waterfront. Or, if not to the waterfront – which, after all, has long been the haunt of smugglers and thieves – then to his death. And whether AD's demise had any connection with the appearance of her latest client, a man whose old-school manners would seem to imply honor, if not exactly honesty. For although this place is a common assembly ground for men of all stripes, the timing of these meetings a bit too much for chance. Even without the knowledge I would give her – that I saw this man, walking deep in thought, as if he had emerged from that low stone building – she has the wit to wonder.

In one matter, what Peter said is correct. The waterfront is not safe, not for a girl like Care. For it is not merely the land and water that clash and mingle here, and that body is not the only one to have disappeared into the depths.

TEN

'I must have just missed him.' Care is talking to herself, rather than to me. We sit on a block of figured stone, the remnant of a building that once must have stood tall and proud. 'I saw him go in not that long before, and the tide is only that low for an hour. Maybe less. He can't have been there long.'

I curl my tail around my feet, enjoying the warmth that has soaked even into this hard surface. The girl has taken her shoes off and squeezes them, wringing a few mean drops out onto the ground.

'But surely someone would have noticed.' She shakes the shoe, as a wave of gratitude washes over me. I may have missed my chance down on the sand, but I am grateful to be dry. 'I mean, if he fell.'

My pleasure dissipates in a wave of annoyance. Surely, I trained her to observe the stages of death better. Surely, she should have noted what I did. Would that I could have found a way to communicate this. I duck my head in shame.

'Unless.' She bites her lip again, then shakes off the thought. 'I don't know, Blackie. I can't see him falling without crying out. And those men – someone would have heard him.'

She sighs. 'Maybe, if he was startled. Or maybe it was the noise of that truck . . .'

I am on my feet. How to tell her what I know? That the man was dead before he hit the harbor floor. I stare at her, willing her to see in my eyes an intelligence akin to hers. A helpmate, if not her former mentor.

Her own eyes are as green as mine, but distant. 'Unless he didn't scream.' She's speaking slowly, as the thought begins to take shape. And suddenly she is present, meeting my gaze with an intensity I know well. 'Blackie, what if he was dead already when he fell?'

It may be inappropriate to purr. We are discussing the demise of a man, albeit an evil one. But I cannot restrain myself, and push my head against her in an outpouring of joy. She is smart, this girl. Even with her inferior senses, she has discerned the truth.

Only, she is not finished. 'There wasn't any blood,' she says now, piecing together the evidence. 'Not that there necessarily would be, with a broken neck . . .' Her voice trails off as she drums her fingers on the stone. It is a self-soothing gesture, much like my own constant bathing. She is thinking – piecing the parts together – and I rejoice.

'I've got to get over to Quirty's,' she says at last, naming the keeper. 'I've wasted enough time and I've got cases.' She gives the shoe one final squeeze and then begins to lace it up again. 'But I'm going to find out what happened to AD, Blackie. I mean, nobody should die like that, and just be swept away by the tide.'

The girl is not looking at me. Her gaze is turned inward, toward thoughts I can only imagine. That body, perhaps, as it floated out to sea. The scrawny gang leader, as she had last seen him – full of purpose and intent. Or earlier, perhaps, when he ran her small cohort of children and teens, manufacturing and peddling the substance known as scat among the despairing of the city. Maybe she envisions something different – the tasks she has before her. I do not know.

What I do know is that her face differs in essentials from mine. Even her eyes, although they share with mine their color, appear dissimilar, not only in shape, but also in the emotion they telegraph to the world. Some of it is her lack of fur. My sleek black coat camouflages many of the ravages of time as well as both injuries and fatigue, while her bare skin – pale to the point of pallor – flushes and blanches at any provocation. Some of it is the very structure of her face, muscles that pull and shape her features.

This is why I stare at her, though she looks not at me. On her face now, I witness the play of her thoughts, if not their content. She is considering – weighing – what she knows, and the options for what lies ahead. When she gives a small nod, her mouth setting in a straight line, I know, even before she turns once more to me, that she has arrived at a decision.

'You're so funny, Blackie.' I blink up at her, in a silent query. I do not understand what she finds humorous, or why she now smiles and reaches for my head. 'Sometimes I think you're trying to read my mind. Our new client liked you, too. Did you notice?'

She rubs one warm palm down my back and then straightens, before I can find a way to reply. As well as I can read this girl, I still fail to comprehend many of her inner workings. I would have her know my confusion. My concerns about this client, the strange, heavy woman who labored up our stairs. But Care is standing, and no longer regards the twitch of my tail, or the slight backward tilt of my ears.

I breathe and compose myself, seeking solace in the knowledge that I have lightened her mood by my presence. As she hoists her bag up on her shoulder and begins to walk, I trot alongside her, my tail as elevated as I would have my state of mind.

It only drops somewhat as she turns down a narrow passage. The printer's alley, once again – a destination as familiar for its scent as for these dark, forgotten streets. I would have hoped, given the exchange at the harborside, that she might have given over this task, this client. But no, this girl has her honor. She has undertaken a case for a client, and I see now that she will put her own need aside. No matter what questions she mulls over about AD's watery end, she will conduct business first. She will, as her cant runs, 'ask the questions'.

Another turn, and the way is shadowed. The afternoon has grown warm, but here the buildings lean close. A pile of bricks draws me aside. It has existed long enough for its honeycombed spaces to serve as a warren for creatures nesting this season. I sniff, but at this hour, it is quiet. The young have already weaned and gone, their dam sleeps until dusk, safely beyond my grasp.

'Care.' One word, spoken softly, but my ears twitch at the sound. A small man, as pale as dust, has emerged from a hidden entrance, several steps down. 'Please.'

He steps aside, holding a heavy door that hangs badly from its latches. She passes inside, but he lingers, surveying the street for signs of life.

He does not consider me, nor the female who shudders and

turns, her dreams disturbed by my spoor. This makes it easy
for me to slip by, a dark shadow on a shady street, as he turns
to follow her inside, and the door swings closed.

'A client, you say?' He has seated himself behind his desk,
while the girl sits opposite. The tools of his trade – a pen in a
chipped mug, his makeshift inkwell; the magnifying glass that
allows this mole-like man to read – are arrayed before him, as
is a sheet of paper, scraped clean, for notes. But his hands
remain in his lap, and as I circumnavigate the room, I make
note of them. Their placement, beneath the surface of the desk
and out of sight to his human visitor, suggest secrets or a desire
to be hidden. Clenched fingers, intertwined, suggest a fear or
apprehension that he would control. Fear of the girl, perhaps?
It does not seem likely. The two have done business before,
and she has served him honestly and well. 'A woman? And I
sent her to you?'

I sniff at his knee, which bounces nervously in place. The
line of questioning has upset him, it is clear.

'Heavy set, with an accent.' Care is describing the first client,
the woman who seeks her brother. 'She said she had received
letters sent by you. Sent by her brother. It contained a bequest.
Her name – the name she gave me – is Augusta, Augusta Blaze.'

Blaze – the fire. The association comes to me unbidden, and
I sit back, considering. This man, the keeper, may have reason
to be disturbed. The woman who ascended so laboriously to
Care's office had an uncanny air about her, as uncontrollable as
flame, despite the encumbrances of illness and of age. The way
she stopped on the stairs, apparently to catch her breath; the
manner in which she greeted me, as if she knew me. As if . . .

No, it's not possible. I shudder to shake off the strange fancy
that had possessed me. I would remember. Besides, the man is
talking.

'She came to see me about an old client, she said?' His
fingers tighten on each other. 'And then I gave her your name?'

Care's body moves as she nods. She does not see his disquiet,
or not its depth. She seeks only to clarify her story. 'She has
lost touch with her brother.' I hear her pause. Consider. She
has begun to question the client's story, perhaps. Or simply

seeks to separate that which she can verify from that which she has been told. 'She believes him to be dead, and she seeks – information. She says you referred her to me.'

'I do refer clients.' The man's voice grows quieter, as if he were weighing his words. Sifting through his memory, perhaps, for such a one as the girl speaks of? Or does he hear the gap in her story – the omission of the object for which she seeks. 'Those I know, at any rate.' A pause. 'I understand that you are trying to increase your trade.'

'And I'm grateful.' She's quick to reassure him, and I find myself wondering why she has not told the man the whole story. Not that I find fault with her caution. 'My business is growing.'

She says no more about his referrals, about the work he sends her way. She doesn't have to. They both understand that they share a particular stratum of this city: those who have papers or items they wish to keep secure, but who lack the strength or the allies to guarantee this. Those who still eke out a living or trade in more than their physical labor. Not many of their kind still exist here, making them natural allies, even if past services did not link them together. 'But I thought that, because you met with her, maybe you could tell me more. Maybe you remember something about her brother or the letter he sent. She didn't give me much to go on.'

A glimmer of insight makes my whiskers prick up. She does not believe in the keepsake the woman says she seeks. Does not believe in its importance, at any rate. Nor does she entirely trust the man seated opposite.

'If I could . . .' He flattens his hands on his thighs now. He inhales.

'I'm not asking you to break a confidence,' Care says. She hears his hesitation. Gleans from it the scruples that bind his profession.

'No, it's not that.' A sigh, or maybe just the exhalation of that breath. 'This woman you speak of – she sounds familiar. I may know her – know *of* her, I should say. She has not visited, nor anyone who could be her. In fact, only one person has come seeking a finder, or one who offers the services you provide.'

She straightens in her seat, waiting.

'A young man came the other day. He was asking questions,

looking for answers about a man who had disappeared . . .' The
hands are still now, resting on the worn fabric. 'I advised him
to seek you out,' he says. 'A young man, pale, with red hair.
He said his name was Rafe.'

'Rafe?' She catches herself and reveals no more. I am heart-
ened. By her own means, she must have discerned this man's
anxiety. The tension of an untruth or something concealed
somewhere among his words. She has experience with this man,
a history that has created trust, but she knew enough to be
circumspect. Now, however, she requires that he be more forth-
coming. 'And – he came alone?'

I could purr. Belated as her words are, she is questioning the
assignment, the man on the wharf – Peter – who hired her.

'Yes.' The syllable comes slowly. He is weighing his words,
this man. Deciding how much to share, much as she did. These
are the ways, the times, even among those who have come to
know each other, to some extent. 'He did, and he described the
man in much the same terms you did. But he was inquiring for
another, he told me.' I hear him swallow. See his body rise up
and relax as he exhales. This, then, is what he has been with-
holding. 'He said he was working for someone. That he would
find the missing man himself, and that he didn't need to hire
anyone. He wanted the custom for himself.'

Now it is the girl's turn to fall silent, and the man seated
opposite her to deliberate and wonder. His hands flex once more
against his legs, but he keeps his peace. Waiting, I assume, for
the girl to offer her thoughts.

'If I did you wrong,' he says at last. 'If I put you in harm's
way in any way, I am sorry. And I—' another swallow, another
flex – 'I will do what I can. I could help you leave this city. I
have contacts, to the south.'

'No, it's not that.' She pauses. 'But thank you. It's—' A sigh
as heavy as the girl herself. 'This man? Rafe? I believe he's
gone missing too.'

The room falls silent, and I prick my ears forward, in the hope
that she will notice what is plainly obvious to me. She cannot
smell him, the traces his body emits that reveal fear or surprise.
She cannot see the agitation I witnessed in the movements of his
hands and his feet. But this quiet, this undue calm – surely she

will hear how unnatural it is. Will question why her statement did not unnerve him, or raise further lines of inquiry.

'You're not surprised.' Her voice so composed, I close my eyes to savor it.

'No.' Another sigh. 'I didn't know, but no, I'm not.'

Silence, but she waits. She is learning, this girl. I may have told her, once upon a time, but she has seen for herself how silence works. The weight of words will pry open the lips of most, secrets being heavier than simple truth.

'I did try to warn him.' And so it begins. 'He wasn't trained in seeking, as you were. He didn't know how to inquire without revealing too much.'

The girl is holding her breath. He is building to something, and she can hear it.

'The man he was asking about – the man *you're* asking about – is dead. Murdered. He was killed because of his own inquiries. Because of the work he did too well,' says the little man, the keeper. 'I gather you did not realize it, Care, but the man you seek is one you knew. He was your teacher. You knew him as the old man.'

ELEVEN

The room spins and then contracts. I open my mouth to wail – my chest filling with the howl – and barely catch myself in time. I am on all fours. My tail extended. The fur along my back and ruff on end in terror and alarm. But for all my shock, I am unnoticed. I am a cat, small by human standards, and I am hidden beneath a desk.

It is as I feared. My world has been upended, but still I can keep my own counsel. I exhale, feeling my swollen sides subside, and listen as the man continues to talk.

'I didn't contact anyone. Not even you,' he is saying. His voice is sad, but easy. I believe he speaks the truth. 'When word got out, I mourned him, in my fashion. We were never friends, not really. But he did use my services. He trusted me, and I saw in him a remnant of the old ways, from before.'

'But my client – the woman . . .' Care interrupts. She has been shaken, as well. I hear it in her tone, her hesitation. 'She said you sent her.'

'No. Though maybe he reached out to her before he – before the end. He had great faith in you, you know.'

I sink back to the floor, grief flooding me. If I could remember . . . but I don't. Only that night – the ambush. I was lured and trapped, the hunter turned into prey. Led as much by my hubris as by the trail so carefully laid to that warehouse and to what should have been – what was – my watery end. A masterful plan, designed to dispose of a formidable opponent. Of me.

This is why I worry so at the girl's too often heedless acts. She sees the world as I once did, a slapdash place of petty thieves and thoughtless thugs. The scavengers who scrap and grapple over the city like some wounded beast. Foes who can be bested, wrongs corrected and made right. She does not comprehend that one will drives them all. A criminal mastermind, the shadow behind so many little crimes. A dark brilliance whom, I fear, has noticed her, who may – in his own way – be grateful for a service she did him unwittingly.

The case touched her heart – a death, a woman hurt, a child endangered – and she undertook it with honesty and courage. But the brute who she exposed, who subsequently faced rough justice at the hands of his fellows, was only a minor player. For although that cruel and petty man was guilty of the crimes that Care would have had prosecuted, his greater sin – in the eyes of those with power – was a betrayal of trust, his perfidy endangering his master's greater plans. For a while after that, he toyed with her, easing her way with clients and with custom, remuneration for services she did not fully understand. Perhaps he hoped to bring her under his sway. He is aware of her now, of that I have grown increasingly confident. She did him a service, it is true, but he is not one to be grateful for long. He is not one to be trusted.

'This line of inquiry is dangerous.' I look up. The man's words so echo my own thoughts as to baffle me. Could I, in fact, have spoken? But, no, I no longer possess the ability to phrase my thoughts in language. And the girl, it seems, will not be persuaded.

'Please, Care . . .' She is rising, and he with her. He would stay her, if he could. Time has passed, and I have missed the details of their conversation. She is gathering papers – her notes, or perhaps his. 'You can't.'

'I can.' Conviction, calm and strong. 'And I will.' She steps away and turns. 'You knew the old man. You knew he trained me. He trusted me,' she says. 'Now people are asking after him, and so I will find out why.'

'First AD, and now the old man.' She is resting against a wall nearby. She has left the keeper, but not gone far. The revelations weigh on her, and she sinks back against the crumbling brick and sits, the ground here newly dried by the late-day sun. 'I wonder . . .'

She looks at me, seated on a slab of asphalt beside her. It is dark and warm, and raised slightly above the earth. I stare back, wishing once again for her to see in my green eyes the aware-ness I possess of her.

'The old man would say there is no such thing as a

coincidence.' She smiles a little, the memory a fond one. 'He
would have me look for connections.'

I flick my ears forward, listening. I do not recall passing
along this advice but it is useful, and I would have her bide it.

'And AD showing up? Coming back now? Could that be
related?'

I bristle at his name. That man – AD – and what becomes
of him matters little to me. He was vermin. Lower, even, without
such purpose as a rat or beetle may have, and I would not have
her waste her time thinking of such a one. That woman, however
– no, I cannot mull this over now. Not while I would watch the
girl and listen.

But she has fallen silent, only the subtle movements of her face
hinting at the play of her thoughts. That sadness – her downcast
mouth – suggests she is thinking of the old man, her mentor, and
his violent death. But as her jaw tightens and she blinks back any
hint of tears, I know she has moved on. Does she ponder the
meaning of these cases, the reasons they may intersect each other
– and her life? Does she question the little man, the keeper, who
conveyed this news? Their history would have her trust him. As
well her nature, which seeks kinship and companions in a way
foreign to my kind.

When she rises, brushing the dirt from her pants, I ready
myself to follow. Back to the keeper's room, I suspect. Back
where she can press him for what he has kept hidden, for the
secrets that weigh heavy on this case.

When she turns, instead, toward the waterfront, I grow
alarmed. As fraught a place as it is by day, as dusk descends its
commerce also changes into that which may endanger the girl.

It is not dark, not yet, as she returns to the dockside, to the
open area where the men gathered and the trucks came and
went. But already the atmosphere has altered. The boisterous
workers have left, seeking solace for their disappointments, if
not rest, for another day. Those that remain are quiet. They
hang by the edges of the open space – by the pier itself, or
over by the stone house – waiting, perhaps, for a summons. For
an order that will brook no argument or negotiation.

Three of them linger by the wharfside, by the place where
the barrier gave way. Hunched over the embers of their smokes,

they speak softly, their manner uneasy. Laborers, ready for any task. The last of the afternoon light reflects off the eyes of one who gives us a furtive glance. He licks his lips and then turns in again. They are waiting, anxious, but the girl is unafraid. She walks toward them, openly, crossing the cobblestones where the truck had idled, head up and back straight.

It is her poise, as much as her gender, I believe, that rouses them. They stand up straighter. One palms his rude cigarette, pinching it out for later. Another sucks the last of the goodness from the weed, then grinds it out on the damp below his feet. The third keeps smoking. It is he who had glanced around, looking for a confederate, perhaps. Or a command. It is he the girl addresses when she reaches them, her voice low but clear, even as I circle the open ground to observe in my own fashion.

'I'm looking for someone,' she says. She is not as tall as the man she addresses, but her confidence gives her stature. 'A man of the docks. We have business with each other.'

The third man nods, taking a drag. The ember illuminates a face drawn and grey. Not as old as his posture would suggest, but hunger of one sort or another has aged him.

'His name is Rafe,' the girl continues. 'He works with an older man, Peter.'

The first man – the one who palmed the butt – starts slightly, his quick intake of breath audible to me. The girl must hear it. Her ears are not like mine, but I see the rapid shift of her eyes – to the man and back. Yes, she noted the telling start but she will not betray her knowledge.

'Lot of guys work here.' The thin man, the leader, makes a show of dropping his own butt, of extinguishing it with one worn shoe. 'What of it?'

'I've been paid to find him.' The magic phrase – the bait. 'And I can pay in turn. For information, if it's good.'

The thin man looks away. To his colleagues, I believe, though more to keep them in line than in consultation. 'He paid you; maybe he'd pay us, too. Maybe he don't want to be found.'

A laugh. Forced, but I doubt they can tell how transparent it sounds. 'Don't be stupid,' Care says. 'Peter and I – we're working together. I know they're a team.' Silence. 'We'll make it worth your while.'

'Rafe was working solo.' The man who started at the name. His leader shoots him a look, but he continues. 'Got a gig off the docks. He had plans.'

'Plans?' Care keeps her voice neutral.

The drawn man doesn't bother. 'Sounds like someone got too big for himself. Didn't know his place, most likely.' The threat is clear, but the nervous man keeps talking.

'I saw him – after. He was going into town.' He licks his lips, his eyes darting back and forth. 'A private job.'

Care nods. Confirmation of what she knows, but also to encourage the man. 'Who hired him?'

'Who do you think?' The thin man, the leader, breaks in. 'Who runs everything down here? So Rafe got an offer. Good for him. He's been carrying that old man for ages, the way he works. He'll come back when he wants his pay. Unless he's done a runner.' He stops and tilts his head, his face now quizzical. 'You with the rozzers?'

'Me? No.' She can barely keep the squeak of surprise out of her voice. 'Not my line. So Rafe had been on a work crew, huh?'

I hear the effort, the way she keeps her voice flat – her face calm. This question matters to her. I cannot tell if they can hear how much.

'He wishes.' The third man, who'd been silent until now. 'The work crews, they get fed.'

'There's only one boss, anyway.' The leader looks away, toward the stone house. He's getting tired. Any moment now, he'll shut her down. 'You know that.'

Care nods. I wish she did. 'Back to town, then.' She stares at the nervous man. Behind the leader's back their eyes connect, and she holds his gaze until he breaks away. 'So I'll be off.'

'Good luck.' The thin man fishes another loosie from his pocket, and the third man leans in with a match. Another glance back, and Care begins to walk away. Across to where the warehouses begin, dark and shadowed as the day fails, and there she pauses.

A moment later, and he's with her – the nervous man. Rafe's friend. 'You'll find him, won't you?' he asks, eyes wide, then glances back over his shoulder. 'He only wanted something, you know, of his own.'

'To get away from Peter?' Care speaks cautiously.

'It's not like that. Not really.' Another glance. The men are moving. One looks up. 'It's just – Rafe's a man now. You know.' He licks his lips. 'And the woman came to him.'

'The woman?'

A fast nod. 'Right away. As soon as she got off the boat.'

'Hey, Naldo!' The leader, looking up. 'You get lost?'

'The boat?' Care reaches for his arm.

'I can't—' The nervous man – Naldo – pulls away. Fusses with his fly. 'Just some boat. From elsewhere. Hang on!' He waddles out of the shadow, hiking his pants up. There's laughter, as he rejoins them and the three of them march off.

TWELVE

I should hunt, once darkness is complete. The girl is sleeping, at long last. At rest having written down her observations from the day. The night air is cool but rich, as full of life as a summer stream to one such as I, and the window beckons. I am hungry, and I should feed, the better able to accompany the girl when once again she rises.

But although I am a beast, a creature of appetite and no remorse, I sit here. I am no longer subject to the anxieties of men, but there is much I would understand. Too much, and I am confused.

This woman – Augusta – is a puzzle. On the face of it, her quest could be simple enough. She sought a man and hired an eager lad on the docks. When he failed – for her appearance here implied he did – she sought another, a more experienced seeker. Care, who now sleeps here by me.

I would not have her fret over his fate. His subsequent disappearance may be of no great significance. It is likely that, as is the custom, he received an advance payment, on commission of the job. Perhaps he did not care to share his earnings with his former partner. Perhaps he is on the job still and will resurface once his task is complete or he has given up. Discounting the man Peter's concern, there is no evidence of misadventure. Yet such stories end badly more often than not, and the bow-legged man did not appear to be faking his distress.

This does not prove his innocence. Indeed, the events on the wharf suggest otherwise. His appearance by the body of the man known as AD may be dismissed as happenstance. The former gang leader was trouble, and such mischief as he was wont to involve himself in can readily be found near where the man Peter works. But both his bearing and his affect suggest otherwise, as he lingered, ill at ease, by the meeting place of those in power. And it was he, not his missing colleague, who had cash to spare – albeit for a seemingly benevolent enterprise.

No, I do not trust that man and would that Care had queried him further before she took his commission. But still, it is that woman who bothers me. And although the girl knows her client has most likely lied – assuming the keeper had little reason to deny a reference – this is not my primary area of concern. It may be that her first investigator, this Rafe, reported back, urging the woman to seek out the girl. It may be that she dismissed him, perhaps disposed of him, as no longer necessary for her search. The girl is wise to the ways of this world. She will come to this possibility, given time. She will take precautions, I believe.

No, what bothers me is this woman's quest itself. 'My brother,' she said. 'A letter.' And yet no letter was sent, if the keeper can be trusted. No package to aid the flight of a grieving relative. If grieving relative she is.

The girl stirs in her sleep, shifting on the sofa. Her fingers twitch, as does her lip, chapped to bleeding. Were she one of my own kin, I would believe her to be dreaming of the hunt. The kill. Perhaps she is, though the prey she seeks is more elusive – not those whom she is hired to find as much as a family of sorts, free from the constraints of poverty and fear.

Family. I maintain my vigil as the girl settles back, the rise and fall of her thin ribs slowing as her breathing calms again. I think of the woman who sat there and of what she said. Her brother. That name . . . The keeper confirmed it.

That woman was looking for me.

No, not as I am now, a large black cat whose preternaturally glossy coat hides the scars and damages of age. But who I once was, before this life. Before this body, which the girl hauled from its own watery grave. A man.

Only I have no recollection of this woman. This sister. Or of any family or anything like beyond the ragtag crew of associates I assembled to do my bidding. The dead man was one once, before his interest in the chemicals he concocted and distributed made him less reliable than others. This girl, whose intelligence was apparent early on. But a sister? No.

Near silent on my velvet paws, I leap to the desktop, the better to examine the papers there. This woman – yes – I catch her distinctive aroma. The man Peter, too, whose sweat and earthy funk denoted his status as clearly as his calloused hands. Were I still my former self, I would read these notes. Review the answers each gave to the girl's questions and her observations, jotted down once each had left.

As I am now, I cannot. But I have other skills and, open-mouthed, I breathe in each document, the better to capture their scent and all it may contain. I do not know the truth about this woman. And as the girl has said, I do not trust the accident that seems to link these cases, clients from two different worlds. I would know more about them for my own peace of mind. I would seek to illuminate the darkness of who I was, before. And more than that, I would understand why they seek to involve the girl, and how. Her sleep is quiet now, and I would protect her.

A moment more of concentration and then I leap. The floor, the windowsill, and I am out. Not to hunt for sustenance, or not merely, for I am a carnivore and I must feed. But for knowledge, and the night is fresh and wild as I set out.

Before the moon moves much behind the clouds, I have satisfied my hunger and have bathed. Whiskers alert, I take in the air, considering where to begin my next hunt – for more elusive prey.

If I could read, I might have noted where the man frequented. The woman, I recall, had not yet a fixed abode. The breeze shifts, bringing with it even here the piquancy of salt. Of course – the harborside. If that man Peter lingers there, I may get more from him. By night, as well, I should be free to examine any vessel anchored close, or at least the barks and barges that passengers may use. If I cannot track that woman to her lair, I may still manage to uncover something of her origins. Perhaps, the thought springs up as I lope silently along the empty street, I may discover something of myself.

Unlike the girl, I am not bound to pavement. Before long, I leave the simple road for a more direct route. Over rooftops; threading rubble now inhabited by those that sense and cower at my passing. Along an alley where polluted water runs, an outlet to the waterside nearby. And then – that gutter. The drain where I awoke to this strange new life.

I am an animal, but still I pause, my ears and tail erect. What does it mean, that I came back? That the apparent ministrations of this girl recalled me? And who was I before?

It is like a wisp of cloud. A momentary dulling of the moon, and nothing more. I am not made for musings like these, if indeed I ever was, more emotion than pure thought. The evidence of my senses, the ratiocination of a disciplined and superior mind. I have always been a hunter, and so I shall continue. A flick of my tail, and I am off, a shadow in the dark and as silent as that cloud.

The waterfront at this hour is quiet. The last of the surreptitious nighttime trade is finished. The muffled oars stilled and stowed. Even the laborers who work at this second trade have gone by now, to the area alehouses or to their own rough beds. Here by the water, the wind is cutting still, a harbinger of the changing season, making any shelter preferable to the open air.

My presence, I am aware, extends the hush still further. There are rodents here that could challenge me in size and strength, raised up on the rich diet of the ships. Other felines, too, I know, from traces in the air. But I am large and male. A black giant of my kind, and while I feel my age, no weakness is apparent in me. Sometime, perhaps soon, I will be challenged. Tonight, however, I pass unopposed.

Aware of the glitter of frightened eyes, I strut, moving boldly from the shadow to the open place where earlier that truck had stood. I raise my snout and close my eyes, the better to sample the air. To me, that current is a banquet. Undaunted by the chill it carries, even as my game left leg twinges, I take the breeze in through mouth and nose for full effect. Fish and other creatures, as life perseveres here, despite the ash that coats the ground, the oily sheen on the water that collects in the drain. The rich, ripe fetor of decay. A reminder of the man we found earlier, I now realize, though his corpse has been taken by the tide. And of my fellow beasts, for sure, and all the effluvia of men that lingers and will last, long after they have gone.

A rustling disturbs my reverie, and I turn. An opossum, her lumbering gait over by that low stone building easily audible. She does not care that I hear her, that others of my kind may be spying from their hidden places. She is large enough to disregard those eyes, her claws useful for more than unearthing grubs. Besides, I catch a faint sweetness. Milk. Her apparent disregard for predators reveals a deeper motive. She would hurry back to her young, too big for the pouch but not, alas, for the sleek rat who also caught their spoor. I see her hunched back as she waddles in the dark.

The squeal that follows surprises me not at all. Here, with such rich fare, the mother did not have to venture far, and the would-be predator, too used to rich pickings, had not the wit to count on her return.

An almost imperceptible shift takes place. A hunt, a kill. A reordering of life. A small dark shape darts from the pier side. And with it, a new aroma is released. More rot – that fleeing creature had been scavenging in garbage – and something else. I close my eyes again and see a green place, blossoming. Faintly floral with an overlay of spices. A memory from older times. Or, no, the other day. The woman Augusta passed by here. The trail is faded, far from recent, and I begin to walk. This much, perhaps, is true. The woman did arrive by ship, leaving some rag or other detritus in the trash that younger rat disturbed.

It was well he ran. I lick my chops at the thought of his tender flesh. But that last kick, toppling a small heap of trash as he took off, did me a service, and soon I am on it, pawing carefully at its edge. Yes, a scrap of paper here, beneath the rinds of some bitter fruit that would have masked its scent. The rodent has earned his reprieve.

I swipe the rind away, the better to take in her fragrance. There is something scrawled on the paper. A letter, perhaps, or contract. I close my eyes. I fight the rush of frustration that I am incapacitated by my current form, incapable of deciphering a simple note. For if I were not as I am now, this scrap would have remained unfound. I cannot read, but I can smell.

If only that rind did not stink so. I can barely abide it and do not know its like. Almost I recoil – and then I do, aghast. Has reason left with the other higher powers of my mind? Steeling myself I approach the peel. Its acrid bite – *citrus* – the word comes unbidden. A fruit not common in these times, in this northern land. With a leap, I am on the wharfside, standing on the tar-soaked wood that serves as barrier and border both. One small ship bobs at anchor, too far for me to reach but not to sense. I open my mouth once more, and shut my eyes. Yes, it is from this conveyance that fruit was brought. That fruit and – I must surmise – the woman, too. She ate this fruit as she was writing. Already, I can picture it, her fingers gripping its dappled surface. Almost, I can taste it – the acid of the juice. The fragrant pulp, reminiscent of another clime.

The letter. The realization nearly topples me from my perch. This woman came from beyond our shores. Summoned, so she said, by a letter. And while I had my doubts as to the keeper's truthfulness, my own senses now confirm, in part his tale. He could not have written to this woman, telling her of the old man's death. Nor is it likely that any other of his loose-knit guild did either, not if I read these signs aright. For in these days of chaos and decay, no service would bring a missive as far as this ship hailed from. Not in the mere months since the old man's demise – and certainly not in time for a bereaved relative to sell up and set sail, arriving here within the year.

I jump down from the low wall and begin to pace, working over the meaning of this realization in my mind. The woman wasn't summoned, then, and yet she knew, as surely as she could, that the old man – that *I* – had died. For this revelation lends credence to the keeper's word – and that the young man Rafe was hired as the woman descended to the dock.

It is too much. I stop and stare. The moon reflecting off the water brings to mind the facts of my demise. The three men, silhouetted against the sky. The water. Drowning. Perhaps this Rafe has met his end. Perhaps he bobbed in the rushing tide, and sank, as the girl's former leader did. Perhaps locating her was his real assignment, and death was his reward.

And the girl? I turn away and begin to move again. One man sought her and is gone. One woman, too, though she will return again and soon. Ahead, the low stone building squats, like a toad, on the wet surface, its back to that brilliant moon. I think of the man Peter. Of the men who watched me sink, and of another who commanded – who commands still, I believe.

My ears flick back and to the sides. I hear no men, no step or breathing. Perhaps inside some answers may be found.

As I myself have learned, the folly of men is enormous. They are tripped up by their confidence and strength. In this case, it is stone that they have put their faith in. Low and heavy, the building sits upon the wharf. But cold stone will not warm them nor fill their bellies, impressive though it may seem. Sure enough, as I slip behind the building, I find a bulkhead, leading to a cellar or other store. A necessary portal for both fuel and food, its doors are made of wood for ease of access. But here beside the water, that wood has grown soft. The rodents that went quiet on my approach have already breached it, and with their passing, I find my own way clear.

The building is empty of men at this hour. I hear no snores, none of the muttered breathing that would give away an occupant. Not that the structure is unoccupied. As I made my way into the basement, squeezing through the gap between the rotted bulkhead and its warped frame and down a rickety stair, I heard the scurry and panic at my approach. Even as I begin to explore – this basement has housed a fragrant variety of stores – I feel their eyes. No matter. I am not hunting, not for the likes of them, tonight.

In this windowless space, my nose is my guide, and I make a careful round. The bulkhead, feet from the wharfside, has clearly been the portal of choice. The warmth of spices and the rich sweetness of foodstuffs – fruit and, yes, meat – have come through there. Have been stacked here, in the cool, for long enough to begin to decay. The essence of one bundle has leached into the earthen floor. I take it in, as images of some other, greener place come to mind. This basement is small, compared to the warehouses across the way. But it is private. It has but one bulkhead, hidden from the common sight. One set of stairs that leads up to the main floor.

I do not know the nature of all the wares that have moved through here, but I can hypothesize. Luxury goods, perhaps, or contraband, the aromas, while enticing, are far from familiar. Only near one corner, where bales are piled against the stone wall, do I begin to pick up a more accustomed smell: bitter, even in its current state. Stinging to the sensitive membrane of my nose and eyes. The drug called scat is stored here in among the bundles.

I raise my head and will my mouth open, to ascertain the truth. Yes, it is the drug, bundled into bales piled higher than a man. A surfeit of the substance, if my knowledge serves as any guide, but packed in oiled clothes that almost contain its stench. That man, AD, concocted such, in just such a basement, by a low fire. But even though he produced the vile chemical for trade, his end results were never so well protected. Nor – another sniff, despite the acid sting – so potent.

I sit and lick my nose. The taste is bitter on my tongue, but the suggestion that follows hard upon it is sweet. AD once dealt in such as this, though in lesser quantity and in quality more dilute. Perhaps he sought an in with those who would produce and distribute once again. Sought, as the boy suggested, to gather his former minions again, and set them to the trade.

Perhaps, as those on the wharf suggested, he fell prey to his own creation while incarcerated. Life in the work camps is hard, and few come back unchanged. The concoction here is stronger than what he could create. 'The scat,' he was heard to yell. It could well be true.

Only, then, why did I not detect this substance on him, on his body, even from the wharfside? It would have been readily discernible – burned for its fumes – if he'd consumed it. And why then did he shadow the girl? He could not think she would return to do his bidding. And, if an addict, he would not bother seeking revenge. No, I lick my nose again – its dampness vulnerable to the biting, acrid air – there is more here than a simple tale of greed or of addiction. It is a riddle that I have yet to solve.

Perhaps it does not matter. Like so much of the commerce that survives these days, this trade is evil and serves, no doubt, that one master who commands these docks. Whatever the dead man's part, I would not have the girl involved. Would staunch her curiosity about her onetime patron. I am not easy in his death, less so in the final actions of his life. But I would keep her from this store, from mixing any further in this corrupt trade.

I sneeze, the slight sound startling in the silence of the cellar.

I salve my nose once more and blink. Despite its careful packaging the fumes are harsh to one as sensitive as I; their effect grows with time in this enclosed space. Time to move on. Ears alert to dangers, I make my way up the wooden stairs and, using the flat of my head as another would his hand, I push the door aside.

Another scent, as well as welcome, fresher air. The onion funk of sweat and dirt. Yes – there it is. The one trace I had expected. That man Peter. I did not sense him in the basement, although it is possible that any tracks there have been covered by the noxious bales. But here – on the ground floor – for certain. And other smells as well.

Smoke, ash, and the heavy spice of tobacco. An office, then, I surmise, looking around. The moon's glow through the windows illuminates one large desk composed of heavy wood, as well as the tall metal cabinets that I once would have opened with ease. Nothing for it now, I am left to sniff at their base. The feet that stood here were cleaner than those below, and they were shod in leather, albeit of a dry and friable kind. Clerks, then, and not management, but still a step above the basement, in every sense.

In search of something more, I leap upon the desk – and nearly come to harm. The surface I have landed on is piled with paper, slick and cheap. Slick as well with wear, I realize as I bend to taste its essence. The tang of sweat and blood and – clearly – fear are on these pages. Not from the hand that wrote upon them. Although I cannot read, my eyes are not so dim as to mistake the even scribblings of some nameless clerk for something panicked. No, these pages must bear witness. *Testimony*, the word comes to me. They sit awaiting action or dismissal, I suspect. For certain, they suggest that violence has been done.

This does not bode well, and I continue my rounds, seeking all the while the distinctive odor of that one man, Care's client. He was here, at least in passing. His feet stepped on this carpet, his hand sweated on this banister climbing to the second floor. And others too. And while I would not have her risk an inquiry, I cannot resist. I climb up to the landing and take stock.

This floor is different, private. A flight above the clerks below, but Peter has been here. This carpet, richer than the one below, is worn with pacing, though not his. He stood quiet, waiting, before a door. As silent in his way as the borers in the walls. My senses are acute enough to detect his presence. His sweat. Fear, again. I recall his mien and bearing, when I saw him on the wharf. He was worried, I believe. Chewing over some turn of fate that did not please him, but, I suspect, that he did not control. I can picture him, here, called upon to wait. It would be an anxious time for him, and I doubt he would have the capacity to refuse whatever task he was called upon to do. A laborer picked from the dock. Older, and now alone, his partner missing. What would his worth be to one of the great of this world?

A slip and scuttle behind the wainscoting calls to mind the quarry I sought earlier. This would be predation of another sort, the man set loose. As hunter? Or as bait? I would find out more.

No men are here, not even on this upper floor. I would hear them, even were they sleeping or at rest. Men cannot be silent, I have learned. I should have known, of course. Unbidden, a dream – no, a memory – comes to me. I am crouched behind a bushel. Contraband, an evil-smelling drug, less refined and less well packaged than the bales below. It should have hidden me from sight, as its odor, now, nearly covers my trail. But I was a man, then, and my confidence my undoing. I had been lured to that place and was expected. And despite my efforts at silence and at stealth, I was exposed and dragged forth to what I know now was my death. I had been careful, to a degree that most are not, and yet my caution did not suffice.

An image of the man AD enters my head unbidden. He, too, is part of this. Was he part of the greater scheme, when I was so entrapped? Could he have been here? I raise my nose and take the air. It is no use. The stench I identify with him – the acrid burn of that drug – has faded. And yet . . . there is something of him, here, or in the air. A dream, perhaps. A memory. Another trap? No, there is no man here. I would surely be aware.

I peer upward at the brass hardware on the door above me. A lock, perhaps, at any rate a knob. I stretch and reach, my claws raking the surface, but they can gain no purchase, and the leather of my paw pads slides on the metal. Locked or no,

I cannot open it. This, then, is the trade-off. A simple entry is denied to me, but perhaps, with scent and sound I do not need to step within to know . . .

I am a large cat, and not as agile as I may once have been. Still, I can press myself near as flat as any of my kind and do so now, my legs splayed out ungainly on the carpet, my snout to the bottom of the door. I am in luck. The building is stone and solid, but it is old. The settling that has set the bulkhead ajar and made it vulnerable to damp and teeth has forced the door off true. The gap allows for air to flow and even, yes, my paw. I reach under to see what I may find and, flexing with my claws, feel fiber begin to tear.

More carpet? I bury my face in the threads that I have retrieved. Yes, likely. A floor covering of some once-rich stuff, but it is old; it came away easily under my talon. It speaks of age and wear and unclean habits: mud and dung and tobacco ash. And something else. I reach again, paw flexing as I stretch to touch, to grab. More fibers. They catch in my claws. I fight the urge to jerk my limb back and instead, stretch further. Grains – soil, perhaps, or something fouler. Sand, maybe, from the nearby shore. My attempt brings more than fibers, though. I have loosened other substances, long trampled into the rug. I pull back my paw and nose it, taking in the tracks of men and trade, the waterfront and all its wares. And something else, both sharp and familiar that makes me bare my teeth. The iron tang of blood was spilled in that room, and although it has cooled, to my discerning tongue it still tastes fresh.

THIRTEEN

I am back before first light. Back by her side, as she sleeps on the couch.

I have the drunkard to thank. It was he who left the door ajar, a piece of broken brick securing it while he went to relieve himself in the alley beyond. He was returning as I slipped in and up the stairs, but he took no more notice of me than of the rats in the alley. It was a moment's work to ascend the stairs and to insinuate myself through the space where the door does not close tight. I leap soundlessly to the arm of the sofa and lean down to sniff her sweet and easy breath. Her slumber is dreamless, and this I am grateful for as well. As I finished my perusal of the building by the wharf and on my silent trek back, I had become concerned. Afraid of what her own inner turmoil might prompt her to, and I am relieved to find her here, lost in the oblivion of sleep.

I myself am far from slumber and settle on the sofa's arm to think. That blood was human. I tuck my forefeet beneath my breast on that thought, as if I, too, could still feel the chill of death. I cannot be certain, but proximity in time and place would suggest that the scarred and scrawny convict – AD – was its source.

Once again, I find myself regretting the hesitation that kept me from descending with the girl. From examining the corpse that lay there broken. Useless emotion, regret, and I flick my tail to dispel it. Such remnants of my human life recur with annoying regularity, and I do not doubt that that woman's appearance has provoked some latent tendency, a regression better left ignored. Particularly in this instance, when my current form restrained me, as much as any fastidious feline dislike of water or of wet.

More useful by far is an analysis of what I know and what logic would suggest. A man like AD may be killed for any number of reasons. His small-time criminality alone would not likely have put him afoul of any larger enterprise, but I cannot rule this out. His capture and incarceration revealed a weakness that more likely would have drawn a boss's ire – or, more plausibly, exposed a useful vulnerability. Indeed – I curl my tail around myself as an idea takes shape – the man's reappearance here suggests a deal was struck. A deal with law enforcement such as once were standard . . .

No, I have regressed. Once again, I am remembering another time, before this city fell so deep into decline. There was evil then, and there were clandestine bargains that linked the state and those such as I now fear. But there was a semblance of order, too. That has gone, and I do not think that such a one as that thin, scarred man would be quite so foolish as to be unaware. If an agreement was reached in exchange for freedom, for the liberty to beg and scrabble for his life back on the docks, it was made with the man in the low stone house. A man, as I recall, he sought first in his old haunts. A man he went willingly to meet, after time spent in the city. Spying on Care, her young friend said.

The girl stirs and turns, and I watch her as she settles, slipping off once again. Her face is peaceful as she sleeps. Although she has begun to show the contours of womanhood – cheekbones accented by her poor diet, a length of bone only recently emerged – she sleeps as if a child, heedless and seemingly untroubled by her dreams.

Would that her rest could always be so calm. For a moment, almost, I am grateful for my mute state. For the change that has left me as dumb as any beast, here by her side. For as such, I cannot share what I have found nor what I infer. Neither the apparent place of that man's death, nor my conjecture that perhaps her onetime leader was killed on an errand for he who runs this city – was killed, perhaps, after reporting on this girl or on some activity in which she has a role.

As a lock of that parti-colored hair shifts as she exhales, I consider and reject hypotheses. It seems unlikely, I decide, that his body was left for her to find. The onrush of the tide, the window of discovery, all would make staging such a scene too chancy.

But his return to the city? His appearance first at a site the girl had staked out and, then, at that stone house? No, I am glad that she cannot read my thoughts – weighing links between her clients and this man. I am glad she sleeps.

What did he say? My tail beats out a rhythm as I run through what I know. Too little. He was seen spying on us, and not just by the boy. 'The scat,' he was heard to say – to yell – within those walls. Perhaps. I do not trust reports given out by men who would dismiss a death so easily. Nor do I believe he was needed to 'cook', to practice his foul alchemy. But the man AD had made his living dealing such wares, as well. Supplying those in need and encouraging consumption, though surely the store beneath that low stone house would supply a larger appetite, a larger market than any he had known.

Was he sought out for some secondary skill, and then found lacking? Did he, in desperation, demand a share? A role in some larger enterprise? Or was the drug secondary to another task – a report viewed as somehow lacking or less than frank?

Or did he in fact complete his mission? Report back what he was sent to find, expecting a reward, only to be discarded as of no more utility? Such usage is foreign to me as I am now. I kill efficiently and without regret, but only for food or to protect myself or my own. But I know of those who take their pleasure in toying with their prey. Who discard the broken object once it no longer serves to amuse. Was AD such a one? I do not know which fate bodes worse for the girl I love, only that I would keep her far from any so engaged.

Outside, behind me, the sun begins to rise. The window, still ajar, admits the bustle of the waking day. The rumble of a truck, its gears grinding from long and sorry use. A shout as some unfortunate is rousted, half asleep or drunk, from beneath a vendor's cart. And somewhere, out of sight, a plaintive call. A bird, driven by instinct, sings out his presence and the day. My ears twitch back. The echo of another life.

I walked these streets as summer bloomed. My senses were not then what they are now, but I had trained myself to listen, alert to such signs around me. I hear him yet again, as I did then, and I am there.

Summer, hotter then, and green. The bird – his braggart cry – falls silent as another passes. He quiets before I can attain his perch, and I know to peer about me. To note what has stopped his call, and why.

I find my reason – a figure, too large for stealth and yet of no apparent threat. I am by nature quieter than that bird, even then, and yet less cautious. I see the figure and approach. She is in pursuit of a certain truth – I know this, though I know not how – and willing to risk communing with others to forward my quest.

A faint flutter, almost silent as the bird takes flight. I notice and dismiss this as the timidity of lesser creatures. I, too, may be viewed a threat, although I hunt elsewhere, purely by my size and strength. The timing of that flight, however, rankles slightly. A question begins to form. And then I realize. The figure on the path does not wait for me, or not alone. Without acknowledging my presence, she lifts her head to greet a man. Tall and lean, his features sharp. He does not note my presence, I believe, as I crouch down on haunches not yet stiff with age. But she does, and as I stand there, transfixed, she bends and then extends her hand to me. I know this woman, and as I stretch my body, whiskers alert for the hint of violence or of fear, I come to realize she knows me – both in the feline form I now assume and as that tall, lean man who sought her aid.

'Blackie?'

'*No!*' I jerk back, as if burned. '*That is not my name!*' The words form in my head, but all that emerges is a yowl. And I wake. I am frozen on the arm of a ragged sofa, claws dug deep in fabric already torn. Above me, stands a girl. *The* girl, Care, her face now knit with sorrow. It is not she whom I'd imagined, transfixing me with her stare. She who knew me – who *saw* me in some vital way. No, this girl, whose brows now gather in dismay, does not even know my name. But she is dear to me, and I, apparently, to her. One hand hovers near me, hesitant. And so, rising, I push my head into her palm and close my eyes. She holds herself stiff and still at first, and then relaxes, and as she cradles my skull, her fingers working underneath my jaw, I unwind as well, and I begin to purr.

'I've had the strangest dream.' She talks as to herself, even after she has settled, once again, upon the couch. 'I was – somewhere – a street that I don't know. You were there, too.' She smiles at me. 'But different somehow. More – a cat, if that makes any sense.'

I gaze up at her, alert. She could be speaking of my past life, though how she would know of this, I cannot begin to understand.

'I think it might have been a memory.' That smile turns inward. Fades. 'The old man was training me. He had me shadowing him, not that I was any good. I think it was a meeting he'd set up. A contact – not a client. Only the woman never showed, not that I saw at any rate. I remember him standing, looking thoughtful. Only, in my dream, he's not alone. He's looking at a cat. At you.'

That's all, but it is enough. A tantalizing fragment of the past with which I continue to rebuild my history. The girl rises to begin her day. I know her patterns well enough to rest easy as she leaves to seek water and to wash. The sound of plumbing barely registers as I mull over what she has said and what it may mean.

A dream, she said. But a memory beneath. A scene that echoes what I too begin to recall. A woman, said the girl. A client, perhaps. So not this woman, who has come from afar. Not this client who claims to be seeking me. And a cat. I extend my paw, as if to make further examination of the leather pad, the fur, the claws that make me what I am. By habit, I begin to wash. Yes, I am a cat. Was that feline she remembered the antecedent of who I am now? Did these two figures – lone hunters, both – somehow merge?

The girl returns as I complete my toilette. Despite my restless night, I jump down to join her, standing by the door. I do not know if she will follow her vision today, will seek to recreate that long-ago scene, or continue to pursue the livelihood I have left her. She is a strange girl, and her pragmatism is colored by her emotions, by the ties she feels to others in her life.

When she heads toward the waterfront, I follow closely. By daylight, the area is busy once again, the threat of violence diminished by the bustle. Commerce takes precedence here, and one girl will be, more or less, ignored. If she goes to observe, to note who speaks to whom, and where they gather, she should be fine. If she makes inquiries, I know she will be discreet. Still, I cannot forget the sight of the girl's onetime leader, his body twisted on the muddy silt. Nor the memory, more closely held, of my own untimely end – my vision fading as I sank into that ditch.

I am relieved, therefore, when Care breaks off, blocks still from the wharf, in an area of large brick buildings neither reclaimed for storage yet nor wrecked for material.

She heads toward one building and my ears prick up. I know this place – its brick, those walls. But some factor – a familiar scent – is missing, and without smell, I may as well be blind. What I am seeking, I do not know. Perhaps those papers she consults would have explained were I still able to make sense of the ink scrawled on their surfaces.

It is not in my nature to brood, to fret over that which might have been. Still, I am mindful – more than most – of the danger of the unforeseen. To better arm myself, I catalogue what aromas I may. The hunters who have passed by here – another cat, whose young reside nearby, a feral dog, near toothless now with age – as well as their luckless prey. Traces of humans, too. A woman who plies her trade in the quiet dark. A drunkard, taking comfort of a different sort. He has slept here and moved on.

As does the girl. As I look up, I see the distance she has already put between us, and so I trot to follow. Around a corner, the building where the drinker slept, she crosses through an open area, past where the rusted hulk of a car lies rotting. And then it hits me.

Startled into action, I begin to run, desperate to turn her back. For all too clearly, I can guess her path. She is heading back to the den of her old gang. Some strange allegiance still to the man with whom she sheltered and whom she once betrayed draws her, I fear. I leap ahead of her. Stop and stare, willing her to recognize the fruitlessness of her search, if not the danger. But she will not pause, and strides past me toward a burned-out shell. The brick a blasted black, its windows gone. Its upper stories crumbling, but its basement, dead ahead, still intact. A burrow of a sort, or warren rather. A place where a homeless girl and the boy that she defended once found refuge, of a sort, and where AD once held sway. Where with heat and flame, he created that noxious substance that held his gang together. That was the element I could not find – the acrid stench of the drug.

Perhaps she smells it too – notes its absence in the air. She slows as she approaches the building, its open windows yawning black even in the morning light. She crouches as she approaches one. Balances herself with one hand on the ground and squints. Her narrowed eyes cannot penetrate the dark, and so I join her, peering deep inside. A figure lies within. Asleep. The woman of the streets, her body rank with use.

I pause, uncertain how to proceed. The figure within poses no apparent threat, and yet, any creature cornered and at rest may lash out. I turn and view the girl. She stares still, as day blind as a mole. I cannot warn her, and so I make my move.

'Get out!' The hand slaps up at me. It pushes me away. 'Shoo!' The gesture has no force in it. The woman barely rouses from her sleep. But my aim has been achieved. By leaping through that window, onto the woman's palette, I have caused her to betray her presence. Care has followed, lowering herself down to the floor, and stands now waiting. Her eyes take longer to adjust than mine, but she can see the movement, hear the voice, if not the matted yellow hair. My task completed, I retreat to bathe. This woman is not as clean as I.

'Rosa.' The girl says nodding. 'You're still here.'

'Who's that.' The woman rises, blinking, her pale face drawn and dirty. 'Care?'

'Who else?' Care watches as the woman pokes around. She finds a sweater of some sort and pulls it on. The sleeve, unraveling, does little to hide the marks. 'How are you?'

Care sees the bruises from rough hands, the burns – she must. Her eyes will have grown accustomed to the dim as Rosa pulls more clothing on. Still, she stands there, waiting.

'Good enough.' Rosa looks up at her. Appraising her, perhaps, for future custom. 'You look good.'

'Come on.' Care holds out her hand and pulls the other woman to her feet. She's tall, this Rosa. Raw-boned and gaunt. 'It's been a while. I know I could use some breakfast. Couldn't you?'

'Breakfast?' Her face narrows as she weighs the words. 'So – you're buying?'

Care nods. 'I was thinking of the Sunrise, if it's still around.'

'You've got scratch?' A spark of interest. Beyond hunger is my guess.

Another nod. 'Enough,' Care says.

'Hang on.' The woman pokes through her pile of rags and adds a few. Adornments, I would guess. Though whether in celebration or in anticipation of attracting clientele, I cannot tell. Perhaps she makes no difference, in her state, but follows as Care leads her to the doorway and the street.

The woman has forgotten me – the stray who woke her – and does not seem to notice that I pace them, as they walk. That I observe, all curiosity. I do not understand the girl's intent. It is enough that she suffers this unclean creature to accompany her. That she returns her embrace when the woman opens up her arms to her. I am relieved to note how Care then frees herself from that embrace. Those hands would search as well as cling, and I would not have the girl's generosity abused. But still, she carries on a friendly patter, drawing the woman out with talk of warmth and food.

'The Sunrise!' Almost, Rosa sounds a girl again. 'I haven't eaten there in ages. I wonder if they have eggs.'

Care laughs. 'Who does, these days? But we can see.' I tag behind, as curious as the tall, ungainly woman who now links her arm through Care's as they walk freely down the street.

FOURTEEN

'So where you get the coin from?' Rosa licks her fingers. Her plate is already wiped clean. 'You on the job?'

'Me? No.' Care looks away, embarrassed. She doesn't want to shame this woman. Doesn't want her to think she has competition, either. 'I'm still working as a finder. You know, the old man's gig?'

'You?' Skepticism in her eyes. 'Alone?'

'I get referrals.' The girl shrugs, not wanting to antagonize. 'There's a keeper sends me work.' For a moment, she pauses, and I wonder just what she will reveal. What she will trade to this Rosa, to gain her confidence. 'And others, too. Right now I'm looking for this boy named Rafe.'

She describes the youth, her voice casual and her expressions veiled. Her gambit pays off.

'Red-headed kid? Skinny as all get out?'

'You know the guy he hangs with?' Care acts casual, like an interested friend. She hasn't told her companion about their former boss, the body that's been swept out to sea not far from the greasy spoon where these two now sit. 'Older guy?'

She's testing her colleague. Checking to see if the other woman is telling the truth, or simply agreeing for the sake of her meal. It wasn't much. No eggs, but the bread and drippings were clearly better fare than the slatternly woman has enjoyed in recent days.

'Uh-huh.' The woman stares. Care has left a crust, and the woman eyes it as I would a fat vole. Rosa licks her lips. She knows there's a price. 'Pete? Peter? Little guy. Bow-legged.'

Care pushes the plate toward her, and I turn away. Rosa grabs up the crust, scraping it over the plate. She'll eat it all before she talks anymore, and I am at ease. Care has made the sensible move: pursuing the easier quarry. That these two cases may be connected, she can surely see, but tracking a local, a man known on the waterfront, is the sensible start. As was rousting the woman for information.

I settle into my niche, a deep sill warmed by the mid-morning sun. It was easy enough for me to follow these two inside. The door is only a hanging strip of plastic, cloudy with age and grime, and although the man behind the grill misses little, he is wise enough to welcome my presence. I confess a moment's trepidation, when I saw his cleaver. But that bread – that's his stock in trade – and the rats cost him more than he can get for meat.

'That guy, Peter, he's kinda weird.' Rosa is sucking her fingers again. The crust was too hard to absorb much, and she runs one dirty thumb over Care's plate before pushing it back again.

'Oh?' Care's voice is noncommittal, and I knead in satisfaction. I never had the chance to teach the girl this part of the job: the grooming of sources. The interplay of reward and, yes, threat that could elicit information. Then again, she was one of AD's gang. Often enough, they were my source – my eyes on the street. Care was different, but she, too started as a snitch. A spy on the world at large.

'Not – you know.' The woman looks around, but the shack is empty. The day laborers who must make up the bulk of this greasy spoon's custom have gone off to their jobs. 'I mean, that's fine, you know? Only, I don't get any scratch for that.' She laughs in a forced way. I suspect there is little she will not do – or find – for hard cash.

'How do you mean, then?' Care's voice, soft, keeps her on track.

'Just, about the kid. You know?' It's a verbal tick, and Care knows it. Still I see the effort she exerts, willing herself not to respond. Her silence will better serve. 'Like he was scared for him. Scared I'd hurt him.'

The sudden grin reveals the missing teeth. This woman is a peer of the girl's, not more than one year or two older, but experience has aged her.

'Was he the timid type?' Sometimes the pump needs priming, but the woman looks confused. 'Peter,' says Care. 'Was he the kind who was always scared?'

A shrug. 'Who knows? But for the kid, yeah. It was like he was his boy or something.'

Care nods and I can imagine her thoughts. The older man is protective of the youth. That's why he sought out Care. Why he hired her. Only Care does not know what I do: that this man has had dealings with those in charge of the waterfront. That he may have been involved in the death of her onetime gang leader, as well. I sigh and shift. My bad leg stiffens if I stay still too long. Perhaps it is better so, I muse as Care takes up her mug. As she finishes the mud-colored beverage within. Let the dead stay buried, I think. Let them drift out to sea.

'So, have you seen AD around?' The question jolts me awake, and I stare at the girl. She is still holding her mug, but her eyes drift up, to take in Rosa's reaction.

'AD? Nuh-uh.' The woman is staring at the mug. Her own is long drained. 'I heard he got out though. Early release, ha!' Another forced laugh. She knows, as does Care, that no legal body authorized their former leader's return. She knows, as well, that Care is interested. 'You gonna have more coffee?'

'Sure.' Care looks up at the grill man. Fishes another coin out of her pocket, and he comes over with his old kettle. Rosa's tit for tat is growing wearisome, however. The strain has begun to show. 'So, what have you heard?' She doesn't even wait for the grill man to retreat.

'Couple of things.' The woman holds the chipped mug with both hands, savoring its warmth, it appears, as much as the beverage within. 'Some people say he made a run for it. Jumped ship, when it got close to shore.'

'Jumped ship?' The question pops out, interrupting the flow. But the woman nods. Keeps talking.

'Uh-huh,' she says. 'Work crew, shipped out. That's what they do with them now. The ships need crewmen, especially if they're to bring back the trade.' She eyes her hostess. 'You thought they just locked 'em up? What would be the sense in that?'

Care merely shakes her head.

'But some people say that's not possible. That nobody comes back from those ships.' She nods, her lips held tight. Care leans in as if to ask. There's something this woman isn't telling. Something she hasn't said.

'Is that what you think?' Care's question, when it comes, is gentle.

'AD is smart. He always was.' A smile plays on her lips, as at a secret memory. 'He knows the score.'

'The score?' The girl's voice is soft.

A quick nod and those eyes flick up, defiant in their bloodshot way. 'Connections, that's what you need these days.'

'I thought AD worked for himself.' Care sits back, and I relax. She hears the undercurrent.

'Times are changing.' Rosa's tongue darts out to lick dry lips. What they taste, I do not know. 'The city's coming back, you know. He's going to make things good again.'

'Who is?'

'You know.' Her voice has dropped, even as her eyes dart around. 'The boss.'

Care waits. There's more to come, and she hears it.

'AD, he was always the smart one,' the woman says. Something like pride in her voice. 'He wasn't going to stay locked up, not like the rest of the crew.'

'You weren't.' It's a statement, but the woman hears it as an accusation.

'I wasn't working at the warehouse the night of the bust. Not there.' A laugh like a bark. 'I got the call. I knew AD wanted us all, but I had a client, didn't I? A private gig. Just like you.'

She looks up at Care as if challenging her, and the girl meets her eyes. She doesn't argue. Doesn't say anything about her relationship with the old man – with me. Doesn't point out that by the time of the bust, when AD's gang was broken up for good, her apprenticeship had already come to its premature end.

'I shoulda been there.' She stares off at some point in the past. 'Shoulda waited till AD could shadow me. You know, be my backup.' More than that, I could have told the girl. In this feline form, I am privy to much. This woman and AD had worked as a team before. Now, however, she shrugs. 'My john was a big guy. I didn't want no trouble.'

'He a regular?' I don't understand what line of questioning the girl is pursuing, although I can hear the urgency in her voice.

No matter. Rosa shakes her head. 'I was hoping. Maybe, if I'd been more careful. The next dude smacked me so hard, my face swole all up.' A shrug. 'A girl can't keep her looks forever. I still see him, sometimes. You know, down here by the pier? But he don't look at me no more. I've heard he don't look at any girl twice anyway. Maybe I should've waited, let AD roll him.'

Time is fluid to her, insubstantial. Almost as if she were an animal. Care ignores the flawed logic.

'You going to work with AD again?'

'I don't know.' The woman slouches. Looks away. She's eaten and drunk and ready to move on. Care's breakfast only buys so much. 'I heard maybe he had something else going on. A job, like.'

'What kind of job?'

A gimlet stare. Care has crossed the line, or maybe she's just bored.

'What kind are there? People. Product. Someone wanting something moved, and AD had all the connections, didn't he? Or he did, anyway. Back before. Maybe he was cooking again. Same old shit – scat, probably.'

'Probably?' Care is focused, but I find myself sniffing. Scrutinizing the air for a trace of the drug's acrid bite. The man on the wharf said AD was shouting for it. 'Rosa?'

A sigh as the woman squirms in her seat. But she's warm, she's eaten. There's another hunger driving her. If her former leader was cooking again, I suspect she would know.

'Look, there's rumors,' she keeps her voice low. Licks her lips. 'A big stash. Pure stuff, too. Better than what AD made. But maybe AD had an in. Maybe he was helping.'

'Where?' Care leans in. To her, the woman's words must sound a fantasy, a rumor. But the girl hears something in her companion's voice, and I remember the bales. The stinging scent that filled the air.

Her question goes too far, though. Touches too near what matters most to this woman, and Rosa closes down. And just then, the stained plastic is pushed back. The grill man looks up. Two men, both large with muscle, stride in, their bulk seeming to fill the space.

'Crazy talk.' The first one turns back toward his companion, as he reaches for a chair.

'Junkie rant.' His companion seems to agree. 'Still, boss said to check.' At that, he looks around, as if realizing that they are not alone. His eyes linger for a moment on Care, a moment longer on Rosa, but then he, too, sits.

'Hello, gents.' Rosa rises in a surprisingly fluid motion. The sweater drips off her shoulders, revealing white and dimpled flesh. 'You looking for some company?'

The grill man comes over, kettle in hand. He looks up at Rosa with cold eyes, but the second man speaks first. 'Yeah, maybe. Rosa, right?'

She murmurs her assent. 'You remember.' Her smile almost looks real.

'Sit right here, girl.' A nod to the stool beside his. 'I know someone who wants to talk to you. May be some business in it too.'

A sound like a purr, as close as she can come, as she takes the seat. But when she reaches for him – one hand sliding up his arm – he turns away, dislodging her. Although his number two has already sized the joint, he scans the room again.

Care. I watch her, my apprehension growing. But she is no rabbit, no brainless creature that bolts at the appearance of a threat. Rather, she takes her time, considering. Although I can hear how her heart is racing, she remains seated. She barely moves. Slowly, almost imperceptibly she turns away, as if her hair were less distinctive than her face.

Maybe it is. He looks at her and pauses. She senses it and freezes. Her intake of breath quickly stifled. Only ears as attuned as mine could hear that gasp. No other nose would detect the sudden sweat that breaks out on her brow and beneath her arms. But his eyes don't linger long enough even to assess the pallor that drains her cheeks or the sudden glassiness of her eyes. As if she were not there, his gaze passes from her. He looks away.

Care seizes the moment to escape. Slowly, carefully, she rises – only I can sense the effort she puts into seeming casual. Into not bolting. I hear her heart racing and feel the warmth that emanates from her. But she moves slowly, throwing an extra coin down on the table as she walks, head down, toward the door. Only when she's passed out of sight from the building – around the corner of the closest warehouse – does she stop to catch her breath. Resting against the damp brick, she closes her eyes. Takes a deep breath. And when she opens them again, I can see the resolution clear and fierce.

Not that she's reckless, not this girl. She hangs in the shadow of the warehouse, surveying the open waterfront before she

moves. The morning's workers – both laborers and hook boys
– begin to gather. The first trucks of the day have been loaded,
and no other ship has docked. But the men who stand in groups
of three or four are quiet. Hopeful, maybe, or resigned. They
barely look up as the girl crosses the cobblestones, toward the
low stone building at the water's edge. The building AD disappeared into, only a day before.

I would stop her, were it in my power. As it is, I dart, anxious,
skirting her legs. That building is a trap. I sense this as any
beast would. Yes, I have entered it, and left it intact. But I am
small and careful, and found access through a portal unavailable
to the girl. Even her former colleague Rosa has means the girl
lacks – her trade buying her sufferance that would not be
extended to Care, were she apprehended. I do not know what
exactly that woman heard, but I am not easy. That building has
known death. Its floors reek still of blood.

I can do nothing, and the girl neatly sidesteps me as I weave
between her legs. She is drawing close. The building itself
seems to wait, lurking, as poisonous as a toad.

'Wait! No.' The girl turns. She does not stop, but she does
slow, even as the short, bow-legged man hurries to catch her,
keeping to the shadows as best he can. 'Where are you going?'

'Peter.' She pauses once she recognizes him. Curious, I believe,
rather than defiant. 'I was looking for you. You took off.'

'Yesterday? You don't have to – that was nothing.' He looks
down at the paving. His hand rubs over his face, as if he could
wipe something away. 'I just— Anyway, you shouldn't be here.'

'But you hired me.' She's staring at him. Looking for whatever it is he's trying to hide. 'This is how I do my job.'

'Yeah, I know I did . . .' He stares off into space. Not, I
notice, at the building. 'But maybe that was a mistake.'

'You don't want me searching for Rafe?' She's doing her
best to read him, read his silence. 'Or just not here? But – no,
it's that building.' She nods toward the low, stone structure.
'Isn't it?'

'Look.' Hands down at his sides, he meets her eyes. 'I'm
grateful for what you did. Looking for Rafe and all. But maybe
we should call it quits.' He takes a breath. 'You can keep the
money.'

'Wait.' Whatever she sees, it has softened her view of this man. 'I don't know what you're afraid of, Peter. But I've barely even started. I'll find Rafe, and wherever he is, I'll do my best to get him free.'

He turns away, rubbing the back of his neck.

'I wasn't even looking for him yesterday.' She's speaking slowly, as if piecing together the words. 'I told you, I had another client. Only – you know more than you've told me, don't you?' He stares at something in the distance. A gull, or maybe just at the sky.

'Look.' His whole body seems to sag. 'Rafe – just . . . Rafe isn't your problem, OK?'

It's where he's not looking as much as what he sees. Care narrows her own green eyes, appraising. 'He's in there.' She nods over at the building. The only structure on the water. 'Isn't he?'

'Don't know.' He's staring at the stones again. 'I only know that's not safe. You can't mess with what goes on there. None of us can. That's . . . off limits.'

'I know about the trade.' There's something off about her tone. She's faking. Improvising on a theme and looking for cues. 'Goods coming in. Going out too.' She pauses, her eyes on his face. 'Scat.'

And it hits me. What I'd missed. The well-packaged bundles, impressive in both purity and amount. This isn't some local stock-pile, such as was once the source of AD's power, only of superior quality. This is something different, much larger. That he would have been a part of? Yes, that would explain his journey here. The words that were shouted. But what did he bring back to trade for a seat at this table? With what was he purchasing access?

Or is there another factor? I find myself going over what we have heard, Care and I, looking for what I have missed. A large stash of superior quality. Clearly, AD's particular talents weren't needed. Is that why he was disposed of? Or had his demands become too insistent? Too loud.

Care has finished speaking, having ventured all she dare.

'Look, I don't know about that side of things.' Distress marks Peter's face. His brows bend upward as if in pain. 'That's not my business. Never was. I just wanted to make a life. Someplace safe, for me and Rafe.'

That catches her up as nothing else has. 'You and Rafe,' she says, weighing the words. 'You really care about him.'

A slow nod. Resigned.

'So why don't you want me to look for him? I could find him, you know.'

The face that turns toward hers is undeniably sad. 'I believe you,' he says. 'But then they'd probably just kill him.'

The import of his confession strikes her almost immediately. 'Wait,' she says after the briefest of pauses. 'You know where he is. You know who took him and why.'

For a moment, there is silence. No movement but for the lashing of my tail. I can almost hear the frantic scrabbling. The flurry of scratching claws, desperate to escape. But then the moment passes. The man appears almost to deflate, his shoulders slumping. He nods with downcast eyes, acknowledging all.

'Tell me,' she says. Her voice is level. Neutral. But there is no mistaking the note of command.

'We do work together,' he begins. 'As a team, here on the docks. And he did go missing three nights ago.' He licks his lips. She waits, and while she does, I work my way around him. I knew his scent, when I found it in that basement. I circle behind him, taking it in. Looking for what else I may find; for whatever this man says, I do not believe it will be the entire truth.

'I wasn't worried,' he says now. 'Not at first. Like I said, I thought, maybe he'd gone off. Found a girl or something.'

'Or something?' Care studies his face. When I glance up, I see the set of her mouth. And although I catch no additional signs of distress – not in his sweat nor in the warmth of his body – I am grateful for her reticence. For her patience, and I will her to say no more.

'I was afraid of this.' The words rush out on one held breath. The truth, then, as straight as he knows it. 'He's been looking— Rafe wasn't happy on the docks.' His eyes search hers, seeking understanding. 'He wanted more.'

She nods but holds her peace.

'I think he got involved in something. Took a job that he shouldn't—' He breaks off. Shakes his head. 'I don't know for sure.'

Care's breath stops. She wants to speak, I fear. To reveal that she knows of the woman, of the mission to the keeper. But she has discipline, this girl. She will not divulge more than she must. 'You know who took him,' she says. 'You must know why.'

It's not a question. Still, he shakes his head. 'I got a message. That's all.' He reaches across his body, one hand rubbing the other arm. The message, then, was painful.

'That he'd been taken?' She sees his anguish and is moved by it. Would that she weren't. She has spoken too quickly. Filled a void for him. He nods again, his mouth a grim line. 'By whom?'

His eyes dart up. The question is too naked and it scares him. 'Not my place to ask, Miss.' He's shaking his head. 'The boss's men, they were. Two of them. That's all I know.'

'Do you know where he was working, for this job of his?' She shifts her focus, and he looks confused. 'Rafe, your friend. Who was he talking to – or what about – that got him into trouble?'

He inhales, as if time were air. The girl knows, of course. Knows what the keeper told her, at any rate. But not what happened after or how the youth's questions – about her, about *me* – may be involved. The man only shakes his head. 'He didn't tell me.' He sounds sad. Spent. 'Only that he'd do me proud.'

He stands there, silent. His head is hanging low, as if he expects to be whipped. Standing so, he doesn't see how the girl looks at him. Doesn't see the softness in her face, but I do. I know this girl, her weaknesses. She hears the echo in his words of her own exchange with the boy Tick. She hears the connection and the love, and she would trust this man. Would accept his tale at its face value, if for no other reason then that he is mourning a loss. She is thinking of the boy Tick, of how his absence would leave its stamp on her. But she is not this man, and she has not pressed him for all he knows.

I leave him to rub against her ankles. Not from affection, but to break the spell she seems ensorceled by. 'Blackie.' It works in that she looks from him to me, the ghost of a smile playing over her lips. 'I'd almost forgotten you were here.'

'Hey, look there.' She turns – we all do – to where a laborer is pointing down at me. 'It's that cat, the black one. I seen him here before.'

Care gasps and would reach for me, to hold me. But I am too fast. I leap back a body's length and wait, appraising the situation.

'What do you want?' Care braces herself, stance wide as the man strides toward her. 'What's my cat to you?'

'Your cat?' The man huffs in some version of a laugh. His colleagues are watching, and he won't be outfaced by a girl. 'That old stray? I doubt it. Fact is, we've got a job for him, that mangy critter. The boss wants something for his cellar. Says the rats are costing him.'

'Well, find another cat, then.' Care stands her ground, arms akimbo as if preparing for a fight. My hackles start to rise. My ears flatten. She will not fight alone.

'Sorry, girlie.' The man is smiling. 'There's a bounty for this one. Black cats are special.'

And then I feel it. The cold steel of a hook, circling around my torso. Hoisting me off my feet. That smile – he was the distraction, while another snuck up behind me. Then darkness, rough-hued. Burlap. A sack. That I could be so foolish . . .

No matter now. No time for self-recrimination. Cruel laughter rises as I hiss and spit, lashing out. The girl's cry over all. 'Let him go!' A cry of pain as one sharp-claw hits home. A shift, and I slash again, claws like talons. Spots of light through the rough cloth. Blood, too. I smell it warm upon the fabric, before I am upended. The sacking tightens, leaving me confused.

'Put him down!' The girl again. 'Stop it!' Frightened, and I fear not just for me. These men are rough, and daylight will not deter them from their petty victory. Their pleasure. They have not worked, or not enough, and too much is on the line. I twist, willing my body to forget its age and injury. A hand presses down, by chance or intent, pressing tight upon my snout. Held thus, I cannot bite. Nor can I breathe, and though I kick and kick again, the spots of light – of sun through cloth – are growing dim. Are fading. That laughter, once again. As if in a dream . . .

'What the—' The laughter stops, and I breathe again. 'Have you gone nuts?'

'Let her go.' A man, speaking through clenched teeth. 'You know I'll use it, Tommy. You know I will.'

'Peter, come on.' The laughing man not laughing now. He sounds confused and distant.

'Let her go.' A growl almost, such as I would make. And then a gasp. The girl. I hear her stumble, and then take two steps. Toward—

'My cat,' she says. 'I'm not leaving without my cat.'

'You heard the girl.' I cock my ears and try to regain my bearings. Peter is standing close by, and Care is with him. Only, no, she is approaching. Coming toward me, in my despair. Only, no, this is not what I would wish. This is wrong.

The one who holds me is a violent man, and I have wounded him. Does she not see this? He will not spare her, no more than he would show mercy to me. He would—

'Let him go,' she says again. I hear her footstep, cheap leather on the cobblestones.

She will not stop, and thus, then, nor can I. I gather up my strength. There is little to brace myself against, upended as I am. But I spread my claws. I ready myself to jump. To claw. To buy what time I may.

A yelp. Short and without words. 'Peter!' A gasp, almost. The girl has stopped.

'You've lost it, man.' A voice, beside my ear, and suddenly the world goes round. I flounder, topsy-turvy, my claws trapped in the fabric a hindrance as I fly. I hit the pavement before I can right myself and leap, with hiss and spit, out into the air.

'You're crazy.' He does not speak to me. Instead, he is eyeing Peter, the bow-legged man, who holds a short knife to the hook boy's throat.

'Go,' says Peter. One word, short. The girl looks down at me, her green eyes meeting mine. And then she turns and runs, and I beside her, away from the dockside and the laughing man.

FIFTEEN

The girl is strong, as am I for my kind and size, but she is young, while I am far older than I may seem. By the time she stops running, throwing herself against a wall, her chest heaving, I am exhausted. Not only am I panting, but my leg is aching. I walk gingerly, barely placing any weight on it as I take the last few steps to join her. She stands doubled over, with her hands spread out on her thighs, but I let her see me, passing beneath her as I rub my head against one warm shin.

'Blackie, thank God.' The hand that reaches for me is trembling. 'When that big guy grabbed you . . .' She doesn't continue, only slides down the wall to a seated position. I move closer, leaning into her warm and fragrant side. She drapes one arm gently around me. For the moment, we are at peace.

I listen to her breathing, as we sit there. I hear it slow and become regular, and I wonder, briefly, if she will sleep. The girl is not a cat, capable of taking her rest where she may, but the times and their usage have had their effect, and she is accustomed to living rough. Still, the child is vulnerable by nature of her size and gender. We have come to rest in an alley, tucked just off the main road. We were not pursued; those men were not built for the long hunt or for stealth. That does not mean we are safe. The girl shifts, her head coming to rest on the arms crossed over her knees. I extend my game leg and begin to groom.

Soon my fur is spotless, nearly pitch black in the shade. The slight variance over my limb, where the hide below has scarred, smooth enough so that it would barely shimmer blue-black in the light. But the sun has already begun its decline, and I see now that the girl has chosen wisely, sheltering in the lee of this building, as its shadow darkens and grows toward night.

She should stay here, I decide, as comforted by that thought as by the rough rasp of my tongue. Rest and consider what steps are best to next take. She is a smart girl and has been well trained, as far as that went. But the intemperance of youth, as well as her early emancipation, has resulted in a rashness that I am ill equipped to counter. Her questioning of the man Peter, for example, was slipshod, and in her haste, she missed an opportunity. Yes, she picked up on his knowledge – that he seemed to be aware that his colleague had been taken as a kind of threat. But she went off on a tangent and did not pursue the most pressing questions. Who took the youth Rafe, and why? And the most crucial of all: what did this have to do with the man's engagement of her services? It seems quite obvious that he was sent to her. By whom and for what reason are what we both now need to know.

'I wonder . . .' She speaks to herself, I know. Still, I pause from my bath. 'If he – yeah, he might have an idea.' She nods, even as she bites her lip. I resume my toilette. This is her process and is not that dissimilar from mine, although I dislike how her teeth have rubbed the corner of her mouth raw. Almost, I wonder, as if she would feed on herself. She needs more than the basic sustenance that she now earns. More than the companionship I, and with decreasing frequency the boy Tick, can provide.

'It would be good to talk things out,' she says, as she pushes herself upright. I am not psychic. Despite my strange antecedents, I am no more than what I once was. In many ways, I am less. And yet I believe I was right in my conjecture. The girl requires companionship of another more like her. She may not realize it, but the girl is lonely.

As she begins to walk, I pace myself beside her. She is aware of me. I have seen her glance down, the faint smile of recognition as I look up to meet her gaze. I keep myself in her line of sight, willing myself to disregard the instincts toward stealth and a more furtive path back to the heart of the city. I do not recall ever regretting the lack of a companion in my life. As a cat, I have no such need. Even the biological drives of a younger animal are faint within me now, and such society as some of my kind enjoy would be irksome to me, at best. Mayhap this is a holdover from my prior existence. Although I must have been at times as other men are, I do not believe I was ever one for society. Certainly not of the chummy pack mentality that drove those thugs by the waterfront, and not of any more subtle kind either. I was a loner, I believe, as I still am by nature and by preference. Even family . . .

That woman, the aged and heavy one who called herself Augusta. I pause for a moment and then continue my casual trot, the thought alone enough to momentarily throw me off my pace. I pore over her words. The claims she made as she hired the girl. The contradictions presented by the keeper, this Quirty.

If she spoke truly, then perhaps she did know me. Perhaps she could shed light on this transformation, or on the enemy who brought me low. The girl turns a corner, and I follow. The day is fading. The shadows grow long, but the timid creatures of dusk and dawn hold back on our passing. My scent, as much as hers, serves as a warning, and neither my ears nor my nose note the presence of any other creature of interest.

She turns again, and I follow. But although some part of me is always alert, I am focused now on the past. On the being – the man – I once was.

Did I – *do* I – have a sister? I have no recollection of such, but I recall so little of any prior life. Too much is emptiness, a void that I cannot explain. Perhaps therein lies the problem. As the girl ducks down a narrow lane, I pause, and then consider. Whatever I was once, I am now a cat. Not some human prone to sentiment. Ties of blood do not bind beasts like the one I have become. I waste no thought on mates or the progeny that may – no, must – have resulted from this once strong and vital form. Nor, I suspect, did they matter much to my previous incarnation. As a man, I do not believe I was much different. The few memories I have recalled are empty of companions, save of those I valued for their utility. Save, I make the exception, of the girl. The hunt – the tracking – this is what drew me on. What draws me now.

The girl! I have lost her. Lost sight of her, I correct myself. For of course in my current form I can both hear and smell her not far off. A momentary panic, then; a sudden reversion to a less capable form. And yet, I realize with some astonishment, I have not been paying attention to our route or to her now obvious destination. Lost in my ruminations, I had assumed a default. That the girl would retreat to her – *our* – lair, and there begin again the laborious process of investigation, mulling over what she has heard and seen and learned.

I had not counted on the resilience of youth. No matter the fright she was given, nor the pursuit that left her winded and hot, she would query another still. The pride I feel in her wells up in a rumble within my chest. She will question this source about his contact. About what he knows, and then she will weigh and decide. She did not miss the gaps in her client's story, and she will persevere.

She is waiting, as I knew she would, around the corner from the building. A recessed door, set down in the pavement. Backed into the shadow, she waits until the shade reaches the portal with no other movement nearby. Only then does she approach the keeper's office.

She raps gently on the door. 'Mr Quirty?' Her voice no more than the rustle of paper blowing in the street.

A creak and it opens. Big eyes blinking even in the dim light. A knife, short but sharp, held in a trembling hand.

'Come in,' he says, lowering the knife, and she enters. The door closes behind her too quickly even for me, and so I make my way around the basement office to where a window, hung with oiled cloth, admits me with ease. I do not even need to conceal myself, as they greet each other by the doorway, and I am beneath the keeper's desk before they approach it themselves.

'You are worried,' he says, as she sits. He picks up the pencil he has been sharpening, the rhythmic scraping of blade on wood filling the space as he waits for her response.

'I have questions,' she says. My tail lashes in anticipation, stirring the shavings around me. Peter. The boy Rafe. That woman. Please, I beseech the air above me, let her be pursuing these and not the fate of her late leader, AD. I hear the intake of her breath, and wait, my own at bay.

'They wanted my cat, Mr Q,' she says, the words deliberate and strong. 'And I want to know why.'

No! It takes all my training, all my discipline, to keep from calling out. That, and the sure knowledge that my protest would only be heard as the yowling of some low beast. Instead, I find myself panting, in my dismay that this girl, for whom I risk so

much, should waste her time or any other resource on concern
for me. I am a cat, and self-sufficient. She, however, is a female,
young and vulnerable. She must not—

But, no. In the pause, as I catch my breath, the scraping
continues. The man has begun to speak again, even as more of
the light tight coils of wood drift down to me. And in his quiet,
measured tone, I hear some semblance of the rationality I would
have the girl aspire to.

'What makes you think they want your cat?' His question is
basic, but no less vital. 'I mean, specifically, as opposed to any
cat?'

She takes a moment before answering. She has learned to
gather her thoughts, to weigh impressions against evidence. But
I fear that she may still allow emotion to influence her unduly.
She is young and she is loyal, and thus, is prone to give affection more influence then is its due.

'They said they wanted a mouser.' I hear the deliberation in
her voice. She is trying to remember and to be precise. 'A black
cat, in particular, for the boss's cellar. They said that a black cat
would be more effective.'

My ears prick forward at that. For of all the axioms I have
heard circulated about felines of my coloring, this one is new
to me.

To her, as well. 'Maybe that's it.' She speaks with a little
more ease. 'I mean, I've never heard that before. But more than
that . . .' She drags the chair closer, a move that makes the
pencil shavings scatter. 'I have a feeling.'

A shift, as the man leans forward too, and she waves off his
response. 'No, I know what that sounds like, and I don't mean it
like that. More like, I saw how they were looking at Blackie, as
if they'd been searching for him. And I know they were offered
a reward – a bounty – for a cat *like* him. Only, there aren't many.
None that I've seen, except him. And, well, it's funny.'

The keeper makes a small sound. A wordless query, as he
waits.

'This goes against everything the old man taught me. I wonder
if I'm picking up something that I just can't quite put words
to. The old man would hate that I'm trusting anything like that
– anything that I can't confirm or explain. But maybe that's

Blackie's influence.' She laughs. The release of tension is palpable. 'Maybe I'm learning to be more like a cat.'

I bristle. I cannot help it. The guard hairs that provide the gloss and apparent uniformity of my coat begin to rise and my spine to arch. It is an involuntary response, and yet I can easily surmise what has brought it about. Anger. Disappointment. And, yes, surprise at her disdain for my methods, for what I taught her. And, I confess, for my current state, in which I have endeavored to comport myself with dignity and reason.

Or maybe, there is something else. For while the girl has chuckled at her own words, she is piecing something together. Conscious, I believe, of the absurdity of her conclusion, the man sitting across from her has not said anything. In fact, his silence is telling. Eloquent, even, and I can hear how Care has stilled her breath, waiting. As, in myself, I recognize the truth of what she has said.

Instinct? I do not like to call it that, conflating as it does the cultivated powers of ratiocination with more basic urges. Rather, a recognition, on some pre-conscious level, of a truth or truths that my senses have been busy compiling. That this man is now silent lends credence to the idea. Reminds me, as well, of that strange unease I had when last we were here – and when that woman, who calls herself Augusta, first climbed the stairs to our shared office and into our life.

'Mr Q?' Care is waiting now, though more for confirmation than for a revelation, I believe. 'What do you know?'

A sigh that would be audible even to ears less acute than mine. He has put down his pencil and his knife both, as he struggles with his answer. With – I realize – his loyalty and priorities.

'I am a keeper,' he says at last. 'My profession is built on trust.'

She nods at his explanation and then begins to speak. The struggle apparent in her voice. 'I understand,' she says. 'But if there is something that would help me – or, no, something that would keep me, or mine, from harm . . .' Her request trails off. Enough has been said.

My heart beats at a faster rate than do those of these two. Still, enough time passes for my agitation to subside and, with it, my upended fur. The girl holds herself still, in the mode of a hunter who knows that any movement may alert the prey. I, confident that my presence has not been noted, tilt my ears forward. A change in breathing, even one more subtle than that voluminous sigh, may be as informative as any words.

'Your questions.' He pauses. Swallows. Licks his lips. 'Your supposition, I should say, may have merit.' The girl, still frozen, does not respond. 'About your cat, that is. I do not say this lightly.' He rushes through these words, anxious to get them out. 'For, as I've said, my profession – my life – is built on trust. Only, you are – Care, Ms Wright, you are special to me. And not simply for the services you have done me, in your role as one who seeks. But because I have known those who loved you and have been honored to purvey their missives, from another time.'

The girl is trembling. She remains silent, but I can feel the emotions that wrack her body. The letter from her father, which this man held. And others, perhaps, of which she is not aware. She makes some motion – assent, understanding – and the man begins to speak again.

'We are not family, you and I, but we have such allegiance that may count as much in these times. And, therefore . . .'

He breaks down. His breathing labored. It is the girl who leans forward, with words to comfort and beseech.

'I understand,' she says. The chair beneath her creaks. She has reached for him – for his hand, perhaps. 'And I understand as well the value of your word. If there is any way I can assure you of my discretion. Of my need . . .'

'That isn't necessary.' He speaks more easily. His mind's made up. 'I only – please, you must understand – I only ask that you appreciate the gravity.'

'I do.' Just like that, a pact is solemnized.

'A woman – much like the one whom you described – came to me here yesterday.' He swallows again. Sighs. 'I believe it was she whom you had inquired about – who had hired the youth and then visited you. But she did not ask about the old man, nor about any brother, missing or gone. She only wanted to know about the cat that follows you about. About how long he has been your companion, and where before he came from.'

SIXTEEN

'**B**ut why? He didn't belong to the old man, if that's what she's thinking.' I must give the girl credit. Although Quirty's words must sound odd to her, she rallies quickly and arrives at what should be a logical conclusion. 'If she thinks he's going to help her find out what happened to him – help her find something that belonged to him, she's mistaken.'

I could argue with that, assuming, of course, that I could speak directly to either of the humans who now sit above me. That I can't encapsulates the situation in a nutshell. It also illuminates a worrisome blind spot in my own logic. When those men down by the waterfront grabbed me, I credited nothing more than the violence of such types. Brutes such as that kill for sport and enjoy inflicting pain, and the hook boys are known for their savagery. To hear that this woman also seeks to learn about me puts their quest in a different light, however, bringing to mind not only that strange dream but also another, earlier encounter.

When the girl found me, I was drowning. She pulled me from the rushing waters of that drain and warmed me with her body, allowing me to revive into this new life. All my memory of that encounter – my salvation – is from a different perspective. From that of my former being, the old man, as I looked up, sight failing, at the evil men above me. They were watching me die. Waiting, I believe, for my final breath. But what happened at that moment of transformation – how my consciousness transmuted from that existence to this current one – I do not know. Nor, I realize now, have I queried deeply into how my feline form came to be struggling in that flood. An oversight, to be sure, and one that I must address. The men by the docks, they were sent to capture me. The one who ordered them— But the girl is speaking again.

'There's something going on down there. Down by the docks.' Her foot jiggles, restive, and I would press against it to calm her, only I would not interrupt her thoughts. Instead, I put my paw out to still one of those shavings, flattening it like a moth. 'Those men, AD, that woman.'

'AD?' The man across from her leans forward, the question tightening in his voice. Care, however, does not respond, so intent is she on her train of thought.

'That man Peter,' she says, biting down on the name. 'He helped me – helped us. But he knows more than he's telling me.'

Good! I could purr, I am so proud. Despite the distractions, she did not miss the gaps in his story – the question he didn't answer. I have trained her, and she is smart. I am so content that I smile – my version of that expression, at any rate – my whiskers smoothing out and my eyes closing. My satisfaction is amplified when I feel the girl's hands on me. She has reached beneath the desk to stroke me, and as she pulls me onto her lap, I relax further, going so limp with pleasure that I almost miss her next words.

'So I'm wondering if I can leave Blackie here with you, for a while,' she says, her hands tightening on my sides. 'Just to keep him safe.'

I cannot help it. I tense, my claws digging into her legs. I hear her yelp in pain, but instead of releasing me, she lifts me high. Deposits me on the desk and holds me there, her hands firm around my torso.

'What happened?' Quirty is standing, his chair thrown back.

'I must have spooked him – maybe I touched his sore leg.' She's standing now too, her weight on her arms, holding me still. 'It's almost like he understood me. But he couldn't . . .'

I freeze at her words, torn between wanting her to understand and revealing myself. In a way, it does not matter. I cannot wrench myself free, and I would not turn and bite her – not Care, the girl who has saved my life. Still, I must make myself heard. I twist and yowl, my eyes searching for hers in despair.

'Blackie, what is it?' Her face could not be more pained if I had struck her. Surely that reflexive clenching of my claws did not cause her serious injury? 'Are you hurt?'

No, those brows are knit in concern and compassion. I temper my voice to beseech her, in my own wordless way. A small, sad whine of grief.

'I don't think—' The man. He keeps his distance, but he is a keen observer. 'I think he doesn't want you holding him. I don't think I should try to keep him here.'

'Blackie?' Her entreaty is quiet, for my ears only. She bites her lip as she awaits my response.

'Meh.' I know my face cannot express my feelings. My eyes may be wide, but they cannot show either my understanding or my sadness, and I can only hope she notes the posture of my ears, the low droop of my tail, indicating my obvious displeasure. I would not cause her grief, not anymore. And yet . . .

Her lip goes white beneath her teeth. I raise my eyes from it to hers and see the tears welling. Behind me, the man is agitated. I can hear his breathing; hear too how he works to calm it. He does not matter at this moment. Whatever he may know or may suspect is nothing to what passes between the girl and me.

'What if I let you go now, Blackie.' She's speaking slowly but directly. My mouth opens, as if to respond, but I hold back, waiting. 'I'm going to let you go, but I hope you will stay here, OK? For your own safety.'

The hands that have been tight around my body begin to relax. I shift slightly – I have been deposited here uneasily and need to get my footing – but when the girl pauses, hands still on my sides, I freeze. I meet her gaze. I blink once, slowly, my eyes on hers.

And then she lets me go.

I do not move, not much. Only to gather my splayed feet beneath me and to sit up, facing her.

'All right then.' She nods once, as if to confirm to herself what she has seen. 'I think we understand each other.'

I keep my eyes on hers, willing her to believe. Behind me, the man moves, though, and my ears flick to take this in.

'Don't—' The girl reaches out, as if to stop him. Or to restrain me, once again. It barely matters. We both freeze in response.

'I'm sorry,' she says, laughing a little. She does not trust her instinct. Not on this, and chuckles to disguise her discomfort.

'But I guess this is as good as I can do,' she says. Then she looks up. 'You'll keep him?'

'I'll do what I can,' says the voice behind me. I sit as prim as a statue, willing her to believe.

'Thank you.' She licks her lips, her tongue lingering on the raw spot, and then she nods. 'I'll be back. Tomorrow or sooner, if I can find out anything.'

She is watching me even as she retreats to the door, and I sit, frozen in my helpless obedience, as she leaves.

'Well then,' says the voice behind me. The man she has left me with. 'What are we to do now, you and I?'

The man's voice is quiet, respectful. It gives no hint of what he knows – or how. But there is a note of something uncanny in it.

What that is is a question for another time. And although I regret breaking my word, my duty is clear. With one leap, I attain the sill of the high window, and although I hear him exclaim – in dismay or shock – as I pass through the hangings that kept out the wind, I am gone.

SEVENTEEN

T
he girl is agitated. Upset. When I find her, half a block
away, she is walking quickly, heedlessly through a city
that should never be ignored. While I am careful to stay
out of her sight, I follow her, and find her path is as expected.
She is heading back to the waterfront. That she wants to confront
her client is clear. That she believes she has left me behind, in
safety, shows the fault in her hasty thought process. Yes, I was
the prey sought, but those predators could turn on her as well.
And before he came to my rescue, that man – Peter – had
warned her about that low stone building and the mystery it
houses.

She is a hunter, however, and that fate of AD weighs on her
conscience as well, I know. But despite all her training, I am
ill at ease. Her pace suggests a recklessness that she can scarce
afford. There is danger in that building. The men who frequent
it are evil, and she lacks the acuity to discover what I have
found. To scent the blood spilled there.

In my solicitude, I would keep her close. The hour obliges.
The setting sun casts long, dark shadows that help obscure me
even as I race alongside her, providing a steady corridor of
shade. It goes against my instinct, to pace her this way. From
the curve of her shoulders, held tight and high, I can see the
tension in her. The hands she has shoved into her pockets must
be clenched tight, and the firm line of her mouth admits neither
fear nor pity. If it were in my power, I would make myself
known to her. Trot alongside her, and let the softness of my fur
comfort her in her distress. But I cannot. She believes me in
danger, and to see me would worry and distract her. Better that
I keep to cover. There will be time enough, if all goes well, to
rectify any sense of betrayal my actions may have caused.

Not being in her confidence has its price, however. When
she veers from the expected path, I am nearly exposed. It is
only my utter stillness that allows me to remain undetected as

she cuts across the avenue and dives into the shadow where I stand. Of course! I follow as soon as she has passed. She has gone to seek that other female from the gang – Rosa – in their former home.

'Rosa?' Care has the sense to call but softly, even as she enters the basement lair. 'You here?' She is alone, I could tell her. No movement to signify the presence of another – not of anything larger than a rat, at least, and even those have made themselves scarce at our approach. No trace fresher than the morning, when Care roused her former colleague and treated her to a meal.

In the space of moments, the girl comes to the same conclusion. With a sigh, she tosses one of the rags her former compatriot has slept in aside, and collapses onto the pallet on the floor. That she has become winded by her rush here is evident. That she is discomfited, as well, by the absence of the woman plays into her apparent surrender. Although her eyes are not as keen as mine, she glances around the dark space – made darker now by the setting of the sun. She seeks a way forward, as much as the onetime occupant of this space. A direction. And I crouch in the corner, unable either to comfort or direct her fledgling inquiry as once I could.

She lingers for so long that I begin to doze. At least, I tell myself as my eyes grow heavy, this place is no longer as foul as once it was. The smell of sweat and unwashed bodies clings to the bedclothes, and the earthy funk of waste comes from the far corner. But the acrid stink of the drug – the scat that AD once manufactured here – is gone, washed out by the passage of time. Without that pollution, it is easy to begin to drift. To dream.

'Old fool.' The voice is soft and low, but there is nothing of gentleness in it. 'Inviting pain, when you could have shed it.'

I look up into cold dark eyes, unable to resist. I am – bound somehow. No, my limbs are held. The men . . . that sack.

I jerk awake to find myself unencumbered – and aghast. But, no, the girl has not noticed me starting, here in the corner of the basement. She sits still, brooding, as if only moments have passed. But then, with a sigh, she makes to rise, pushing herself off the low nest with her hand and pausing, as she does.

'Wha—?' The half-formed word explains her actions as she turns and begins to flip through the clothes so rudely assembled there. What she pulls forth is not at first recognizable to me, although she turns it to and fro. A weapon of some sort, rudely forged. A wooden handle, taken from some other tool, stained dark by the usage of many hands. Attached to that, a blade. Long and slender, even from where I sit, I can see the sheen of its sharpened edge, the filing that has given it a needle point. A shiv, such a thing is called, and I remember AD, as he ran, shoving just such a weapon in the waistband of his pants, where his ragged shirt would hide it.

And as she examines it, she runs her hand along the flat of the blade and then inspects her hand for signs of blood. I cannot smell any, not from here, though if I were closer, I suspect I would find such where the blade and handle join. A weapon such as this is made for use, and I am puzzled by the appearance of such a deadly tool here, in the bed of this woman. AD would not likely have forgotten it, no matter how beguiling the woman. I do not think she has either skill to have stolen or cajoled it from him. A man does not carry a weapon lightly these days, nor abandon it for a fancy.

That he did not have it on him when we spied him, watching us, may explain why he did not choose to engage the girl then. Despite the advantages of size and age, he would prefer certainty. A weapon. Its absence may also explain his death, although such a blade would not necessarily have saved him. I do find it curious that he went to a rendezvous without it. Perhaps he had another such on him, lost in his final struggle. Or some means of defense that in her hurried search, the girl was unable to find. Or perhaps he went to a meeting deliberately unarmed, a possibility that raises questions of its own.

In my prior life, I would apply reason to this puzzle. I would gather more information and look back, as well, over observations I have made. In this life, I have begun to accept that other, more subtle senses have a role. Some of these are feline – the scent, or lack thereof, of the drug, for example. Particularly in light of the hunger I could see too clearly in the woman's eyes.

Also, I wonder at the import of my dream. In the past, I would have dismissed such a nighttime vision as fantasy.

Insubstantial and unimportant. But I have learned in this life that in such dreams I may find deeper truths. That such fancies may hold the keys to memory, and that this was no mere reverie. Instead, I consider it as a snippet of that last trial, perhaps, before I was discarded and left to die.

'*Inviting pain*,' he said. The words ring in my ears, which twitch back in alarm. '*When you could shed it.*' I do not understand this memory, and it disturbs me, as does its timing now, in this place. Almost as much as does the realization that, while I pondered that brief vision, I have been oblivious to another sound. A rasping sound, as in something dragged. The slap of a hand against a wall, and then a dark shape in the doorway.

Care looks up and gasps. Her hand moves quickly, secreting the knife much as AD did, down the back of her worn jeans. 'Rosa,' she says. The effort entailed to keep her voice steady is obvious to me. It would not be to a human's ears, I believe, and in this case most certainly is not. Rosa stumbles forward, blinking in the dark. But not alarmed. Not even at finding someone in her refuge, on her bed.

Care stands and steps forward, as if aware of the trespass. Or, mayhap, as she prepares to leave. And then it hits me: the chemical stench. Sharp as bee sting, or as smoke that burns and blinds the eyes.

'Care!' The one word, perhaps all that she can muster, as she stumbles forward into the arms of the girl, who then lays her on the bed. 'I should've known you'd come back. I'm so glad.'

EIGHTEEN

'Rosa? Are you all right?' Care stoops over the prone body, one hand on her bare arm.

The mumbled response does little beyond provide proof of life, but Care has clearly had experience with intoxication of this sort. Kneeling on the palette, she pulls the limp woman over, until she is lying on her side, and props her there using the rags and dirty blanket that appear to make up Rosa's bed and wardrobe both. The woman does not resist, appearing as pliable as a fresh kill, though even from my corner I can hear her breathing. Smell the warmth of her body. In the dim light of the basement, I doubt Care can see the bruises forming along her bare arm, the cuff of raw flesh around her wrist where the skin has worn away. But after she has her arranged and then covered – her airway unrestricted but her vulnerable body under wraps – Care draws back in surprise and holds her hand to her face. It is wet and even in this light, she must see that the substance on her palm is dark and growing tacky. To me, the sharp iron of blood is obvious, even with the burnt fumes of the drug filling the room.

'Rosa.' She shakes the limp woman, urging her to wake. 'Come on. Do you have a candle or a lamp or anything?'

'Sleepy.' The woman protests, before she pulls away and flops forward, her mild resistance draining the last of her strength. Care begins to rummage through the bed clothes, patting the area near the palette for what she can find. It is not full dark yet outside, but the last of the twilight barely illuminates this cave-like room. To me, this presents no problem, and it only is my awareness of what additional distress my appearance would cause that keeps me from advancing on the girl and guiding her hand to that which she seeks. I realize I have tensed, as if ready to leap, by the time she finds the thick candle, which she lights and sets on the crate that serves as both table and storage.

'Rosa, wake up.' The yellow glow has confirmed her suspicions, and she turns from her hands to the unconscious woman. 'You're bleeding.'

She shakes her again, more roughly this time, panic in her voice. 'Wake up.'

'I'm awake.' The woman pushes herself upright and blinks. 'Care!'

'You're bleeding.' The girl keeps her voice low and calm, as if speaking to a child. 'I want to examine you. You may need help.'

A flash of something – concern or confusion – passes over the intoxicated woman's face and then departs. She checks her own wrist as if it belonged to someone other. Rubs the raw place and winces, before releasing it. Her fingers are sticky with blood, but even from where I observe I can tell that it no longer flows fresh.

'This?' She conjures a smile, almost a laugh. 'That's nothing. Besides, I got paid, didn't I?'

'Those men, the ones in the café.' Care sits back on her heels. 'You've been with them all day?'

A shrug almost unbalances the befuddled woman. 'We had a party,' she says. 'I gave 'em what they wanted. Poor old AD.'

'What about him?' The girl is losing patience. 'Rosa, tell me what you know.'

A toss of her head sends her dirty locks back. Her face shines in the candle light, but in the half-closed eyes there's a spark. Rosa is waking from her daze.

'I guess I know why the boss got rid of him, don't I?' Pain or the lessening of her intoxication have left their mark. She's sounding mean, almost resentful of the dead man. Care stiffens at the change of tone.

'The boss?' She hasn't drawn the weapon. She's waiting, I can tell, to hear what the woman has to say. 'Are you sure it wasn't something else, Rosa? Did you two have a fight?'

'Me 'n AD?' She snorts and shakes it off. 'Nah, we had an understanding. I brought my clients around, and he kept me supplied.' She wipes her nose on the back of her hand and pauses to inspect the abrasions there. She is beginning to sober up, the effects of the drug wearing off. Still, she seems too inebriated to lie.

'Maybe he'd stopped being so generous.' Care is spinning a scenario. Making it sound reasonable. ''Cause I can't imagine AD not cooking.'

'You don't know the half of it. AD tried, you know?' Her words are slurred, the eyes that blink up at the girl unfocused. 'He wanted in again. He was going to deliver, only someone tripped him up.'

Care is silent. Waiting, I assume, to hear what the other woman knows. If she can tell her who killed the man and left his body for the tide.

'Poor old AD.' She sniffs and wipes her face with the back of her arm. 'He just didn't know no other way. You'll stay, though, right?'

She reaches up for the girl, as if to draw her down onto the filthy pallet. Disgust, or maybe frustration acts as almost like a blow, turns Care away from her onetime colleague. She scrambles to her feet and would head to the low door, only Rosa stops her, calling out her name. She struggles as if to stand and then gives up, propping herself up on her bruised arms. 'You should think about it. You'll come around to it. They always do.'

Care doesn't respond. I suspect she can't, and as she stumbles through the door, I follow, unconcerned about the laughing woman who has fallen back on her slovenly bed.

But if I had thought the girl would retreat, I was mistaken. Although her gait is uneven, the result of the tears she brushes from her eyes, she is driven, this one. And I keep close as she continues on her path – down to the waterfront that she fled only hours before.

By the time she arrives at the wharf, she has regained control. It is full dark now, and yet she hugs the building, making sure not to betray herself with movement or sound. The open area where she was detained – where I was grabbed – is empty now. The only sign of life is a small fire, down past the dock. The men who sit around it cast dancing shadows, but they appear to be still, as if settled in for the night. In the other direction, muted voices betray the presence of a bar – some low shebeen where men with a coin to spare can seek oblivion. But the cobblestones before us lie quiet and still.

Care cranes forward, eyes wide. She is listening, as well, I can tell from the intense concentration on her face. She is looking for Peter. Or, more likely, some word about him, for she must realize the price he will have paid for defending us. For holding off those who would have taken me from her. She is thinking, I imagine, about AD.

I glance up, wondering if this is the time to reveal myself. There is much I could tell her – that while the stones are neither slick with blood nor wet from recent washing, violence has been done here. Spatter and tears and sweat augment the age-old fetor of decay and rot, but the blood shed here is not life's blood – not yet. The body she found was brought from elsewhere, from inside.

It is just as well. Such information would act as catnip to the girl, and I do not want her following the trail as I did, inside this building and up the stairs. Not that this is likely. Despite some inkling of consciousness, of connection, she sees me as a dumb beast. Then again, this could prove useful, if need be. If I make myself known, she would hesitate, out of fear for me. She would sacrifice her own hunt to save me.

I am debating this move. Weighing the pros and cons, when she acts. Keeping low to the ground, she runs. There are no shadows on this open space, but the uneven paving dapples the light, and she is still small and light. Her footsteps are near silent, as close as her kind's can be, and the laughter of the pub provides cover. The men by the fire do not look up, and she crosses undetected. From my own perch, I see her sidle up to the low stone building, flatten herself against its wall, to reduce her own silhouette. It is a matter of moments for me to join her. A sharp squeal announces my presence, but she ignores it, rightly attributing it to the kind of creature that will not raise any further alarm.

Moving slowly, each step deliberate, she follows the line of the building. It is as I have feared. She means to enter – to follow the path of her onetime leader and uncover the cause of his death. What she hopes to achieve here, I cannot tell. She owes nothing to the dead man, and will gain nothing from such knowledge – nothing that will avail her, I fear. But when she reaches behind her to draw forth the shiv, a shudder passes over me, causing my fur to ripple. It is good she has a weapon, for these are dangerous times. It is the way she eyes the blade, weighs the handle in her hand that unsettles me. She is not following a case nor seeking knowledge. She is thinking of the body she found on the sands below here. She is remembering AD, and the damage he once did.

The groan alerts her. A sound more animal than human that causes her to start back into the shadow before she peers cautiously around the stone wall. A low pile, still warm, shifts a little and moans again. A man, or the remains of one, left for the night like so much refuse. My ears go back as she approaches him, for I had hoped she would not notice the smell of blood, the heat of a bruised body beginning to cool.

'Peter?' She moves quickly, once she ascertains that nobody else is nearby. 'Is that you?'

The slight movement could be a nod, and she kneels by the battered face. Blood oozes from where the neck and shoulder join. A hole the size of a coin. A hook.

'Oh, Peter, they did this to you.' She bites her lip, remembering. 'You saved me, you know. Me and my cat.'

'They would've killed you.' The words are barely audible, even to me. 'I owed you.'

Maybe she doesn't hear. She's too focused on his wounds. She removes her jacket and rolls it into a cushion for his bloody head.

'I've got to get help. Get you somewhere warm.'

He shakes her off when she tries to move him, however, raising one hand in protest.

'I'm sorry,' he says. 'They made me.'

Care looks down at the man before her. I cannot read her thoughts, but I fear they do not echo mine. That she does not plan on plumbing this man for answers while he is still able to speak.

'It was a setup,' she says, and my ears prick up. Perhaps my training has been retained. 'You hiring me to find your friend. You know who took him. You know where he is.'

A sigh that seems to deflate him. 'I got him into this. I told him to take the job. Wanted him – out of here.'

'But you two were a team. You'd worked together.' She is trying to understand, but I would that she ask more and speak less. His time is running out.

'They're taking the young men. The strong ones. It's no kind of life.' He licks dry lips, his eyes fluttering. 'I remember.'

'Remember what?' Since she can't raise him, she leans in. 'I don't understand.'

'The boss wanted you busy. Working, so I could follow.'

He pauses, and she shakes her head in confusion.

'To find him. Your partner. He gave me the marker, so I could see . . .'

Another pause. The tip of a tongue. The man is fading.

'They said they'd release him. They wouldn't make him go.'

'Go where?' It's the wrong question. 'What partner?' It no longer matters. In the silence, she repeats her final question, even shakes the man's shoulder ever so slightly. But it doesn't take senses as acute as mine to ascertain the truth. Care can read it in the way his arms hang loose. In the way his head falls back. Her client is already gone.

She releases his shoulder. And then she carefully removes the folded jacket from beneath his head. The economy of poverty informs her actions, but I believe she also has the sense to know not to leave any sign of her presence here. Besides, the night has grown cold, and she is shivering as she dons the thin coat again, as she sits back on her heels by the corpse.

I would comfort her. I would press my body against hers and share my warmth and the softness of my fur. Besides, I, too, would pay respect to the dead man, now that his utility is past. Were it not for his interference, I might have met my end in that dark sack, or soon thereafter at the hands of those thugs. I have my reasons for holding back, but I am at the point of abandoning them.

I begin to approach, when footsteps from the other side of the building cause me to freeze and Care to draw back in alarm. She barely has time to seek shelter, crouching beside the bulkhead, when the two men appear. They have been drinking, the reek of cheap whiskey precedes them, as does a faint whiff of that bitter smoke – scat. I hunker down at their approach. In such condition, it is unlikely they will be overly perceptive, but they are not so intoxicated that they would not be dangerous to one such as Care.

In the dark, their vision is limited. The girl's is, as well, but I see her raise her head slightly to peer over the brick bulkhead. Even without my sensory acuity, their gait should make it obvious that they are inebriated. That does not mean they won't notice the movement or see the reflection of her eyes. At least she holds still. Even her breathing, as I can hear, is soft and level. She is on her guard.

And they are careless. Two men, one larger, but clumsy with it, as he stumbles, his boot caught by the body of the man who expired only moments before.

'What the—?' He rights himself, only to bend over to peer at the dead man. 'It's the cripple,' he says. 'The one who pulled a knife on Sarnsby.'

'What's left of him.' His friend has an evil laugh. He kicks at the corpse as his friend looks on.

'Damn, that gave me a start, though,' says the larger man, considering the body at his feet. 'Why'd they leave him here?'

'Had other jobs to do, didn't they? Besides, the boss had an interest in this one.' The smaller man crouches by the body, his hands inside Peter's jacket. 'Here, give me a hand.'

His colleague hesitates, though whether out of distaste at robbing a corpse or some other, more primitive concern I cannot tell.

'Come on.' His friend looks up, and I can see the sallow cast of his skin. 'It's not like he's got any fight left in him.'

'I don't know, Mack.' He has put his hands in his pocket. He would leave, I believe, if he could. 'If the boss wanted him for something . . .'

'Not going to be doing any jobs for him now, is he? Give me a hand.' He is patting down the dead man, running his hands up his legs. 'They probably left him here to go over later themselves. Now, do you want a share or not?'

The big man sighs and bends to help his friend. 'What's a loser like this going to have on him anyway? Sarnsby took his knife, I hear.'

'He got called in by the boss.' A whisper, now, but urgent. 'Had a big commission, I hear. But he never checked back. And the boss – he's on a rampage.'

I sense, rather than see the girl start at these words. The men are too involved in their low task to notice. Mack – the smaller one – grunts. He pulls a wad from Peter's shoe, currency wrapped in a torn sheet of paper. The bills he pushes into his pocket. The paper he examines and throws to the ground.

'Damn it.' The smaller man looks around. 'The others'll be back soon, and they'll want a cut. Here, Nudge, pick him up, why don't you?'

'Pick him up?' The big man hesitates, but something in the other man's tone is not to be questioned, and so with a grunt, he bends once more over the corpse. Taking it by the waist, he lifts the lifeless body.

'I want him upside down. Hurry!' His companion is growing impatient. The alcohol wearing off, perhaps. But although his friend is large and strong, he is clumsy, perhaps again the result of the drink, and it takes several tries before he manages to get a firm grasp on the dead man and lift him. Only when he has him suspended, holding onto his knees, does his friend rise. A rattle and clink follow as several small objects fall to the ground. The coins Mack pounces on. A small round object – a rock, perhaps – he picks up, too, although he discards it once he has looked it over.

'OK, now in the drink with him.'

'But the others – if they left him.' Nudge pauses. Adjusts the weight of the corpse.

'Are you daft?' His friend's voice has become a hiss. He holds up a coin, its sheen obscured by filth and blood. 'Look at this! I'm not taking a chance that the boss wants his cash back. No, let Sarnsby and the others answer if anyone comes looking.'

'Do it,' he says, as the other man hesitates. 'Tide's changing anyway.'

The big man – Nudge – grunts and heaves, and a wet thud follows. The girl winces, and I know she's remembering her onetime leader, on the sand. This one will follow shortly. The tide has already turned. I can smell the fresh salt rising, even if it has yet to reach this far.

Maybe Nudge can sense this. Maybe he looks for something else, out in the dark, over the water.

With that, he undoes his pants and relieves himself over the edge. I hear, from behind the bulkhead, a soft sob. But the two men have not my ears, and besides, the bigger one is clearly preoccupied, his gaze directed over the low wall, to the harbor floor below.

At least, they do not linger. And once they have left, the girl rises. She wipes her face with her sleeve, but makes no more sound. Her grief, if grief it is, has gone silent. This time, she is careful. She peers around the corner of the building, to the open space before it, and waits, before returning to the bulkhead.

I still have not approached her, wary of either startling her or causing her distress. Still, when I see she would enter, I reconsider my decision. Evil has happened in this building, and despite the current quiet, evil lurks there still, imbuing the very atmosphere with its pungency.

It is with rare indecision that I linger, tail lashing, as she fusses with the lock on the bulkhead door. At least, I realize, she is too large to find entry as I did, through the rotting brick. And the shiny new lock, of a more recent vintage than the rest of the building, withstands her efforts to pick or break it. Finally, she sinks back to the ground, her back to the brick wall. Her breathing is ragged. She is near tears, and I cannot hold back any longer.

'Blackie. How did you . . .?' The advantage of being deemed a lower creature is that I am not held responsible, and there are no recriminations prompted by my presence, by my obvious escape.

Instead, she greets me with open arms, holding me close as I rub against her warm body. I do not like her arms wrapped around me. They hinder my movement and, I fear, dull her sense of the world around us. But at this moment, for now, I am still. I let her hold me and then rest her face on the thick fur of my ruff. Her tears do not penetrate, but I feel their warmth, the shuddering of her sobs as she cries. I wait, listening and smelling the approaching tide. The body is likely gone, the moon full risen by the time she releases me. But its light catches a small object, overlooked in the darkness. It is that small stone, which now I see has been crudely carved.

The girl is sniffing, but even as she wipes her eyes, she looks about her. Sees the scrap of paper the smaller man discarded and reaches for it, holding it close to inspect it in the pale moonlight.

Such objects no longer appeal to me, beyond the odors they may convey. Instead, I find myself drawn to the carving. I nose it gently, turning it over as it lies on the ground. Not stone, I realize as soon as I am close enough to pick up its faint scent. Ivory, perhaps, or bone – the faint trace of an animal is still discernable, revived by the fading warmth of the dead man's body. Its charcoal color, which helped obscure its fall, must be due to age or use; the incisions have been worn nearly flat by handling. Still, in the grooves and edges, I can smell the lint of his pocket, savor the tang of the blood that was shed. It must be the piece's animal origins that so compel me, for somehow it intrigues me, in ways I cannot otherwise explain.

'What have you found there, Blackie?' Her warm hand slides beneath my wet leather nose, finding the object and lifting it. 'I know this,' she says. She holds it close, to better see it in the dim light, and turns it this way and that. 'It belonged to my old mentor. He kept it on his watch.'

NINETEEN

I am dumbfounded. Worse than that, I am mute. A dumb beast,
incapable of asking the most basic question. Of communi-
cating in the simplest language. At her words, I sit back,
blinking, as a parade of images flash before me. The carving
– an *amulet*, the word returns, as if from deep under the nearby
water – between my fingers. I rolled it back and forth, examining
engraving that was, while still worn and ancient, more distinct
than now. A face – a cat's face? I can't be sure – and symbols
that even then I could not read. In memory, I recall both curiosity and frustration, as I rolled the small, round, bead-like
object between digits that were thinner-skinned and more flex-
ible than what I have now.

The frustration nearly won out, I now remember. I was sitting
at my desk – Care's desk – and had opened a drawer, ready to
toss the small thing in. Some impulse stayed me, and instead
I clipped it onto my watch chain, utilizing the hole drilled
through the small piece's center. And then? I cannot recall, just
as I cannot my initial finding of the piece, whether by purchase,
gift, or luck.

How it came to be in the pocket of a dead stevedore is another
question. One that Care is now pondering, I believe, as she sits
back in the dirt. In one hand, she holds the paper, in the other
the carving. I can see her trying to draw connections between
the two. I would warn her, if I could that the leavings may bear
each other no relation. But she seems to see one, as she looks
from the carving to the paper and back again.

'Could this be what Augusta is looking for?' She shakes her
head. The piece is small and seems of little import. The paper,
however, holds her attention.

'My address,' says Care. 'The old man's. Could Peter have
known her – could he have known the old man?' She shakes
her head again, as if weighing the thought. No, I could tell her,
I had no contact with this man before, in any form. Unless—

I jump. I cannot help it, leaping backward as if to avoid attack. The memory comes too quickly to control. A shadow – three – the central one taller. Looming. He towers over me, even as I fade and sink. Feeling, the last shreds of sentience, is leaving me. My sight is fading, too. And, yet, I know his hands were on me. Pressure and then a sudden jerk, of something snapping. A chain link torn. A trophy taken for no reason, but to exhibit control.

'Blackie?' The girl's voice brings me back to the present, and I regain control. Willing my fur to settle, I approach her once more. 'What a funny cat,' she says, and returns to her examination.

'Could he have been a client before? A friend of the old man's?' The girl's voice, seeking an answer, brings me back. 'And I didn't know? This writing – I don't know it. But if Peter was one of the old man's clients, wouldn't he have said?'

She holds the bead still, but her gaze is elsewhere, unfocused, as if she were in fact looking into the past. I lean into her, offering my soft warmth as comfort. She loved the old man, the person that I was, and misses him still, I know. And I, mute in the way of any animal, am unable to tell her that the sentiment was shared. Is shared, still, although I no longer inhabit that form.

We sit this way in silence, and I begin to relax. She must sense my affection, my allegiance, despite my inability to communicate. Despite her time on the streets, she is not so jaded as to devalue either loyalty or love. In fact, she appears to be thinking of it now. My ears perk up to catch her half-spoken words.

'I know he was hired to lure me out, to fool me; but still, he saved you,' she says. 'Maybe he was another one – another one like me. He didn't tell me everything, of course. I knew that, even before the end. But he was a friend – and loyal, too, I think.'

She sits up, her hand clasping the round thing as if it held her word. 'Maybe that's why I found this. It's a reminder of a promise.'

Something in her words resonates. Not the memory I have recalled, but something older. A hand passing this piece to me. Placing it in my then-pale palm.

As I did then, she opens her fist and gazes at the piece anew. 'Maybe this is Augusta's, I don't know. But until she comes back, I'm going to hang onto it.' She falls quiet, her mouth set firm.

'I'm going to find his friend, Blackie,' she says when once she speaks again. Her voice is quiet, still, but suffused with determination. 'Find Peter's friend and help him get out of whatever trouble he's in. Not just because Peter paid me, but because it's the honorable thing to do. I'm going to finish the job I was hired for.'

Mute in my disbelief, I stare up at her. If she were to gaze down at me, all she would see is an animal. Mouth open, my fangs must catch the moonlight, but my voice, what voice I have, is ineffectual. How can I explain the error in her thought? Share with her the memory of that tall man, the evil one, who tore this charm off my dying body? It was only that last encounter that taught me of his utter treachery – the guile and cunning that could overpower a man such as I was. What hope has this girl, who sees the best in one of the tall man's minions? Who wishes to honor her contract with a man who has been killed and discarded, slaughtered perhaps for no reason but to entrap her in such a mission as this?

With a nod, she rises, and then looks back at me. I lick my nose. It is a reflex, but it serves to refresh my acuity. I see her smile, a sad smile, and I know. She understands the danger, at least to some extent. She knows she is at risk, as was this man, and she would safeguard me, if she could. Would try again to place me out of harm. Does she see that in my eyes which signifies that I will not leave her? Does she understand that her mission is mine, as well?

I am a cat, and I cannot ask her this. All I do know is that when she sets out, walking swiftly through the night, I am at her side. And when she looks over and sees me there, she smiles.

TWENTY

The girl is young and growing still, and the day has been both long and difficult. Still, having stated her intent, I am somewhat surprised as she makes her way back through familiar streets to the building that has become our home. She does not appear fatigued. Indeed, with the moon illuminating the rutted streets and the sounds of human commerce falling behind her, she begins to run, and it is all I can do to lope alongside, keeping pace silently by her side.

I am pondering what else could be motivating her return when she slows and then suddenly stops paces short of the building entrance. Standing at the entrance of the alley that I use most often as an egress, she pauses. And although I hear her panting, as am I, I do not believe it is breathlessness that has caught her up short. She is watching – looking for something – and I in turn scan the air, closing my own eyes to better focus on receptors more sensitive than hers.

For despite the apparent stillness of the night, it is alive. The warmer weather has brought out creatures that have spent the colder months in slumber, or near to it anyway. I mark their passing – the opossum, which awaits a litter of new kits. The rats, whose frenzied scrambling to mate and feed may just make them vulnerable when next I have a chance. A young tom, which has doubtless picked up on the same clues I have. He may not know of my presence, not yet, and I consider whether I will have to fight him or whether he will move on, when I notice that the girl has quieted her breathing. She holds herself still, but not, I suspect, in thrall to the aromas of the night. No, she is insensible to the full range of stimuli the world offers. And I must remember how she perceives the world.

I look up to follow her gaze, and immediately understand. For all my superiority of perception, I have allowed myself to become distracted. The warmer weather, in this way, has had its way with me as well. For despite the panoply of life around us, she is staring up at the window – our window – where, now, I can see a low light moving around the room.

Sight alone cannot avail her, though, and the open window grants me a modicum of peace that I am unable to share. A scent I know wafts out. It does not put me entirely at ease; however, as there are other strains upon the breeze, and I am grateful at her caution as she does finally enter the building, as she cautiously climbs the stairs. She knows this building, after all these months. And if she cannot go as silently as I, she still knows how to minimize noise. She keeps to the edge of the stairs, where the worn treads are less likely to creak or groan. And she pauses by her own office door. When she opens her mouth, ever so slightly, I almost wonder if she has learned to take in the air, as I do. To taste the history it carries.

No, I realize as I finish my own ascension. She, too, is panting after the run, her pulse most likely quickened by apprehension. She waits, the door ajar, and I see my chance.

Ignoring the quick intake of breath – the slight gasp of surprise that she cannot control – I make my move. Tail high, I push my way into the room, opening the door with my body as I pass.

'Oi!' The voice is higher for being startled, but recognizable still, and does the trick. Care bursts in behind me, all caution forgotten.

'Tick.' She reaches to embrace the boy, nearly knocking the small torch out of his hand. 'So good to see you.'

'Care!' He laughs, knowing his outburst betrayed his nerves. 'That cat of yours – I should have known. I thought maybe it was a ghost or something.'

I freeze and stare up at him, but he keeps talking, unaware of the impact of his words. 'I'm glad you're here, though. Look, I've got something for you.' He reaches into his pocket and pulls out a round object. It is puckered, much like that amulet, and gives way slightly to the pressure of his fingers as he holds it out to her. That pressure, along with his warmth, releases volatile spray – obscuring all the other traces in the room with a sharp tang that burns my eyes and nose.

'An orange?' Care takes it, even as I draw back in disgust. 'You shouldn't have.' She digs her nail into it, as if to claw it, and then stops. 'Where did you get this, anyway?'

'Got a bonus, didn't I?' His satisfaction informs his words, as if they swaggered with him.

'A bonus?' She begins to peel the thick hide off the orb, releasing more of that sharpness. Oil, I realize, which is being sprayed around the room. It is a heady scent. Near intoxicating, and it makes it difficult to concentrate. I back up, my nose nearly numb. Was this what I had sensed – the strange taint that had eluded me before? I keep my eyes on her face, however, and see that the stench is bothering her as well.

'Uh-huh.' The boy sounds proud. His stance is not one of ease, though, and I realize that this might be what the girl – so centered is she on sight – reacts to. 'The boss noticed me.'

'The boss?' Her hands are still. I hear that in her voice which I would recognize as my own hackles start to rise. 'Tick, what are you doing?'

'It's good, Care. Really.' The boy licks his lips and then begins to speak, his words tumbling over each other in their haste. 'That thing – that *orange*,' he says the word as if it were strange to him. 'We'll be seeing more of those soon. They're opening up the trade routes again. Getting ready.'

'New trade routes?'

Another nod. 'A schooner's due – a new one, from the south, and now everyone says the trade's going to be regular again. Fruit like that and – and all kinds of things. Not just for us, but for the outer lands, too. Necessities, like, for the islands. And, Care, they're looking for crew.'

'No.' She's shaking her head. 'Tick, you can't.' She puts the foul fruit on her desk and walks toward him. She would take him in her arms, I think, only he backs away and begins to speak again.

'It's going to be great, Care. There's a real chance to do something. To see—'

'Why do they want you?' Her question comes out hard, but he barely blanches.

'I'm growing fast, Care. In case you hadn't noticed.' It is true; the boy has shot up several inches in the time I have known him. Thin and reedy, he has begun to resemble the man he may one day become, rather than the half-starved infant the girl once saved. 'And now's the time to sign up. They've only got like half the crew together, and the ship will be here soon.'

'The crew—' Care stops, her brow knitted. 'Where are they staying, this crew?'

'Down by the docks, of course.' The boy scoffs, and then catches on. 'This is my chance.' He looks over at the desk, at the uneaten fruit. 'They go south, Care. They say there are wonders there, and that everyone will come back rich.'

'I don't think they're telling you the whole truth, Tick.' She shakes her head, which appears to have grown heavy with misgiving. 'I spoke to a man recently who was very worried. His friend was caught up in this.'

'He was probably jealous.' He nods toward the fragrant fruit, his pout making his face look childish once again. 'Aren't you even going to eat it?'

'Here.' She passes it back to him and musters a weak smile. 'You're the one who earned it. But, Tick, in the morning? Take me to where these other sailors are gathered, will you? I think there may be someone there who I've been meaning to talk to.'

The boy sleeps soundly, as the young do. The girl less so. Although she pretends to bed down with the boy, giving him the sofa while she makes a nest on the floor, she is soon up and at her desk. This, then, was the reason for her haste. By the light of a small lantern, she pores over the papers I recognize by their scent as her notes. And although their contents have less meaning for me than do the scratchings of the sparrows in the dust, I can judge their significance by her expression. Illuminated by that one small lamp, her face is drawn, the poor light playing up lines of worry that age her beyond her years.

I could stick with her, scrutinizing her for clues about her intentions. But I am as I remain, a beast. As best I can judge, she will not leave this room – those papers, the boy – before morning, and I do not know what the day will bring. She barely glances up as I jump the windowsill and quickly returns to her studies. I do not think she notices when I squeeze beneath the opened frame and leap first to one outcropping and then again, to the alley down below.

I hunt immediately and with success. Creatures grow careless of their own safety as the seasons change, the coming cold provoke a kind of madness, and they are lucky that I am efficient, swift, and clean. But as I sit back to groom – the leavings of my hunt quickly grow repugnant to me – I am struck by a thought. I have long mistrusted the boy as weak, if not deceptive, and have recognized the girl's attitude toward him – uncritical and protective – as her greatest vulnerability. But even if his appearance here is, as she doubtless believes, innocent of ill intent, that does not mean it is harmless. As I swipe a paw over my velvet ear, I consider my own recent hunt.

The boy may believe he has been rewarded with an exotic treat. He may decide to share it with the one who has protected and nurtured him for years now. That does not mean that biting acid fruit came at no cost, nor that the girl's determination to know more is anything that has not been anticipated.

I cast my eyes up at the moon. It has sunk in the hours we have been inside, in the time it took for me to kill and eat. But I can see it clearly still, settling into the space between two dark buildings. It does not look so dappled now, unlike when it was at its zenith and bright with strength. It does not so clearly resemble the strange bone carving that the girl has found. But I feel reassured, somehow by its presence. As if something that was stolen from me has been returned. A piece that – yes! I remember – once was purported to be protective of me in some strange, undefined manner, it has come back to me now, when I would assert myself to keep another from harm.

I am not so limber as I once was. It does not take either memory or imagination to know this. But while the path down to this alley was easy enough for even my stiff hind leg, my return to the girl is facilitated by those who have fewer resources than I. The drinker who makes his home under the stair is cautious, and within an hour he has slipped out again, leaving a brick in place to defeat the simple latch. Even by daylight, I am no more than a shade, when I will it, and pass by him easily as he relieves himself. A slip of darkness in the night, a shadow that makes its way up the front stoop toward the opened door.

'Hey!' The voice startles me, and I freeze, a whisker's length from that brick. 'You – I don't know what to call you.'

Ever so slowly, I turn, aware as is every hunter of how movement can betray one.

'You!' Across the street, an answering movement. An arm,
beckoning. That voice – the whisper is familiar, though not of
recent vintage. If it were a voice, I think, I could place it. I
hunker down, staring through the dark for surely my sight will
match or better that of any human eyes.

The drunkard wobbles back, his mission in the alley done,
and I relax. Of course. It was he who was hailed so. One person
– a woman hoping for custom, I believe – to another. A woman
of the night, most likely, seeking a client or, in these foul times,
merely shelter and some warmth.

But as he makes his unsteady way back to the stoop where
I now cower, pressed against the topmost step, I hear again a
hiss. A summons. 'Please.' A whispered plea. And when the
drinker turns, with stumbling step as the movement threatens
to topple him, the voice – if voice it is – falls silent. The figure
retreats slowly, and disappears. The man blinks and shakes his
head. I can smell from here how soused he is, and know from
observation that he most likely doubts his own perceptions. I
back carefully away as he staggers up the steps and pulls the
door wide. He is too close for comfort. His careless feet could
do me injury, even if he did not mean me harm, and I draw
back.

This creature – this woman – I could follow her. For whether
she did indeed summon me or not, she holds some mystery that
I would know. That last syllable, pleading, betrayed her as Care's
client, Augusta. The one she seeks, and who has lied about her
purpose and her origins, arriving here before the prescribed date
and seeking not the girl, but – can it be? – me.

I raise my head to catch her perfume. Her warmth – a bit of
spice – is fading. Only then do I recall my own foreboding,
and how vulnerable the girl may be. The drunkard has passed
by me and now kicks the brick away. But in his tipsy clumsi-
ness, he has thrown the door open wider than needs be. It is
only now swinging to its close and I make my move. The door
clicks closed a hair's breadth behind my tail, and I am in. The
man has headed for his nest and so I race up the stairs and find
my way inside our battered door. The smell of the boy's strange

offering has dissipated, leaving only an odd bitter aftertaste. The girl is at her desk still. But her head is on those papers now, and her breathing, deep and even, matches that of the boy upon the couch.

I do not understand how she can sleep so soundly with that stink so near at hand. But she stays this way till morning, while I, on guard atop the windowsill, ponder the mysteries of this city and what the day will bring.

TWENTY-ONE

'No.' The boy is firm. 'It's men only. Besides, AD's been hanging around.'

'AD?' She pauses. The boy will hear soon enough. They are talking, the two children. And I – well, I must have drifted off and now stretch in the warm of the morning sun.

'Look, Tick, I'm not worried about AD.' The girl stands over her desk, shuffling through papers. She appears to be looking at them – sorting through them – but I suspect it is misdirection, an attempt to distract the boy from the import of her request. 'Just tell me where the crew is being mustered.'

'No, Care.' He shakes his head. He has washed, after a fashion – the girl has seen to that – and now dons his clothes again: worn pants, a patched shirt. He takes the wool cap from a pocket and then shoves it back again, mindful, perhaps of her generosity. 'You don't get it.'

'Tick, this is what I do.' She looks up from the papers with a faint smile. Pride tempered with affection. 'I find people, and I need to find this guy, Rafe. And if men are being rounded up for the ships, then I'm running out of time. He's in danger.'

Tick doesn't return the smile. 'Care, you don't get it, do you? You're the one in danger. I told you, AD is looking for you.'

'Oh, Tick.' She pauses, weighing her words. 'I don't have to – we don't have to worry about AD anymore. AD's gone, Tick. He's dead.'

His eyes widen. 'Care – did you?'

'No.' She almost laughs, although her voice is sad. 'I found him, though.'

'And – you're sure?' He leans in. Clearly, the scrawny gang leader still looms large in his imagination.

She nods, her mouth set in a grim line. Her eyes are distant, remembering.

'Do you know who did for him?' The boy, his brow furrowed, sounds older than his years.

'Could have been anyone,' she says, with a shrug, and returns to those papers. 'Another dealer. Someone he ripped off.' She pauses. Frowns as she flips one sheet and shakes her head. 'Maybe one of the old crew.'

'No.' The boy looks thoughtful. 'None of them would. He was protected, Care. He was on a job. A job for the boss.'

She looks up at that, her eyes focused on the boy. 'What do you mean, Tick?' I know she's thinking about what Rosa said, about how nobody escapes without help. Is she remembering the shiv? Yes, she must be.

Another shake of the head. Though whether he doesn't know or won't tell is unclear.

'Tick?' I can hear the effort she is using to hold her voice steady.

'Look, I told you to watch out for him.' The words seem to pain him. 'I knew he was looking for you. Asking about you – about who you were spending time with.'

'Because of the bust?'

Another fast shake. 'I don't think so. Not that he wasn't angry, but it was something more. He was asking about what you were doing. Who you were seeing. If there was someone helping you, you know?'

'Helping me?' Her voice has gone soft.

'Yeah,' he says. The word comes out in a rush, as if he is relieved to finally give up the secret. 'Someone who was connected with the old man.'

She lets him go after that. Her questions on behalf of the missing Rafe abandoned in the flood of new information. She barely seems to notice as he takes his leave.

'I'll come back, Care. Before I go for good,' he says. She's staring at the window, but her eyes are not focusing. 'The ship's expected tonight or tomorrow. Maybe you can see me off?'

'Tick, you don't have to do this.' She turns, but he's already gone.

Whether in pursuit or in response to some other cue, she rises and readies to leave, grabbing the jacket and her canvas bag. This grants me the opportunity to examine the desktop that has so engaged her since waking. I nose the papers she

has perused, regretting yet again my inability to make sense
of the cryptic glyphs scrawled thereon. My eyes close on finding
her perfume, so warm and familiar. It is not quite obscured by
that bitter oil, and I would indulge further. There are other
odors here, as well. Clues I may read as easily as she does
that script.

'Blackie?' I look up; she is standing by the door. I cannot
resist. These papers are dead things and will remain. I jump
down to join her, slipping by her as we make our way to the
street. But if I'd thought she might go after the boy, I am taken
by surprise. It would be easy to track him. To seek out the small
factory where he once worked, assembling cheap clothing for
the export trade. To follow him on his rounds. Nor does she
head for the waterfront, to search for where this Rafe must be
held. Instead, she veers into the old industrial district, into the
warren of narrow streets, where the buildings – those that remain
– lean so close together that the morning sun does not reach
through. Now, indeed, I regret my decision, made in haste.
There was something amiss about those pages, something
beyond the acrid bite of citrus. I suspected as much, and yet
rejected this hypothesis before I had properly tested it. An
animal's response, dismissing the written word as of little importance. Or, worse, a remnant of human pride – unwilling to
accept that which I have lost. Now, though, this much is clear.
She would not come this way were it not a matter of papers or
of the written word.

'Mr Quirty.' Having arrived at a familiar doorway, she calls
softly. 'Mr Quirty, are you there?'

Her voice, though low, is urgent. She has observed the usual
precautions on her way to the basement where the keeper may
be found. Despite the apparent urgency of her mission, she has
paused to surveil her path, stopped and waited at several corners
in these close-packed streets. Now that she has arrived, she
seems ready to abandon such safeguards. Raising her arm, she
bangs on the door with the flat of her hand. 'Please,' she calls
through the door.

'He's not there.' At the sound of the voice, the girl whips
around. I, standing on a pile of bricks nearby, freeze in horror.
How can it be that I have been taken by surprise? That this

woman – for it is she, Augusta – has managed to sneak up on me? On us. In her hand, she holds the keeper's short knife.

'You!' Care is taken aback as well. She sees the knife and looks back up at the woman, her eyes narrowing. 'Is that Quirty's? Did you follow me?'

The older woman shakes her head. 'I've been here since dawn,' she says. 'I was waiting – hoping to speak with the keeper again – but he's not been around. I looked—' And here she turns toward me. 'I looked in the window, and it's dark. And then I found this, out here.'

'Damn,' says Care, her brow creasing. 'I wish I hadn't left him. I wish . . .' She glances toward me, as well, and my ears prick up. 'I wonder if he went after my cat?'

'Your cat?' There is a note in the woman's voice not easily explained.

'I left Blackie, my cat, with him.' Care doesn't hear it, or dismisses it as curiosity. 'And he got out. I'm thinking that if Mr Quirty tried to find him, he might have exposed himself to danger, somehow.'

I cannot comment. For all I know, her supposition is correct and I am at fault, having left that good man open to danger or, worse, led him into it. All I can do is dismount the pile of bricks and approach the girl, rubbing my cheek against her shin in penance and regret. I hope to offer comfort, if nothing more constructive.

'Maybe Blackie could have helped him, if he'd hung around.' Care sounds downcast, and I brush against her again, conjuring a purr as she massages the base of my ear. 'Maybe he could've saved him.'

'Keepers are often at risk.' The woman's voice is low and even. It reminds me of a letter, hidden in the wall. Of secrets that he has held for others.

But I am wrong to dismiss the girl's powers of perception. Her retention of all I once taught her. 'Why are you here?' She looks up at the woman, waiting. 'Really? I know you hired someone else – before you came to me.'

'I did.' The woman nods, as if she is not surprised. 'I needed to check you out. To see if you were who I thought before I approached you. And he was on the docks.'

Care tilts her head. 'The boy you hired, he's been taken.'

'I know. I'm sorry, but that wasn't of my doing.'

The girl stands and stares at her. Appraising her, I believe. The woman waits, as if expecting such, and after a moment the girl speaks again.

'You didn't have a letter, did you?' Her question is in fact a statement. 'The keeper – the man they took – he had no package for you. Nothing from a brother to a sister. You lied to me.'

She nods. 'I did, about the letter. But not about everything.' She does not mention the carving, and I glance up at Care to see if she notices the omission. But she holds her face still, waiting, as the woman continues to speak. 'I was desperate, you see,' she says this as if it were evident. 'I needed to find what happened to him, the person you knew as the old man.'

She sighs and her body loosens. A lie is a rope that binds the speaker, and the truth can cut it free. 'Things are bad, where I come from. They're getting worse.'

'But if you knew he was dead . . .' Care begins the sentence, prompting her. Has she noticed the woman's phrasing? That her quest is mentioned as a thing of the past?

'I didn't come seeking his help,' the woman says, stressing the last word. 'Not exactly. But I helped him once, and I thought . . . I still believe there might be something.'

'You thought . . .' Good girl. She tilts her head, as quizzical as any kitten, and waits. 'What?'

Bother. She is waiting for the conclusion of the sentence. Not, as I'd hoped for the reason for the assignment to be cancelled. An assignment that unnerves me, as so much about this woman does.

She is perceptive, this woman. Even as my ears go back in frustration, I feel her turning toward me. Looking at me, as if she could see my struggle to remain calm.

'I thought,' she says, 'perhaps, your cat might be involved.'

'My cat?' My ears prick up at Care's tone. But the woman only shakes her head.

'It's not likely, but you never know. People are panicking. They say it's starting again. The raids. The roundups. And now that I'm here, I see all the signs.'

'Signs of what?' Care speaks softly, as if she dreads the answer.

'The trade.' A whisper, barely more.

'That's why—' The girl's voice is not much louder. A thought voiced aloud. 'The scat. "Export quality," Rosa said. The ship coming into the harbor.'

The woman nods once, slowly. 'I fear it's going to begin again.'

The girl's face goes blank as realization hits. 'Tick,' she says.

TWENTY-TWO

'Wait!' The woman calls, even as Care rounds the corner, racing, and I am at her heels. Augusta has turned to follow, but she is large and aged, and her lumbering gait is no match for the girl's. I hear her labored breathing fall behind us, and then I must focus on my own. The girl is driven by fear, by love, and even in my youth, my strides would not match hers.

I have one advantage: I have surmised her destination. This talk of trade and of export, the boy and a ship. She is heading toward the waterfront, where all these factors come into play. More to the point, she is heading to the pen, where the child was held. The mother spoke of sailors, and also of the relative emptiness of the enclosure. I have only the faintest sense of what such a space may be used for, but I have an animal's inborn distrust of the cage. I believe this same instinct has been roused in the girl as well.

Suspecting her purpose, I am able to pace myself, to make use of the shortcuts available to one of my size and ability. When the girl rounds a corner, racing around the perimeter of a wreck that once housed a factory, I am able to leap over the rubble and cinders to meet her on the far side. When she must detour to avoid a fence, a barrier of wire erected around some small freehold, I can slip beneath it. No stakeholder will note my passage any more than he would that of a bird or rat, and were it not for my midnight coat, most would welcome my presence for the services I provide.

Still, I almost miss her when I arrive, panting and winded, at our destination, not a block from the river basin. I have come by a back alley, a narrow passage letting out toward the back of the enclosure, where the walls, tall and windowless, block even the midday sun.

A trickle of water, making its way to the harbor, runs the length of the fencing, and I pause, thinking to refresh myself.

The water is unclean, I know, and I lower my face to it gingerly. This form, I have learned, is resilient in many ways, but I am not immune to sickness or to poison. Jaws open, I breathe it in. Waste, which I expect. The faint oily tang of industrial residue, not surprising down here by the docks. And something more – yes, blood. I drink my fill, but not with fervor. The blood I am tasting has a particular taint. It came from men, and it was shed under great stress and pain.

Once I have slaked my thirst, I begin my exploration. The girl must be here, I know, and although I trust her to conceal herself, she cannot hide from me. Sure enough, I smell her before I see her. The run has warmed her body, and although she does her best to keep her breathing silent, her exhalations spread her scent in the warming air.

With my nose as a guide, I quickly locate her across the main thoroughfare from the pen, crouching in the same alley we availed ourselves of the other night, one that affords her a view of its entrance – and of the guards. I pause where I am, across the street. It may be risky for me to approach her. Not only may I, or another of my ilk, still be sought, the two men on duty look bored and dull, capable of cruelty even without the added impetus of profit. A small gang nearby talk loudly of their exploits of the night before. I study them, weighing the signs, and it is as I hoped: some member of the cluster engages the two on guard. A rude jest causes them to laugh. Their heads back, mouths open, they are as heedless as they will ever be, and I use their distraction to dart into the street toward—

Blat! The blast of sound sends me flying, its blare almost physical in volume and force. But instinct serves me well, for I am across, and the truck that rumbles past, a hair's breadth from my tail, provides cover as I join the girl, who now stands, white-faced and shaking.

'Blackie.' I allow her to gather me up in her arms and hold me close. I, too, felt the chill of death just now. But in a moment she releases me, and hunkers down again. And I by her side lend my focus, taking in the guards and their cohort. The walls, and the one gate that stands closed and barred. It must appear impenetrable, I think, to one such as the girl. Those walls stand higher than any man. Higher than some buildings, these days, and the guards will not be so careless a second time.

The girl is small for her age, and thin. I take her size into account as I gauge the wall and the wire atop it, coiled and barbed. If it is the boy who is inside, they might both make it. Provided, of course, that the guards did not detain them, and they could gain sufficient leverage to top the barrier. If it is another – I think of the man Quirty and of the lad Rafe, whom she has sought – then I am less sure. The man is slight, but well beyond first youth. The lad I have not seen. I sniff the air, pondering other options. Walls may be breached. That streamlet may have done its work, loosening or undercutting what looks like plaster upon stone. I consider returning to that back alley. To seek a weak spot, where the ground is soft.

'Tick.' Her whisper distracts me, and I look up to see her staring back toward where she has come. A sense beyond mine – born from affinity or long association – has alerted her. It's the boy. Shoulders back, the knit cap pulled down almost to his eyes, he's walking down the street toward the group of men now roughly queued outside the pen. He's moving quickly, lengthening his loping gait as more men gather. But not running. No, as if he'd put such childish moves behind him, he strides in haste, and his lengthening limbs – this new posture – presage once more the man he may become.

'Tick,' she calls, louder now. Perhaps she sees this too. 'Come here.'

'Care.' He sees her and pauses in the street, his eyes darting from her sanctuary in the alley to the men and back. 'What are you – you can't be here.'

'I'm so glad I found you.' She stands and doesn't seem to hear the import of his words. 'I thought – I was afraid . . .'

'I've got to go, Care.' He steps back, turns to look at the men again. 'They're lining up.'

'No, wait.' She reaches for him. Takes his arm and pulls him into the shadow. 'Tick, you don't know what they're doing.'

'You're the one who doesn't know.' His chin is up, his voice full of pride and bravado. 'You want to keep me a kid, but this is my chance.'

'Tick—' He starts to pull away. 'Look, I'll make you a deal.'

Her face, always mobile, sets. She's changing tactic. Changing
her priorities too, perhaps. 'I need to get in there. Let me take
your place – just briefly – and I won't fight you on this. Not
anymore.'

'Why?' He squints in the shadow, trying to make out her face.

'It's a job,' she says, putting her quest in language the boy
will understand. 'Like I told you, I'm looking for someone, and
I think he may be being held against his will. Press-ganged.'

'I don't know. I don't think they're doing that this time.' He
looks over, eager to be gone. 'I could see if I could find out.'

'No,' she shakes her head. 'I'm going in and I need you to
stay here.'

'Care . . .' His impatience is giving way to frustration. 'You
can't go in. They only want boys.'

'And who's to say I'm not?' She grabs the hat, the one she
gave him, and jams it over her own head. As I look on, she stands
and slumps forward. With her shoulders arched, her slim form
could be that of a boy's in first growth. Could be Tick's older
brother, in fact. 'That's why you need to stay here. In case I need
you to get out.'

'But I'll miss my chance.' He whines, his rising voice
revealing his youth. In response, she reaches for him once again.
Holds him close, and I consider that she has heard what I do
not, an unspoken plea. A regret and a request.

There is little of logic in what she has said. Little, I suspect,
the boy could do to free her, if she does indeed manage to make
her way inside. And I am compelled to consider if by this ruse
she merely intends to keep the child from hiring on, for I little
doubt she would sacrifice herself. Will she also find the other lad
– this Rafe – or answer the riddle of the keeper's disappearance?
From up the block, I hear a limping step. A panting breath. The
woman Augusta has found us at last. Care turns and sees her
coming. She pulls the cap low almost to her eyes and, with a
swagger that befits a would-be seaman, saunters toward the gate.

I will not panic. It will serve no purpose to run after her, like
some dog, as she queues up with the men across the street. But
I am stymied, as I stand and stare.

She is wise, this girl, and she has observed the men carefully.

Although she has joined them, she does not engage. Her goal is to gain access to the enclosure, not to gather information, and so she slumps against the wall, as several of their party do. Her arms are crossed across her chest, a further barrier to conversation, but this pose only makes me more aware of her changing body and of the risk she runs, putting herself at their mercy.

Beside me, the boy grows restless. I do not know if he worries for the girl or if he is simply regretting the opportunity he has surrendered. I have little patience for him and would leave him behind. Only, this alley, nearly opposite the entrance to the pen, offers the best vantage point. The girl chose it well, and I would not leave it until I have a plan.

'Don't worry about her.' The voice, close to my ear, makes me start. I have been so focused on the scene across the street, I had not noticed the final approach of the woman Augusta. She crouches now beside me, lowering her profile and putting herself almost on my level, as I sit, head up and ears erect. 'She can take care of herself.'

I cannot help it. My ear flicks at her voice, an unconscious acknowledgement of her words. I will not reveal that I comprehend her words, even as I find her declaration encouraging. Nor will I be distracted from my watch. But she has noted that movement, or perhaps some other sign that I am not what I would seem. I have been careless and now fear becoming embroiled in an exchange I do not understand when I have neither time nor energy to expend.

'Who are you?' The boy saves me, without meaning to. His question, edged with annoyance, will not be ignored.

'Me? I'm a client of your friend's,' says the woman. 'I knew her mentor, you see.'

'The old man?' I can't help it. My ear twitches again, turning to catch her words. The boy is curious. Eager to be distracted, I suspect, rather than see his chance be squandered by Care. The man she speaks of was known to him, but the boy was too young – and too compromised by a growing weakness for the oblivion of drugs – to be of much use to him. Still, the boy recognizes his importance.

'Yes, he and I had dealings once. We had an agreement.' I do not respond. I observe as the line across the street begins to move.

The guards are talking to the first men. Asking questions and taking their measure, I gather. One has passed the interrogation and goes inside. The next is not so lucky. A guard – the shorter one – pushes his shoulder and he sways back. I wait, expecting a responding blow. A brawl, a punch, but the man keeps his hands by his side and, recovering his balance, stands straighter. A test then. A few more words, and he too is waved in. Care stands and takes her place as the queue assumes a more formal order.

'You know he's dead, right?' The boy, disappointed, is distracting himself.

Care steps up. She is three from the head of the line.

'I do,' says the woman. 'That doesn't negate our agreement.'

I will not listen. Will not turn, at any rate, although I cannot help but wonder at her strange statement. Her words were meant for me, I have little doubt. The boy's question merely providing the excuse. An agreement. Of what sort? There is the distinct possibility that the woman is lying. She had originally told Care that the keeper sent her – a story she appears to have given up, if her confrontation with the girl is any indication. That she knew him, though, I am inclined to believe. Knew *me*, I correct myself, as I once again regret the gap in memory and understanding that keep me from accessing more of that previous incarnation. Of whatever encounter we may have had. It does not escape my notice that she has been party to the disappearance of two men – the youth Rafe and now the keeper. Whether she was instrumental in these or is herself racing against some other, larger force, I cannot tell, but I do not like the way she hovers, waiting, as Care takes another step toward the guards at the gate.

'He made me a promise.' The woman's voice, low but clear. Another step, and Care is talking to the guards. Her hands are on her hips. Her chin is raised, mimicking the bravado of a young man. If only her slight build, the delicacy of her features do not give her away. A girl – a young woman, really – in their hands . . .

'My need is great,' says the woman behind me. She is ignoring the boy now. Speaking directly to me. 'Or I would not have come here. Would not ask.' Across the street, the gate opens, and Care passes in.

I cannot stand it. Cannot wait. I leap from the alley and race across the street, ducking beneath the wheels of a truck that slows as it nears the enclosure.

'What's happening?' the driver yells.

'We're signing up help,' the larger guard calls, turning toward the street. 'We're back in business.'

I take advantage of the distraction to slip behind him, behind his mate. The gate behind them is closed and latched. But it is a gate – not a door – and stands ever so slightly above the jamb. If I can squeeze beneath it, I will be able to follow the girl. To save her perhaps, or at least to share her fate. I lay my head upon the jamb and press my muzzle forward.

'Hey, what's this?' A hand wraps around my tail and pulls. And I, despite my scrabbling claws, feel myself being lifted. Hoisted against my will into the air as, around me, the waiting men laugh. 'A cat?'

I hiss and claw, catching flesh. I smell the blood. 'Whoa! Watch out.' The hand releases me and I drop, landing secure on all fours. The laughter has died down somewhat, as I spit and snarl. Not that my growl – an unearthly whine emanating from deep within my chest – will hold them off for long. I remember the sack and the brutish handling. But all I hear is laughter and imprecations. Nothing of a summons or request. Still, I know this type. Their cruelty. I wait for the first rock.

'Hey, what's the hold up?' A voice and then the squeal of metal from behind cause me to jump and twist, readying for the fight. Another man, fat and florid, stands in the open gate. 'Keep 'em coming,' he says, looking not at me but at that guard who now nurses his bleeding hand. 'We haven't got all day.'

'Sorry,' says the guard and looks away. No, word has not come down to these low scoundrels, or else the hunt is off. If he has other thoughts of me, of exacting retribution for his scratched and bleeding limb, he is too late. In the moment when the newcomer spoke, his round, red face peeking out to address the guards, I saw my chance. Wary of his thick black boots, I slipped through the open gate and raced to conceal myself before the cry could be raised. So that when the gate closes once again, with a clang, I am inside. I am trapped. This is a cage, and I fear it. But I cannot abandon the girl.

TWENTY-THREE

have been lucky, dashing in beneath the gaze of those guards. Lucky, or no – it occurs to me, I have been sought. I may have been purposefully let in . . . No, it does not bear thought. Though if the hunt for such a one as I has been abandoned, I do not know what has taken its place. Two hunts – if I recall the boy's words. First, for a black feline. Then, for a colleague of the girl's.

I pause. It is possible. But if the missing keeper has been picked up in this sweep, perhaps in my stead, there is little I now can do. Nor can I count on fortune to sustain me, I remind myself as I survey my surroundings, all senses alert, as the reverberations of that slamming gate fade.

I am standing in an open space, but not – I see as I back up to the nearest wall – as large a one as I had expected. The space I have entered is not, as I had surmised, one vast pen, open to the air. Rather, directly before me is a wall – a barrier of similar construction to that outside. It is a baffle, I realize, directing traffic to the left or to the right and blocking any view of the interior from the gate.

I am panting, more from agitation than exertion, and the odor of many men overwhelms me. Still, I raise my muzzle, searching for a trace of the girl who passed by here not moments before. Her warmth, her sweat. The gate beside me swings open once again, and I am out of time. The heavy tread of boots enter and turn toward the right. I do not see if their owner has been beckoned or told to proceed this way, but it is all I have. Once more, the gate swings shut with an awful metallic crash. Ears back, to protect against such noise, I turn as well, and follow the boots. They lead me to a yard, a kind of open corral where boys and men mill about, talking among themselves. Low buildings – reaching only part way up the surrounding walls – line the yard. The doors to these are closed, for the most part. But as one opens, the men look up. A small bald fellow with the swagger of authority steps out. Behind him, another figure – a giant of a man. It is he who calls out for silence.

'Yo! Quiet here.' His voice as big as the rest of him, and all conversation dies away. 'Listen up, if you know what's good for you.'

A pause, as he gathers their attention, and then the little man begins to speak. His rhetoric is empty and, worst of all, needless. He talks of adventure and reward, when these men would work for a hot meal, most of them. But it serves my purpose well. The men are rapt. Mouths gape open as he describes the sea journey – the exotic lands they will soon know. I make my way behind them unobserved, all the while hunting for the girl.

A hiss, almost like a sigh, and the creak of a door cause me to freeze. I have been circling the perimeter, making use of what shadow there still is to conceal my search of the small crowd. At this sound, I cock my ear and dare a glance. A door behind me is off the latch. A sliver of darkness shows against its frame – the interior unlit. But my vision is not hindered by the lack of illumination. I can see the movement within, furtive and quick. I push my head against the door and it gives way, with another small squeak. Against the dimness, Care's face shines like a beacon.

'Blackie?' I race to her, overjoyed at finding her, especially here, away from the crowd. She looks at me with alarm. 'What are you—'

Her frantic question, interrupted, goes unanswered, drowned out by the sudden rise in volume of the speaker outside. The door has been pushed open, and Care steps swiftly sideways, as if to block me from view. I have already ducked into the shadow. Before us, in the light, the silhouette of the man who stands there looms large.

'What's this?' He looks from the girl to the desk behind her. Papers in disarray. Drawers open. Care must have been rummaging through them before I interrupted. Before I opened the door further, exposing her to this brute. 'Some little sneak thief thinks he can pocket our goods without the work?'

My ears swivel, taking in the room and seeking other exits. The door beside me, where the man stands, is the only one lit. A further door, off to our left, leads into darkness. Another room, perhaps, or storage. Care has seen it. Her eyes dart to the side. But the man does not appear concerned. A store room, then, without egress even to the yard. He steps inside, and reaches behind him to close the door.

All this passes in a moment and in that time, I make my preparations. Care glances about, aware that she is cornered. In her haste, she did not plan for this eventuality, and my appearance has further distracted her. I am a worry and a bother. But I will make amends. I crouch, my hind quarters wriggling as I gauge distance and height. I will have only one shot at this man – his hands, perhaps, if not his face – and I wait until the ideal moment. He steps again, away from the door. One more step and I will launch myself. In that moment, I trust, the girl will make her move. She will be able to evade him, if I can hold him long enough. She will gain the door. And although she will find herself back in the yard, there then will be the chance that she could lose herself. Lose him, and join the crowd. The man has only seen her here, in the dimness of this unlit room, and coming from the sunlit yard he must still be partially blinded. If I can reach his eyes . . .

'There you are!' The man turns as I ready to jump, and my chance is lost. But as I hear Care's intake of breath, I see that suddenly the situation has changed. 'I've been looking for you.'

Another figure enters, stepping to the side of the guard. Shorter than the guard, though not by much, and slimmer, but his deepening voice reveals his gender. Male, but still a youth, with a spring in his step at odds with this room, this place. His vitality is apparent as he advances into the dark room and extends his hand. 'Come on,' he says, his tone familiar and not unkind. 'They're waiting.'

'Hang on here.' Uncertainty has crept into the guard's voice. Irritation, too, I think, at having his intentions foiled. 'What's this?'

'Carl.' The youth smiles, a broad grin that lights up his pale and freckled face. 'Carl sent for him.' And then I see it. The tension. He is holding himself back, this tall young man, but he is coiled like a serpent. His apparent nonchalance a bluff. Unnoticed in the shadow, I do not relax. I do, however, stare up at the girl, hoping to see in her a spark of recognition for the ruse.

'Oh, yeah.' She forces a smile on her face, but she must hear herself. She coughs and clears her throat. 'Yeah,' she says, her voice a half-octave lower. 'Sorry. I thought I'd get that list for him.'

'He's got it.' The youth takes her forearm and I see their eyes connect. 'Come on. He's waiting.'

And with that, he ushers the girl back out into the courtyard, walking quickly as if they were indeed late to meet a boss. Beside me, the large man grumbles, his hands now fists against his hips. Whoever this Carl is, he must have weight, for the guard not to question them. Or perhaps the youth simply moved too fast. I watch the big man, gauging my own next move, and when he steps back into the light, I am ready. If he decides to follow. But, no, he simply stands and looks on as two young people walk away. And so I take advantage of his distraction, slipping once more through that door into the courtyard to await my own opportunity to follow the youth and the girl, as soon as I may do so unobserved.

It is not easy. The tall young man moves quickly, ducking slightly, as if he would hide among the crowd. The girl struggles to keep up. I see her stumbling step – half jogging – as he propels her, his grip still firm on her arm. She turns to look at him and nearly falls, tripping on some unevenness in the ground. Only that grip keeps her upright, and he does not slow.

I am losing them, waiting here in the shadow by the wall. I follow the perimeter, cloaking myself in the slight shadow of the wall, and I speed up, desperate to remain in sight.

'Oi! What's this?' The cry alerts me, and I dash ahead, just missing the boot that comes down hard. A hook man, one from the night before.

'Hey, boy!' I press into a door frame, seeking to disappear in the slight shadow it provides, but the sailor's eyes are on me, even as he calls for assistance. 'You see that cat? The boss was looking for a cat like that.'

He gestures, and I whip around to see a young boy, Tick's age, approaching. He must have been hanging back from the crowd. Bored by the speech, perhaps, or hoping for escape. I offer, at least, the possibility of diversion, if not a chance for a reward. A wicked grin spreads across his dirty face as he focuses in on me. My ears go back, flat against my skull. I hiss and spew spittle toward him, but he is unafraid. Gleeful, even, with his new-found commission.

It is his eagerness that proves his undoing. In his spiteful enthusiasm, the cruel child lunges for me, grubby hands extended. And although I am sorely tempted to claw those hands – to see their pale and dirty flesh bedewed with blood – I have other concerns, beyond this boy. Although he believes himself to be swift, he has not thought out his attack. Most likely, he is incapable of the physics governing our movements, but his age and education make him particularly ill prepared to capture one such as I. As he runs forward, it is an easy matter to leap aside. And although I hear him grunt, as his matted head hits the closed door where I sheltered, I do not turn to look.

A cackle of laughter follows me as I run. The hook bearer clearly believes his domain to be secure, the boy's mishap merely a momentary delay. And as I race, seeking both the girl and sanctuary, I fear he may be right. The buildings that line the yard may not stand as tall as the outer walls, but without a moment in which to determine a means of access, their low thatched roofs do me no good. My route along the perimeter has been noted. The hue and cry is raised. A crate, which might afford a means of approach, is snatched up as I race toward it, and a leg extends, blocking my way. A rapid detour saves me. Even at my age, I am more agile than these men.

'Blackie! In here.' Her voice, even at a whisper, reaches through the crowd. Ahead, where the encircling rooms have turned in again, I see a hand – *her* hand – gesturing from within a dark space. And I freeze.

I want to run to her. To see her safe and free, away from that strange young man who escorted her so roughly away. For safe she must be, if she is able to call to me. And yet I am loath to draw attention to her. I am the quarry now. The game of all these men. Boot treads following the lighter footfall of that boy. I peer into the darkness, willing her eyes to meet mine – green on green. A voice cries out. 'Get it! Quick, you laggard.'

My choice is obvious. It is no choice at all. I turn and run into the crowd. I will draw the men away.

I am in luck. The speaker still holds their attention. He is describing some kind of sorting process. The bunks the men will occupy while they await the ships. Explaining meal times and the rules that govern them, things of importance to poor souls like these. My presence does not register at first – a low and darting thing around their feet. The ones now chasing me – two men, perhaps a third, and, still, that boy – add to the havoc, careening through the crowd. Their eyes seek me and not their fellows, and more than one gets pushed aside. Voices are raised in anger, as one man pushes back. I weave around the scuffle, hoping to draw more in, and hear above me a change in tone.

'You there,' the speaker calls. 'That's enough.' Complaints quickly muted, as the guards begin to push their way into the melee. The brawlers stop – or are stopped – as one of them is thrown aside. He falls across two other men, who quickly prop him up.

'Sorry, sir.' He dips his head, fearful of being ejected. Of losing what he deems opportunity. The guard just growls and turns away. Sticking low to the ground, I slip away. After such a reprimand, the men will not let my pursuers go so easily, and I can make use of them. A buffer between me and those who would seize me.

I pause at the crowd's edge, cautious about being exposed. Those roofs are promising. If I could gain access, their thatch would offer traction. The wall is high above, but it might be possible.

'There he is!' I start, lowering my body into a defensive pose. But it is not the man who calls out, nor even the boy who does his bidding. The youth – the one who took Care away – is standing in a half-opened doorway. Staring past me, he points toward a distant corner, beyond the fighting men. Away from where I cower. And, yes, behind him, I can make out Care. Her beaming smile catches the light.

It works. The men turn away. And, goal accomplished, I dash across the open space and through the opened entry. The youth stands back as I make for the girl, and though I hear him closing the door behind me, I do not heed it. Instead, I launch myself at her as she throws herself down on her knees to greet me, wrapping her arms around me and nuzzling her face into my fur.

TWENTY-FOUR

S he holds me close in her arms, and I consider her as dispassionately as only a cat can. I do not like to be constrained, not even by one I love. In circumstances such as these, her embrace serves neither of us well, restricting both our movements when danger may come from any side, but it does keep her quiet. And it is not disagreeable. Plus, as she buries her face in my ruff, I am at least able to survey our surroundings. To take stock of what we face.

The youth, at least, appears to pose no immediate threat. He stands and studies us thoughtfully, as if pondering the nature of our bond. I peer at him over the girl's shoulder and, satisfied, scan the room. We are in a long space, one that seems to run the length of this stretch of wall. Rows of cots extend outward. The bunk rooms, then, of which the speaker told.

'I was so scared,' she says. Her breath is warm on my fur. The sensation pleasant. Reminiscent, I imagine, of when my dam must have washed me, a rough tongue in place of the girl's soft lips. My eyes begin to close – and snap back open as the youth begins to speak.

'It's OK now. You're OK.' His voice is soft, as if he would comfort us both. 'Those men – I don't think the boss is even looking for a cat anymore.'

'Who *are* you?' The girl reacts, holding me tighter to her chest, and steps back as he raises his hands, but he only holds them there, as if in surrender.

'I'm – I'm sorry,' he says. 'I wanted to get you away. Big Dan's a savage.'

She nods, but stays silent, willing him to tell her more.

'I recognized you, you see. As soon as you came in. Despite the hat.' One hand goes up to his own head, as if his words were not understood. I do not think that is why the girl holds her peace, however. She has been startled out of her ruse and been speaking in her normal voice. This must have occurred to her, and now she would resume her subterfuge – if it has not already been revealed.

'I knew about you, about how you work.' He keeps on talking. 'So I wasn't too surprised.'

'But who *are* you?' She pitches her voice low, but not unnaturally so. In the dim light, she could still be taken for a boy. After all, nothing he has said is definitive, though she must have the same suspicions I do.

'I'm Rafe,' he says, as if the answer is obvious. 'I was told to look for you, you see.'

What follows next is curious, not least because of how the girl reacts. She lets me down, for which I am grateful. Her arms loosen as of their own accord and I jump to the floor. I am quiet, I know that, but the soft thud is clearly audible in the silent room. And yet the girl does not move her head. Does not make her near automatic confirmation of my landing or where I would go next. Instead, she stares still at the freckled youth. Almost, I think, she would approach this lad. That she doesn't leaves me grateful. Although his voice is soft and he appears to pose no threat, too many questions hover around him. How he came to be here, for example. His late colleague admitted some complicity in the effort to entrap the girl, and here he is, in this evil place. Surely, Care must question this. Even her apparent rescue should not be taken at face value. Not while we remain here, in this enclosed space, at least.

'I was on a job.' He starts again after the moment's pause. 'I – my friend was urging me to look, to find something else to do. We work on the docks together, but it's getting hard for him. I let him think I wanted that – to go off on my own. And at first it was fun. A woman hired me for an errand. I went to see some little guy, works out of a basement—'

'Quirty,' she says. Then, with some urgency: 'Is he here?'

'I haven't seen him.' His skin is fair, beneath the freckles, and he does not color as he speaks. A sign of honesty, perhaps, or of long dissembling. 'Why?'

'He's missing.' She bites her lip. Unwilling, I believe to say more. But her eyes reveal her distress, darting back and forth.

'I don't think he'd be here,' the youth says, and there is

something conciliatory or consoling in his voice. A warmth, though that may be affected. 'They wouldn't take a man like him. His age and, well, his sight would make him – he wouldn't be of use to them. Unless . . .' He shakes his head. 'No, they don't know.'

'What?' Care seizes his hand.

'It's nothing. Rumors. Things they say. What I do know is he told me to look for you. That you do this kind of thing for a living.' He stops then and I see that he is staring at her, his mouth agape. 'He said your name is Care.'

There is a moment then that I do not understand. A communication of some sort I cannot decipher. I look from this tall youth and follow his rapt gaze. His eyes are brown, plain as mud compared to hers. His hair unkempt and shaggy. Still, there is a connection. A magic – a meeting – that I do not comprehend. He stares at the girl, and she stares back. Both pale and far too thin, even if labor has put some wiry muscle on his bones. Both of an age. I would study them. Would understand. The silence in the room is palpable. The noise outside seems far away, and then suddenly it isn't.

'Hurry!' A man yells, right outside the door. 'You laggards, hurry up!'

The spell – whatever it may be – is broken. Both the youngsters start, as if bracing for attack. Care turns toward the door and then looks back up at the youth.

'Is there another exit?'

He shakes his head. 'Only back into the courtyard. They lock us in at night.'

'Yo! Over here.' Another voice, and footsteps racing. Some tumult in the yard. The girl drops back. She runs her hands along the far wall as if looking for a weak spot or a door. A crash, as of a body, hits the wall beside the door and both jump. But there is no follow-up attack. Whoever fell is off and running, amid shouts for aid, for water.

Water? I, too, have been bewitched. My attention stolen – diverted by this young man. But now the danger has become apparent. A low growl starts deep within me and my fur begins to rise. I go to Care to stand beside her, even as she continues her slow progress, running her hands along the far wall. When the youth – Rafe – approaches, my growl grows louder. This may not be his doing. I care not. This slim young man has trapped the girl in here. Trapped us both as a predator I cannot fight bears down. She does not know this yet – cannot smell what I do and does not hear the hiss of its approach.

'*Fire!*' The cry is raised. 'Fire! All hands now!'

The girl spins round to face the red-haired youth, but he is too fast. He reaches for the door. His hand touches the knob and with a yelp jumps back. 'It's hot,' he says, shaking his burned hand. Behind him, the girl gasps. She sees now what I have scented – the faint stream of smoke that worms its way inside. Pulling the thin blanket off a cot, the youth wraps his hand and reaches once more for the door. He winces as he turns the knob and begins to pull it toward him.

'No!' The girl is beside him, pushing the portal closed. With reason. Her senses may not be as keen as mine, but she could see the ash and flames beyond. The inferno waiting merely for an opening. That crash – whether by intent or accident – has brought the danger to us. Whatever burns is propped against the bunk room's outer wall and door.

'Up.' The youth now eyes the ceiling. Uninsulated, bare, it shows the thatch upon the beam. The girl looks, too, considering, and as she does, her companion acts. He grabs one cot and pulls it over. Throws it on its mate, ropey muscles standing out on his wiry frame.

'Come on.' He motions her to climb. To mount the teetering pile, and when she hesitates, he jumps up there himself. 'I can boost you,' he says. 'I bet we can break through.'

She joins him then and reaches up. He clasps her around the waist and lifts her. 'It's soft,' she says, pushing against the matted straw. 'It's rotten.'

'Hang on.' He lowers her and together they stack another cot upon the pile. For sure they must both smell the smoke. See how the thatch has begun to smolder, the red of embers crawling up the straw.

'I'll push you,' Rafe is saying. 'You can climb up, on the beams. They'll hold you, I think, and you can scale the wall.'

'No, wait.' She scans the room. Between the darkness and the smoke, I do not think she sees me. 'I need to find . . .'

I would not detain her and, gathering my courage, make my

move. I leap atop the cot beside her. She rewards me with her smile.

'Boost me up,' she says. 'Then hand me Blackie, and *then* I'll help you up.'

He looks at me but doesn't answer. Only joins his fingers together and crouches, waiting for her foot. A heave and then she's up. The thatch is old and damp and shreds where she pushes at it. Coughing, she breaks through. And as I watch her go, I feel his hands upon me. Hoisting me. I hiss and I would fight. But then I am raised high as well and, scrambling, find myself upon the roof. The thatch has caught at last. Flames lick at its edges and smoke rises thick and black from its damp rot.

Care coughs, crouches forward, and I suffer a moment's fear. She will fall. Back into the barrack, into the flame. But she catches onto the beam. Wipes her streaming eyes with one free hand, then leans forward again.

'Rafe!' she calls, as loudly as she dares. 'Come on.' She extends her hand.

'Go.' He's shouting to be heard over the cacophony of the yard. The fire crackles. Smoke is rising. 'I'm sorry.' His voice cracks.

A crash from below sends smoke billowing up and the girl starts back. Voices call out, and among them I hear the young man cry. Whether in pain or joy, I cannot tell. I would not linger and instead leap and find my perch upon the outer wall. Where I wait an anguished moment, as the girl, thrown back by the thick grey smoke, appears to hesitate – to question.

Go! If I could command her, I would. *Flee!* Instead, I cry, lifting my head for a heartfelt yowl. And as my wordless protest dies away, I turn to see her staring. Her face fraught with concern.

'Blackie, are you hurt?'

I am not above dissembling, and lift one paw in response. It works. She scrambles up toward where I sit, and as if spooked, I leap again, landing in the alley below. It is only as I step back that I remember to limp, and I am rewarded as I see the girl swing her own feet over the barrier and then drop, with only a little less grace than myself, onto the dirt below.

It is only then that we see someone running. The boy – Tick – and right behind the woman called Augusta.

TWENTY-FIVE

'Care! Over here!' The boy waves madly and the girl rushes to him. 'You're safe! I was so scared.'

He hugs her, his eyes closing, and the girl holds him close. I stand back, fur still on edge. He stinks of smoke and stinging ash. As do we all, I know. Even the girl, whose joy shines through her smutty face. 'Oh, Tick,' she murmurs, lips close to his unclean hair. 'Tick.'

It is my nature to stand apart at such moments, shunning such embraces even when tendered with love. Still, I cannot help but wonder at the timing of the boy's appearance. I had seen no open flames inside the enclosure. Smelled no cooking pits or forges.

I would know more, and gingerly approach, sniffing for further clues.

'We can't be seen here.' I catch myself at the voice and see Care start at the sight of the older woman.

'What's wrong?' Tick pulls free from the girl. Looks down the narrow alley, hedged in by high walls. 'We can't stay here. Come on.'

They follow the boy away from where Care has dropped down, along the pen's outer wall until we come to an alley, leading up to the street. The shouts are louder here. More men pass by the alley's mouth, coming at a run, heedless of our small crew. The smoke is thick and oily, but we are risking exposure, and then Augusta begins to cough. Soon she is bent double, with Care supporting her, they maneuver her up the alley and onto the street. Together, they move down the block, a victim of the fire and her helpers, disregarded in the panic.

I linger, unnoticed in the shadow of the curb. The runners do not pause or turn as they pass by, their attention taken by the fire in the enclosure. The gates have been opened, I see, but men pour in, rather than the reverse. Their efforts are paying off. Although the air remains bitter with smoke, the quality has changed. Steam – the smell of wet straw of saturated wood smoldering – gains preponderance. The fire is coming under control, as I rejoin the small crew in the alley, not far – certainly not far enough – off the main street. But even were my lashing tail insufficient as a warning, I would note the tension here, between these three. The level of strain is dangerous, as it keeps the girl here, too close to the street, and vulnerable.

'Come on.' The boy is frustrated. He takes Care's hand and would pull her along.

'No, wait.' The girl stops and would turn back. 'Rafe. We have to wait for him.'

'What?' The boy looks up puzzled.

The woman, however, reaches out. 'No, go. You have to.' Her eyes are clear and there is no trace of hoarseness in her throat. 'You were lucky to escape,' she says. 'He won't be far behind.'

Her meaning is clear to the girl, at least. She shakes her head. She would object, I believe. Would ask for explanation or some elaboration of the process that has clearly been elided over. I would that she would query their arrival here as well, so synchronous with that conflagration.

Perhaps this has also occurred to her. I see doubt cross her face.

'Care!' Tick pulls at her. Perhaps he spots it, too. The boy has not had a great deal of education, despite the girl's best efforts. But he has learned much of how to survive on these streets, and that means honing instincts others might disregard.

'No.' She looks at the boy, then at the woman standing calmly by. 'I need to know.' I await the question – the one I myself would ask. It does not come. 'Augusta,' she says at last, turning toward the older woman, 'did you hire Rafe?'

'I did.' She nods once, in assent.

'Why?'

'As I told you, I seek that which was my brother's – or news of him.' This second bit follows fast. She is not quite comfortable saying this. She is hiding something. 'This lad was on the docks when I disembarked, and he had an honest look about him. But then, when I didn't hear from him . . .' An eloquent shrug completes the thought.

'He was grabbed.' The girl sounds angry. 'Taken. And then I was hired to find him, much as I work for you.'

'You were hired to search for a youth.' The woman repeats the words. 'When his location was already known.' Care does not argue. 'Have you given thought to why?'

'It doesn't matter.' The girl shakes her off, but I still hear Peter's words. To keep her busy, he said. So she may be followed. 'The man who hired me is dead.'

'Loose ends.' A sharp note in the woman's voice causes the girl to look up. 'And the man who sent him to you – the keeper?'

'Quirty,' Care fills in the rest. 'You know that. And now he's missing. But he's not in there – in that pen. And Peter didn't – he said he didn't – tell anyone about him.'

'You guys!' Tick interrupts again, urgency raising his voice almost to a whine. 'It's not safe here. We have to go.'

'We'll go down there.' With her chin, Care indicates another alley, running off the street. Even from here, I can smell flowing water, the ditch that flows past the enclosure. A good choice, then, with outlets on both sides. Hidden from the street and sheltered, shadowed as the day grows older, but not right by the pen – and not boxed in. Like any vulnerable creature, Care has learned a fear of traps.

Dropping her hand, the boy breaks into a run. The women follow, picking up their pace.

'Someone is looking into you.' The woman speaks softly, as if sharing a confidence. She could be speaking to the girl; she could be addressing me. 'Looking into your secrets.'

I freeze as if the shadow of a raptor has passed over me – and with much the same feeling of dread. Of course. That scent that put me off. The papers on the desk. Someone had been there. Searching, only I in my animal ignorance had not thought through the possibilities. That one might read and learn, and then retreat, without removing anything. And the boy, with his foul fruit that masked any scent? Was he complicit?

The girl will never make this leap.

'Quirty wouldn't give anyone up. Maybe he's gone into hiding.' She remains defiant. An image of a mole comes to mind. Small and blind and secretive, but not so small nor so trusted as another, closer still. 'I hope he's gone to ground.'

'Care!' A whisper – loud – from the shadow of the wall. Tick snatches the girl's hand.

'Sorry,' she says, as she lets herself be led into the alley, where the boy relaxes, with his back to the wall. The woman hovers, pacing. She peers down the alley, along the trickling watercourse toward the enclosure. The pall of smoke hangs heavy in the air, but the cries have died down. Out on the street, men are standing, no longer racing too and fro. And another, at the alley's mouth, slouched against the brick.

'Is that? Yes.' Care stands, as if to hail her onetime colleague. For it is Rosa, standing – one hip out – on the street leading to the enclosure gate.

'Care, no.' At Tick's protest, she stops and turns. The boy has scrambled to his feet again. 'That Rosa? She's a skank. I don't like her.'

Care frowns at the boy. 'Tick, don't talk like that. You've been spending too much time with those men. Rosa does what she has to – what she can to get by.'

'It's not that,' the boy protests, and I find myself listening. Remembering the way that woman licked her fingers. The way she spoke to those men. Care is lonely, I know, and I fear this has made her susceptible. I recall the way she looked at the youth, and I would lend my protest to the boy's. It is too late, Care is waving. She catches the woman's eye. Rosa turns and looks around, blinking into the shadows where we shelter. She wobbles as she does so, and staggers against the wall.

'Care?' A grin breaks across her face, and, still blinking, she pushes off. Begins to make her halting way.

'What luck,' I hear her say. Her mouth opens as if in greeting. As if she would call out more. But her words are lost.

One voice, then many, from the street beyond and echoing down the alley.

'The ship!' they cry, though in wonder or in fear, I cannot tell. 'The ship is here! It's come!'

TWENTY-SIX

Augusta reacts first. She starts and turns as if to run back to the street. I dash out of her way. I do not fear her, but a headstrong woman may trample any creature in her path and our narrow sanctuary is deep in shade this late in the day. She does not get as far as where I crouch, however. Instead, she reaches for Care's arm. The girl's own forward motion spins her round, one foot slipping on the wet gravel where the rivulet still runs.

'Don't be a fool,' the older woman hisses.

'I know her.' Care protests. 'She's a – a source.' She would say friend, I think.

'That woman is a whore – she'd sell you for a hit of scat.'

'Not you too.' Care shakes her off. 'You're as bad as Tick.'

She looks around. We all do. That's when we realize: the boy is gone.

'Tick!' The girl calls out as she pulls herself away. She would race off in pursuit of him, without another thought, but the woman once again reaches out – for support or to restrain her.

'You can't go out there,' she says, catching hold of Care's wrist. Standing alert by the girl's side, I am grateful for these words of sense. Grateful as well that Rosa has disappeared, though whether caught up in the excitement or for her own reasons, I do not know. 'They'll catch you.'

'But it's not safe—'

A short and bitter laugh. 'He works with them, does he not? He's expected.'

'I don't care.' The girl snaps out her retort. Only I can hear the fear that makes her protest tremble. 'He's just a kid.'

'If he wants to go, you can't stop him.' Suddenly the woman sounds unutterably sad. 'A lot of boys want to go to sea. They won't force him – not this way.'

Care pauses in her fretting. Looks up at the woman. 'What do you mean?'

'Did you learn nothing inside that pen? They're taking on sailors.' Her voice is low. Resigned. 'The men have been queuing up for days. They're being promised a voyage to a warmer clime. The chance of fortune.'

'Fortune.' Care turns away, disheartened. I would go to her, to lend the comfort of my fur, only I wish to observe. To study this woman, worn to the breaking point for a quest I do not understand. A holder of secrets, ready to burst.

'I can't just let him go,' the girl says, more softly now. I recognize that set of her mouth. That tone. The old woman, though, remains cryptic. I would understand the tension coiled inside her.

'You can do better than to rescue him,' she says, her lined visage grim.

'What do you mean?' Care whips around to face her, the fury now foremost. 'You don't understand.'

'I understand well enough,' the woman says. Even more than her body, that ruined face, her voice reveals her age. She sounds tired. The day has been too much. 'Children put at risk. Families broken. No, you can do better than to simply rescue the boy. You can help me stop that ship.'

A stunned silence holds for a moment, and then is broken by the most unlikely sound. A bark of laughter. A snort that dies away into a sigh.

'That's good,' she says. 'Stop the ship. When we can't even save our friends.'

With that, she pulls her arm free. Donning Tick's old watch cap once again, she starts down the street. Toward the waterfront, following the crowd of men who have moved on from the enclosure to gather and gape at the new arrival to the wharf.

It is huge, this ship. Black with tar or wear, its masts spiking to the sky. Perhaps with sails unfurled it is a thing of beauty. A vague memory of such conveyance tickles the back of my memory, much like the ash that still clings to my nose. But now, as the ship draws up to the pier, it has no such softening feature. Nor any saving grace that I can see. The deck looms awkward and enlarged: high railings and an enclosed roost break any elegance in its lines. Huge nets stretch along its sides. A cage it seems, or trap – between the bars and those long nets, this ship is fitted to keep all in. The smoke in the air takes on the bitterness of brimstone or of blood.

There is something terrible about this ship, looming large and dark. The girl slows as she approaches. Hangs back from the crowd, and for that I am grateful. But even as I look on I see her gather herself up. She alters her gait. Arms swinging, she emulates the stride of a tall boy and makes her way toward a figure at the edge of the crowd. The slatternly woman stands there, head hanging, almost as if she would sleep.

'Rosa.' She speaks softly, but my ears pick her voice from the general turmoil. 'Rosa,' she repeats the woman's name a little louder. I brace, fearing that other, more perceptive listeners will turn back toward her. 'Rosa, it's me.'

Finally, the yellow-haired woman turns. Under half-closed lids, she sizes up the newcomer. Lifts her jaw and pouts her lips before suddenly – with a widening of those heavy-lidded eyes – she stumbles back. 'You? You're still here?'

'Yeah.' The girl moves closer. 'Rosa, I'm looking for Tick. Have you seen him?'

'Tick?' The woman blinks, confused. I am too far – the air still too thick with smoke – but I suspect she is under the influence of alcohol or drugs. 'Oh, you mean that kid.'

Care nods. 'He was just here. Only I – lost him.' I do not think, in her condition, that the frowzy blonde notices the pause in Care's explanation.

'He wasn't with that keeper guy. Was he?' She is attempting to focus, I believe. Struggling, perhaps, with either her words or a concept she cannot quite elucidate. ''Cause that was business. I mean, you understand.'

'The keeper? Quirty?' Care's voice grows tight. She would shake the woman if she could. Much as I would a rat. 'What happened with Quirty, Rosa?'

'If AD hadn't screwed up. All that talk about the scat and all.' She looks away, as if uncomfortable. Back toward the enclosure. The crowd by the gate is dispersing, and with it, her chance of custom. 'A girl's got to look after herself,' she says. She would move on.

'Where is he?' Care snatches her arm up. 'Where did they take him?'

Rosa steps back. Stumbles and would fall but for the hold Care has on her. 'Like you care. It's you they're asking about, isn't it? You and whoever you're working with. Why don't you go talk to him yourself then?'

'Talk to Quirty?'

'Talk to the boss.' The blonde is angry now – the drug or drink is wearing off. 'They say those stones only make the screams louder.'

TWENTY-SEVEN

There is no time to formulate a response, for with that Rosa lurches, pulling her arm from Care's grasp. Almost, I think the girl would reach for her again. Detain her and question her some more. But the blonde woman has had enough.

'Hey, there.' She hails a straggler. A man who has hung back from the crowd. 'What you doing?' He is poorly dressed. Nearly as poorly as she is, but she stumbles up to him and throws an arm over him. His arm goes around her waist, and she laughs. Care, meanwhile, has caught herself. She turns, and making as if to adjust her cap, would hide her face. Shoulders hunched, she makes her way to the side of the road. Hunched in the shadow, almost she would make herself invisible, I see. Almost it works. Her age and modest clothing do nothing to attract the eye of those who pass us by.

We are in luck. The street is nearly empty now, the arrival of the ship having drawn the attention of those who fought the fire – and those who gathered merely to enjoy its havoc. That crisis must be past, it seems. No more cries for water or assistance echo out of the enclosure, and when we pass that big front gate, it has closed again, although no guards stand by.

'They won't be manning it until it's clean and loaded.' Augusta has come up behind me once again. Perhaps she has been here all along. She speaks as if to herself, and yet – I cock my ear to listen. 'Supplies and then the goods for trade. We have three days, I'd guess. Or maybe four, but then at turn of tide, she'll sail. That is, if we don't stop her.'

I turn toward her. Almost, I feel, she would understand me, and there is much that I would know. Why must we stop this ship? And who is she – to me and to the girl? But perhaps my memory has played another trick. For without further comment or reference to my state, she has stood up straighter than I have

seen. As if age has fallen from her she walks past me – up to
the crowd and the girl that I hold dear.

I cannot risk it. This strange old woman has goals of her
own, and I fear what she would sacrifice for them. Keeping my
body low, I trot behind to listen and perhaps to intervene.

'Tick's not here.' Care turns on her with the ferocity of any
dam. 'What do you know?'

'They won't take on crew, not yet.' Augusta talks as from
experience. 'Not till the wares are stored. Maybe he's gone
back to volunteer. They'd need a boy like him, to help them
clean.'

'Back to that pen?' Furrows crease her forehead. 'But the
fire . . .'

'It wasn't much.' The woman shakes her head. 'A diversion,
nothing more.'

Care stands speechless. As, I confess, do I.

'I knew you'd get away,' the woman says. 'You're strong and
smart, and you have help.'

Care glowers. 'I should be grateful,' she says, after a moment's
thought. 'I guess. But still . . .'

'Look, if you don't want your friend to take ship, then help
me stop it.' The old woman speaks with force, for all that she
keeps her voice low. Speaks with an energy that belies her years.
'Stop it once and for all.'

'But how?' Care seems resigned.

'They can't set sail without goods to trade,' says Augusta, a
small sly smile beginning to bend into her cheeks.

'No.' The girl's response is clear and firm, and I am glad. I
do not understand who this woman is or what she knows, but
there is that about her which makes me uneasy in her presence.
'No way,' the girl repeats.

The woman leans back, eyeing her. 'You know the best way
to save your friend is to stop that ship,' she says. 'You know this
in your heart.'

'I have another obligation.' Care speaks slowly and with weight.
'To the keeper – Quirty. If through his association with me, he
was taken, then I owe him. What Rosa said . . .'

'The stone house.' The woman finishes her thought. 'Our
goals may be aligned, you know.'

The girl is silent. Her eyes sink to the ground, to where – if she would focus – she would see me staring up. I seek to meet her gaze, to match my green eyes to hers and thus, perhaps, embolden her. She knows this quest is futile. The boy grows more independent every day. The man was taken, and may already be dead. And in her heart, she must recognize another truth as well – an animal truth, which I would remind her of. Her own survival is at stake. She has been caught up in some larger web, and for the moment has fought free. Instinct should guide her now to save herself and flee.

It is no use. I lash my tail in frustration, but even as it whips about, stirring up the ash again, it does not catch her eye. Despite her downcast gaze, she does not see me. And I, a beast, cannot speak my mind. I cannot inform her with my knowledge or my fears. All I am able to do is share her trials. And so, when she nods once, a quick, curt gesture of capitulation, I stand and take my place beside her. Ready to accompany her wherever this rough quest may lead.

TWENTY-EIGHT

should not be surprised, I know. With instincts deeper than I understand, I have suspected we would come back here. The low stone building on the wharf sits, as noxious as a wart, and draws all evil to it.

At least the woman comes to it with care. Although the building is not far from the pier, where the hulking ship is tied, we take an indirect route. The woman leads, hugging the warehouse opposite, and as the day grows old, making use of the lengthening shadows to mask her steps. The smoke is clearing, the ash has largely settled, as she makes her way, but the growing shadow gives cover and she moves soundlessly, despite her age and girth.

The girl follows in her own grim silence. Now that she has a purpose, she will act bravely and without hesitation. I recognize the determined set of her face, her mouth closed tight. If she would talk, however, I believe she would voice questions. How Augusta comes by her knowledge, for example, and what her role may truly be. Perhaps she wonders, too, about the youth she left behind. About whether he survived and what strange machinations brought him into her life. For now, though, she is set on the task she has undertaken, driven in part by trepidation that her actions have put the gentle man in harm's way.

'Quirty shouldn't be here,' says the girl. We wait across the open dockside as the sun begins to set. The woman turns toward her, the lines in her broad face deepening with concern. Care's voice is soft. 'If I hadn't said anything to Rosa.' She bites her lip, remembering.

'Hush.' The old woman quiets her as one would a child. They squat. Two men, their clothing grey with ash, lumber by.

'You lucky dog,' says one. He coughs and wipes his sleeve across his mouth.

'If you'd kept working, they'd have picked you too.' His

companion stops his swagger. Waits for the other, now bent double, as he hacks again. 'I told you the whip was coming by.'

'It's the smoke.' His friend stands up and shakes his head. 'I was working as hard as you. We got that lean-to down, didn't we?'

'Yeah, we did.' Expansive, he claps the other man's back. 'So let's get drunk while we still can. I don't ship out till Wednesday.'

The two pass on. The woman turns and stares at Care, her dark eyes eloquent in their silence. She doesn't have to speak. We've all heard. Two days, and then she sails.

By the time the darkness is complete, the dock is silent. Even the usual nighttime revelers have gone to drink or to their beds. The fire and the ship's arrival have made their mark. The city waits with bated breath. With surprising alacrity, the woman darts across the open cobblestone, and the girl and I follow, finally stopping on the water side of the squat building.

'This was where I found him.' Care speaks softly, her voice little more than a whisper, reaching out to touch the cobblestones as if she could still feel the warmth of blood. The woman looks up, some distant fire reflected in her eyes. 'Peter,' Care explains, in a voice grown sad.

'There will be others.' The woman's response is grim, as cryptic as her face. 'Best not to linger.'

She cocks her head, as if listening to voices beyond my ken, even as she speaks, and I sense her watching. Waiting, as if for some preternatural cue. Her eyes catch mine. She stares at me, more boldly than I would have thought.

It is too much. None of my kind suffers such a direct approach easily. Even my attempts to catch Care's gaze are only bearable for love. From such a one as this, this is a challenge. An imposition, if not a threat. I look away, even as she mutters something about an idea. Even as she asks her younger companion to wait. That she will return.

I am grateful she is leaving, even if only for a brief respite, and I keep my head down as she slinks away. I am thinking about her, rather than the dirty pavement before me. I do not need to scrutinize the ash and dirt to find the residue of bodies, of blood and waste from those whose remains rested here before the end. I do not need to examine the slime on the remaining stones to find traces of both pain and death. Still, I feel my whiskers tickled by something loose upon the ground. More ash, I think at first, raising one paw to brush it from my fur. But even as I do, the fragment curls back up and bounces, recoiling on itself. It is leaf-like but not a leaf.

A sudden exhalation, quicker than a sigh, and I look up again. The girl has laughed, just slightly, a soft sad smile now playing about her lips.

'Look at him,' she says. Her voice is gentle. 'Playing like a kitten. What do you have there, Blackie? Is it a bug?'

I am affronted. No, ashamed. For she is partially right. I was distracted, my attention diverted instead of centered on our current plight. I bow my head and nose the curling fragment forward. An offering of sorts.

'A moth?' The girl kneels to look.

'No,' she answers her own query. The eyes that rise to meet mine are large and round. Did I not know better, I would call them full of wonder. 'It's a pencil shaving. Blackie, does this mean Quirty's here?'

Of course! I look up, my own eyes wide and as dumb as any beast. But now I understand. The dread I felt – the unease. These were not simply memories, or the residue of two bodies, both long since taken by the tide. Humans, like any other animal, emit pheromones. But I, caught up in useless regrets about the life I lost, had ignored my most basic of feline senses: my awareness of the smell of fear. Of a small man taken against his will.

That does not mean I can condone the girl putting herself at risk. And so I leap, desperate to take back the telltale shaving. To destroy it, before she can show her colleague. She has not yet made her decision. There is time—

'Look at that! Just like a kitten.' She laughs and strokes my head, still cradling the curled peeling in her other hand. I am too late. My foolishness – my pride – has put the girl at risk.

A rustle of movement. The woman has reappeared, in her arms a bundle of debris: half-burned faggots dragged free of the enclosure as it burned. Half burned and still smoldering. I recoil at the bitter ashen scent.

Care sees this, her head swiveling from me to the woman. 'What are those?' She holds her suspicions in check, her question level and calm. 'What are you planning to do?'

'Torch the place.' Augusta looks around. Kneels by the bulkhead, where she dumps the armful of wood. She pauses as she crouches lower, as she blows on a charred stick, urging a faint glow from its end – an ember that fades away. 'The cargo is probably stored in the basement,' she says, without looking up. She blows again, the red creeps along the blackened wood.

'You can't.' Care grabs her shoulder and pulls her back. The move is sudden and strong, and the woman nearly falls, catching herself on her hand.

'I have to.' The woman rises with a swirl of her skirts. Faces the girl with the same intense stare she had given me. As I look up to see what the girl will do, my acute sense of smell tells me that that question has already been decided. The smoldering embers on that stick, fanned by the sudden movement of the woman, have flared. Not to flame, not here, but enough to eat away at the charred wood. And whether because of that movement or the underlying destruction of the previous burn, a piece has broken off. A chip, perhaps, no more. But it is enough. The character of the smoke has changed already. It is not wood that burns, nor the charcoal that the branch had near become. No, there is something fresh and chemical in this smoke. An ember or a spark has fallen through the cracks and warping by the bulkhead door and found there drier fare. A fire has been lit in the basement of the low stone house. And these two females stand here arguing.

'I'm sorry,' Augusta says, her conviction clear. 'There is no other choice.'

'There has to be.' Care's voice is rising with concern. 'They have Quirty. He might be in there.' She stops and swallows. Fear of fire is ingrained for a reason. 'He might be trapped like I was.'

She stops, as if surprised by her own words. 'You knew that might be possible. At the pen – when I went in. Tick wouldn't. He might have thought it a distraction, but he's a boy. A child. You *knew* that we – that people could be killed.'

'People will be killed.' The old woman doesn't deny the

accusation. Barely reacts at all. 'I need to save as many as I
can.'

'I don't understand.' Care shakes her head, so caught up in
this confrontation she cannot sense what has become increasingly obvious. The smoke is catching. Spreading. Soon, it will
be too late to smother or contain. We must flee, not only from
the conflagration soon to come but from the men who will
muster here to fight it. We must—

'Help.' A voice so soft as to be little more than breath. 'Help
me.' The words followed by a cough.

I cannot restrain myself. I move by instinct, the small cry
of something underground exerting its primal lure, urging
me to focus on the bulkhead, on the opening from which the
cry emanated, and the woman marks my shift. I should have
expected her to notice, uncanny creature that she is, and she
pivots too, turning from the girl, who follows her gaze to
see that I am in my hunting crouch – snout extended, whiskers
forward toward that tantalizing sound. Too late, I recall the
reason for that cry – the stink of smoke. I catch myself and
draw back, opening my mouth to take in what I may. But
even as I breathe it in, doing my best to gauge the extent of
the fire beneath us, Care is upon me. Kneeling beside me,
by the bulkhead.

'What is it, Blackie?' She sees the smoldering twig and
knocks it back. It rolls across the cobbles to land harmless
several lengths away. And then she sees it: a thin white line
snaking from the crack.

'Is someone there?' The voice again, and once again, a cough.
Now that she has been alerted, the girl hears this – or hears
enough. She crouches by the bulkhead, her mouth to the cracked
door.

'Hello?' She cannot help inhaling after she speaks, and that
close to the bulkhead she gets a mouthful of smoke. She gags,
choking, but recovers quickly. 'Is someone in there?'

Another cough from within, and the girl sits back on her
heels. It isn't the bad air. Nor that voiceless hacking. No, she's
thinking. Planning how to proceed. I know the set of her mouth,
the way her brows pull together. As she pulls AD's knife from
her pants, I know she will seek entrance. Will endanger herself

to free the trapped, whoever he may be. I recognize her determination, and see in it the end I have long feared.

'I'm sorry. I didn't know—' The woman starts to speak, only to be cut off.

'You didn't care,' the girl barks back. She throws herself down again by the bulkhead. Works the knife into the worn place and begins to lever it, back and forth.

'It doesn't matter.' The woman is preternaturally calm. 'I am sorry, but it doesn't. One life in the balance . . .'

'Hello?' The voice, faint, from below. 'Help me, please!'

'It's Quirty,' cries Care. And at that moment, the board cracks further. She drops the knife and grips the edge, pulling with all her might.

'You can't go in there.' Augusta has caught on to her actions and reaches for her. 'Please, hold off. There may be another way.'

She doesn't even look up, so intent is she on widening the gap. 'I can't wait,' she grunts.

She doesn't, of course. Once she has decided to act, the girl will not hesitate. Scraping her hand inside the narrow opening, she clutches the outer board and pulls. I retreat – the violence of her action alarming – and as she braces herself, feet against the brick and pulls once again, I hear it – the harsh crack that I feared. Even with my ears flat, the sound is assaultive. Worse, it signals success. Bracing once again, the girl attacks the second board, and with another sharp snap, it too is fractured. The opening she has created is narrow, fit only for a creature such as myself, but the smoke it has released is spur enough. Sliding one leg in and then another, she pushes her way through. I hear the rasp as clothing rips, and smell the blood springing up where her skin has been torn as well, her slender hips still a squeeze for that tight space. Her face betrays no pain, her grimace only sets harder as she raises her knife in a fist above her head before squirming the rest of her slim body through. For a moment, I wonder if she will drop it, her hand already scraped raw. But she holds it tight. And then she is gone.

The thud as she drops down hard, the stairs below removed or ruined, brings me forward. I peer inside, concern overcoming my distaste for the noise. For the bitter fumes. But that smoke obscures what light may remain, defeating even my superior sight. All I can sense is movement. The girl righting herself, I will myself to believe. But either that movement or the improved ventilation of the broken boards has fanned the smoldering embers. A billow of smoke rises up, causing me to step back, eyes smarting. More coughing – from two throats this time. And the telltale crack and snap of flames, as the fire springs to life.

As I watch, a spark rises from the opening. Wafting on the heated air, it climbs uneasily. A firefly that I could swat down in a moment.

'She made her choice.' The voice behind me sad but calm. 'She's smart enough to have understood the risk.'

That spark enthralls me. I stare at it as it rises.

'The chance to come again is not given lightly, and it must not be sacrificed without reason.' The voice would have me turn. Would have me join in. 'Not when there is another, higher purpose, and not when debts are owed.'

Debts. I think of a young girl, distraught and alone. Homeless and hungry, who shared her meager meal with a dying feral creature. Above me, the spark wavers and burns out, and I dive into the dark opening. I will not abandon the girl.

TWENTY-NINE

The smoke is thick and oily. I feel it on my fur and whiskers, even as it stings the wet leather of my nose. Unlike the girl, I have landed quietly, my innate agility and sense of depth combining with my memory to help me gauge my leap. Not that I did so with conscious thought. For surely, any higher reasoning would have stopped me from such commitment, such foolishness. I love this girl, and more, owe her allegiance for my life. But there is little I, a cat, can do in such a hell as this.

A hell it is. I am lucky to be so low and hold my position until I can reconnoiter. Before me, I hear a roar. A monster has sprung to life, devouring the air let in from above. Down by the hard-packed dirt, some oxygen remains. The moment I raise my head above my paws, I too shall start to succumb. Already, my eyes are burning, my ears flick back. The fiend before me howls with rage at being so restrained, and I crouch mesmerized before it.

'Mr Q.' A crash and I jump – too close to the flicking flames. The heat stings my paw pads, it singes my whiskers. But it is just the girl, off to my right, who has startled me so. Bent double, she is working – one hand holds a piece of her torn shirt over her mouth. With the other, she grabs a packing crate. Pushes it aside. 'Please.' Her plea, half smothered by the cloth, would be inaudible to any but my ears. Certainly, the small man slumped before her hears her not.

'Come on. Wake up.' She kneels beside him, shaking his thin shoulder. But his collapse has served him well. Down on the floor, he must have had a chance to breathe, and now his eyelids flutter, open, and then focus.

'Care?' The word provokes a coughing fit. The girl responds by ripping free another strip of shirt, which she ties around his head, covering his mouth and nose. At least she pauses then, to affix her own rough mask.

'Can you walk?' Even as she asks, her voice muffled by the

cloth, she tries to pull him to his feet. He stumbles, and she pulls his arm over her neck. Her eyes – and mine – rise to the narrow moonlit opening where, finally, we both can see Augusta's hands, pulling to widen the gap.

'It's no use.' Augusta calls down to us. Her round face obscures the hole, blocks what little light there is. 'I'm going to try to find something that I can use to break the lock.'

She disappears and, too late, I recall Care's knife. In the restored moonlight, I see her glance around, doubtless with the same object in mind. She must have dropped it in her fall, or when she reached for the prone and coughing man. She pats the ground, seeking it now, but the smoke is too thick, and she cannot find it.

'You should save yourself.' The keeper gazes up at his would-be savior. 'My leg.'

'No.' She clasps him to her and half drags him toward the hole. At least, the air here is breathable. If only it were not also farther from the stairwell. From the door.

Of course. I whip around, willing my eyes to function through the smoke. The girl has never been down here. She does not know about the stairs and cannot see them through the ash and grit. I pause to get my bearings – and feel my whiskers with my spirits sag.

The stairwell is behind us, back where the fire burns the brightest. And even without seeing it, I can tell from the pooling of the smoke that the door at its top is closed tight.

'Hello! Augusta?' The girl has gone to shout up through the bulkhead. I see her balance on the ruined stairs and reach up for the door. 'I have a knife. I just – hang on!'

The moon illuminates her filthy face, striped with ash and sweat and beautiful to me. 'I just have to find it,' she calls out. But rather than resume her search, she waits there for an answer, wreathed in oily smoke. If I could boost her through, I would. If I could leap up past her and find a rope, I'd do so, returning to her here even if it meant the fire took me whole. But the gap is too high, and I too small. I hate this helplessness more than I fear death, unable even to explain.

'Augusta?' she calls out once more, before she staggers back, her body sagging in defeat. It is no use. The woman is gone.

I go to her, for comfort if naught else. And then I see it – dim but clear. The blade of AD's shiv catches the last bit of light, not a body's length from where she stands. If only I could tell her.

'Go.' The man is dragging himself forward. 'Maybe I can boost you up. Or you can stand . . .' He collapses choking.

But I've seen my move. I dart past him to the girl. Stand on my haunches, imploring with my paws.

'Oh, Blackie.' Sadness suffuses her face, and pity too. 'You didn't . . .' A sigh that sets her coughing once again. 'Hang on.'

As I had hoped, she bends for me. She would save me, lift me up, as the man would do for her. Only I am quicker. I dart away – just out of range – and hear her heart-felt sob. 'Blackie, come here.'

She stumbles forward, toward me. And I dart again. Only this time, as she reaches for me, her hands find the metal on the floor. Her fingers run along the blade. Grasp the handle. Raise it. Good girl! She has the sense to follow, as I lead her back – not to the blaze but near it. And then she sees what I would have her see: the stairwell, still intact, up to the ground floor.

'Mr Q, come here.' She rushes back, but this time I do not follow. Again, she drapes the man's limp and bleeding arm around her and half carries, half leads him forward. His head lolls, and I do not believe him conscious, which may be just as well, for as we near the fire, something catches with a crack as flames shoot out. But she is brave, this girl. Doubled over from her coughing and eyes streaming, she drags him, drags herself up one step. Two. And then to the top, where indeed the door is shut.

At first, in frustration, she bangs on it. I hear her sobbing and it breaks my heart. But then the cooler processes of thought prevail and, settling her companion against the wall, she fits the knife – its edge now pocked and dulled – into the frame and pushes. It does not budge. She sets it again and tries once more. The coughing has grown worse and she must pause to spit and wipe her eyes. A final time, she slams the metal in, pounding on it with a hand that must be raw and burned. And then with a cry – half yell, half groan – she throws her full weight on it, pushing against the stair frame. Against fire, against death. And with a crack, the blade snaps off.

She falls back, as do I. There comes a time . . .

But low creature that I am, I find it hard to simply surrender. Indeed, I feel my whiskers tickle. Could it be? Yes. I scramble to my feet. Paw at the door where – yes – that last desperate push has cracked the frame and a breath of cleaner air slips through. I stretch and scratch. I yowl, rousing the girl. And, coughing, she rises to throw herself against the door. Against all odds, it gives. She stumbles forward gasping and then reaches for the man beside her, dragging him up onto the floor. I wait till they are clear, my whiskers shriveling in the heat, and then I leap beyond them to land, blinking, in a room lit only by the moon.

'Mr Quirty, please.' She shakes the man, who lies beside her on the floor. Slaps him across the face. 'Please.'

I lash my tail, impatient. We have escaped the blaze below, but it is an insatiable foe. Although she has closed the door behind us, already, the air around us grows thick with smoke. The warmth unwelcome even after the evening's chill.

'Wake up,' she pleads. The window, near at hand, offers an option. It is closed, and I cannot in this form operate its latch. But the girl could – or could break it – easily enough, and then we would be free of this place. If only she does not hesitate too long.

The man beside her stirs. He groans and coughs and struggles to sit up.

'Hang on.' She reaches round him, propping him with her body.

'Care?' He blinks up at her, his voice a rough rasp. 'I thought it was a dream.'

'No.' She shakes her head and, as if wakened from a reverie, takes in the room. It is as I recall, a clerk's space of desk and paper. 'Can you stand?'

He tries, and stumbling they make it to the window. A crash from down below is all the spur I need. I leap up to the sill and wait.

'It's locked.' The girl's hands slip and fumble at the catch. 'Well, nothing for it.'

She turns back toward the desk – and hesitates, her face perplexed. The smoke, I think. The fumes have gotten to her, for she is seeking not for a weapon or a tool but for a paper. A printed sheet that lies atop the surface, one of many I recall.

'AD's report,' she says aloud, her attention caught by her onetime colleague's name. His fate is history, I would remind her. Sad, perhaps, but not undeserved. I would she move. Respond. Make haste to leave this place.

'Miss Care.' The man slumped against the wall exhorts her too. She doesn't listen.

Instead, she picks it up. Her lips move as she reads, softly to herself.

'It took a while,' she says. Her voice, distracted, sounds puzzled and yet calm. 'We—' She winces and keeps reading.

'He wouldn't change his story though. Said he'd followed her for days. "The scat," he kept on yelling. Only after he was broken did we realize we'd misheard him. "*This cat*," he meant, when asked about her contacts. "This cat."' She turns toward me. 'Blackie?'

How can I respond? What is there to say? Our lives are intertwined, but none of this will matter soon. Her human ears are dull to it, but I can hear the floorboards creaking – the joists are giving way. And so I do all that I can: I throw back my head and howl, caterwauling all my pain and loss and fear.

It works. She starts as if newly woken and, hoisting up the chair, she swings it, smashing through the glass and muntin both. The air that rushes in intoxicates. I almost close my eyes to savor it. To drink it in. Only, we are not the only creatures fed by it. A roar below, and the door behind us buckles.

'Go.' She pushes the man through and pauses. I would not have her wait for me, but I am in no position to argue or use reason, and so I lead. With one leap, I am through and stand, rigid, on the damp cobblestones, until I see her, too, emerge, coughing and stumbling as the room behind her bursts into flame.

THIRTY

Slinging his arm over her shoulder, Care props her companion up. Together they hobble across the cobblestones, across the open space. But if she feared the breaking of the window would call attention to their flight, she need not. Already, as they make their way, the remaining windows begin to crack and burst. From one the smoke has started to billow. Soon flames appear. The hue and cry will soon be raised.

'A little farther,' she is urging him, his body bent by wracking coughs. 'Just – to the alley.'

He nods in response and they make it past that first building – over toward the wharf where the black ship looms large – and back into its neighboring alley before his strength is spent. The keeper slumps forward. The ordeal has been too much for him, but once she drags him, panicked, into the dark, he starts to stir again.

'I'm sorry.' She stops him when he would start to rise.

'No, rest.'

He nods, but he would speak, I see. 'They wanted to know about the old man,' he says. 'They think there's someone still—'

'I know,' she says. 'They don't believe the trouble that I've caused them.' A rueful smile. 'They're certain I have help.'

The two are quiet, and I would give much to know their thoughts.

'First they set AD on me,' she says. 'They didn't like his answer. Then, I think, maybe that redhead who came to you.' She shakes her head and sighs. Almost a laugh, but there is no humor in it.

'I found him honest,' says the keeper. 'As far as I could tell. And I – I have some sense of such things.'

'Maybe.' The smile returns, if a bit forced. 'It doesn't matter now. I'm sorry I got you into this. I think that – Rosa, a girl I knew. I think she spoke to them.'

He raises his hand to interrupt. 'I knew the risk when my old friend . . .' He pauses, his breathing labored. In the distance, the shouts of men. 'There is a letter, hidden still. I don't know how they knew.' Care tilts her head, confused.

'It tells of a – a promise, made long ago.'

'To Augusta?' Care's brow knits in thought.

'In part,' the keeper smiles. 'But also to a purpose. He was another like your father, Care. He sought justice.'

'To right the wrongs . . .' She recites the words.

'Exactly.' Quirty, quieter now, as if at peace.

They are still in the alley, resting, when Augusta finds them. Although I, of course, had noticed her approach, she takes the two humans by surprise. Quirty starts like a small animal. He would flee if he could. The girl stands, ready for a confrontation. Her face reveals both anger and disappointment.

'What happened? Where did you go?' Her voice quavers with the hurt.

The woman shakes her heavy head. She looks exhausted. Near to death. 'I told you. I had a mission.'

'But . . .' Care stops, her question dies on her lips. 'You would have let us die,' she says instead.

'There will be deaths. Many of them, before this is over.' The woman's eyes are dry and hard.

There is nothing left to say, and the woman slumps against the wall, joining Care and the keeper, whose regular breathing reveals that he has slipped once more into slumber. I would be heading that way myself, having found a niche in the wall, an indentation where once a window stood. Now it is bricked up, but the sill remains, a sturdy perch above the damp of the alley floor, with the security of the bricks at my back.

From this post, I muse over the woman's words. The ship, I know, bodes ill. How I know this, I cannot quite remember. That it ties in with this woman – with our long-ago exchange – I suspect but cannot affirm. I was different then. A man. I viewed the world differently. Through other senses, primarily, and with other prejudices. I recall reading, vaguely. The belief that I could understand much through those scratched out symbols. That they explained matters of life and death for which I now rely on scent and sound. Were the limits of my perception, then, the reason for my lack of certain aversions? Did I not fear fire for that reason?

I am remembering the girl, warming herself in an alley not far from here, while I hung back unnerved. And the fire that she did well to fear and flee – and the youth she left behind.

I am deliberating on this – on the mystery of those flames. On that youth and what appeared to be a selfless act – when I hear the cries. 'Fire!' someone is shouting. 'Fire! Hurry! Help!'

'They must have just . . .' the girl mutters, her voice drained. 'Finally.'

They are responding to the stone building at last, it seems. They will try to salvage the stores, holding the goods at greater value than their lives. Only something more is happening. I sense it. A memory or a dream, perhaps. I slip into the dream state easily these days, a condition of both my feline form and my age. The emotions of earlier rising into articulate form. The calls grow louder. Closer, almost, they sound.

'What—?' The girl stirs herself, and I open my eyes to see her standing. She peers out at the street – but not back toward the building we have fled. No, she is looking toward the water. Toward the pier, and with some haste, runs to the alley's end. After only a moment, she turns back toward those of us who wait. But I do not need her panicked visage to inform me of what my nose now senses. This is no dream, nor is it the fire we have fled. Another conflagration has started. A different one. I smell wood and ash and the sharp stink of pitch as well.

'It's the ship.' She's yelling. The noise out on the street has risen. Still, I blink at the girl in dismay. Another fire? Could a stray spark have flown that far? I hear a sigh and turn and look. The old woman is staring past her. Down the alley, toward the ship.

'They called me Blaze,' she said, the fire reflecting as if it were a spark in her eye. That's when I see it, a vision – or could it be? – a memory. The old woman disappears and in her place I see a fiery young girl as wild and passionate as her brother was cool and cerebral.

'It had to go.' The woman pulls herself to her feet, heavy with age once more and weary. She shakes her head and makes to walk away. 'You know that.'

'Not this way.' Care is yelling. 'Not like this. There are people on that ship.' She freezes, her eyes wide as if she has just heard herself. 'Tick,' she says, and breaks into a run.

THIRTY-ONE

'No!' The woman grabs, reaches for her too late. The girl is yards ahead. And while the man, who's newly roused, struggles to his feet, I find myself frozen in mid-calculus. We are safe here. Far removed from either fire or running men. The girl may not know this yet, but I now hear as well as scent the scope of this new conflagration. A veritable inferno, it feasts on treated wood and canvas and roars for more. Already, it sends billows of thick black smoke skyward. Nor will its floating berth save it. The ship will burn to the waterline, and fast.

If I had still the power of speech, I would follow. I would reason with the girl. The boy may not have taken ship yet. He may have exited, or jumped ashore. The darker truth compels me: if he is doomed, she cannot save him. Her actions only endanger herself. First, there is fire and then, the men who gather. For they will know that the blaze was set, and they will seek a scapegoat. It is in their nature.

As it is in mine to hold back, here, in safety. To avoid the flames, and all the concomitant furor. And yet . . .

'I warned her.' Beside me, Augusta speaks. Her voice is low, but I do not think she merely voices aloud her thoughts. I glance over and her eyes meet mine. Hers are immeasurably sad. 'I tried.'

I turn from her to face the man, the keeper. His mouth hangs open, his breathing rasps. I cannot voice my thoughts. Not in a way these two can hear. And yet – the man nods once, his own voice stolen, so it seems, by his emotions as well as by the day. It is enough. I leap from my perch on the makeshift sill. I sniff the wind to gauge its flow – the smoke, the men, the trucks they've summoned – and I take off, running low and quickly, following the girl.

I find her wharfside and would go to her but for the crush of people who make such an approach dangerous. Instead, I leap

atop a coil of rope and tangled canvas. It reeks of smoke and
has just been salvaged, I deduce, from the burning vessel.

'Quick, man,' someone yells. Already work have jumped
aboard. Volunteers? I cannot tell. Their features dark with soot
and smoke, their eyes wide with panic, they grab at fittings on
the ship and toss them to others, on the pier.

'Here!' one watcher calls. His arms are wide, inviting those
on board to fling their bundles toward him. 'Throw high!'

The job is complicated by the nets, which line the sides. If
once they kept the crew – or others on the journey – safe aboard,
they are a hindrance now. A laborer shoulders a box – heavy
from his posture – and braces to hurl it toward the pier. It
catches in the net instead and weighs it down, the deck dipping
in response. 'Come on!' They shout from shore, but he turns
back to seize another, unwilling or unable to venture onto the
ropes. These, too, have begun to burn. Smoke rises as embers
start to curl.

I shift on my own perch, aware of how the conjoined fila-
ments each feed such a predator. How the glow will climb and
spread.

'Oh, no.' The girl's voice is not audible to most. She speaks
in a mere sigh amid the shouts. But I, whose hearing makes all
others dull, pick out her cry, and following her gaze I understand. The big man – the one who tossed the box – is shouting
orders. Sending someone hidden in the smoke below. A bundle
of some sort, it seems, has been deemed too important to be
left. Through the smoke, I see it – wrapped in canvas, tied in
rope. It rises from a hatch upon the deck. And yes, beneath it,
almost obscured by its size, is the boy. It's Tick, working to
empty the ship.

'Go on.' The man's voice is hoarse and loud. His command
nearly incomprehensible. He has taken the bundle and heads
toward the ship's side. The boy stands staring.

'The others,' the man yells out – or something like. Arms
full, he gestures with his chin back toward the hatch, from
which now smoke is rising. The boy turns back, but the man
will not wait. He steps atop the gunwale, the bundle in his arms.
Reaches for the rope as if to climb over the netting. To evacuate
with this last treasure in his arms. With one arm, he clutches

the upper line of the restraining net. Steps forward onto its webbing – but he is too late. Too late or too heavily laden. Like me, he must hear the tearing sound – a rough snap that causes him to start. He drops the bundle, which falls with a splash to the water below, and then he too is gone. The ship sways with the weight, leaning in to hit the pier. I cannot hear him surface.

'Tick.' The name is a lament. She cannot see the boy, I think. For although I can make him out, standing transfixed by the hatch, the smoke is thick now. The timbers groan and creak. The ship is breaking up.

She turns away. But a voice amid the clamor pulls her back. She starts as if she would jump forward. Perches on her toes. Out on the pier, a pale figure – thin but tall – is pushing through. He leaps onto the net and, light enough, scrambles over the fraying lines to tumble to the deck. And there is lost in smoke and chaos. I stand as well, rearing back on my haunches and, for the moment, unconcerned with exposure or the bounty on my head. I do not breathe, nor, I think, does she.

And then she gives a cry. A man on the pier is brandishing a pole – a boat hook – his grappling iron fitted to a wooden shaft. A hook boy, then, readying for violence. With a sweep of a muscled arm, he throws the deadly projectile, and it disappears, into the smoke.

And then comes out again. The youth – Rafe – holds it aloft in one hand, the boy bent double under his other arm. They reach the gunwale, and with the hook, he pulls apart the torn and smoldering net, and then he pushes through. He jumps and lands upon the pier and together they fall and roll, the men there stepping back. The boy stands, coughing, and looks around. Rafe takes a moment longer. But by then the girl is running, pushing by the men assembled. She pulls the boy into her arms and half drags, half carries him to shore.

'What were you thinking?' Fear turns to anger in the girl. I've seen this shift before. The daring rescue over, the men have turned back to the sinking ship. None now dare board, but some use hooks to try and snatch the goods that remain on the deck.

'How could you?' Her voice near to breaking.

'I had to, Care!' The words eke out between the coughs.

'And now they know I'm good at it. That I work as hard as any.'

'Oh, Tick.' She peels off her jacket. Wraps it around his skinny frame. And in the process, something falls – small and round. I jump down from my perch to nose it on the ground. It is the carving.

I am sniffing it. Trying to remember, as the youth walks up.

'Rafe.' Care looks up at the young man, her arms still around the boy he has saved. 'Thank you. I didn't know— When you wouldn't leave . . .'

The tall youth shakes his head. 'I couldn't, even if I wanted,' he says. 'They have my friend, you see. My buddy Peter – more than a buddy, really. He raised me.'

Rafe's words trail off. Something in Care's face alerts him and stops him speaking.

'I'm sorry,' she says. 'Peter's dead.'

He shakes his head, confused. 'No, he's working – that's what happened.'

She bites her lip and stands, letting the boy go. 'He was killed, Rafe. He died defending me.' In a few words, she tells him of the fight, not far from where they stand. The words nearly break him. His pale face goes even whiter beneath the grime and soot, and he hangs his head in sorrow. Together, they stand in shared silence.

'Hey, boy.' The crowd on the pier has begun to disperse. I duck behind the coiled rope as a thick-set man strides forward. He's holding a boat hook, the same one he had tossed to Rafe.

'Yes, sir.' Tick stands. Chokes back a cough, even as the girl reaches for him.

'No,' she says. 'You can't.'

'Can't hide behind your apron strings for ever.' The hook boy – now a sailor – affects a hearty laugh. 'We saw you out there. You too, kid.' He turns toward Rafe, a grin transforming his visage into something open, almost. 'You want a berth, you've got it.'

Still chortling, he puts an arm around the boy. Leads him away – toward where the men have gathered.

'You can't stop him, Care.' Rafe's eyes are inexpressibly sad.

'He's right.' I turn with a start. Augusta has appeared, her silence surprising in one her age and size. 'There will always be another ship,' she says.

'What can we do?' Care looks from one solemn face to the other.

'Don't worry.' Rafe nods as if to himself. His mouth now set and grim. 'I'll look after him. I'll bring him back. You fulfilled your promise – the one you made to Peter,' he says, his face twisting into a sad smile. 'And I will, too.'

For a moment, I think they will touch. That he will embrace her. But down on the wharf, a sailor laughs, and with that the youth turns to follow Tick.

'Where do I sign up?' we hear him call.

And for a moment, I fear that she will join him. She takes a step, and then Augusta raises her hand to stop her. She'll speak, I think. She'll talk of the youth and his return, of Care's duties to herself and others. Only the movement has turned her toward me. She sees the small pebble, which lies between my paws.

'What is that?' Her voice is hushed. She turns and crouches before me.

'Blackie.' I look past her, grateful to hear a faint note of joy in the girl's voice. To see that she, too, has turned back. She kneels before me. Picks up the piece. 'I almost forgot – I must have dropped it.'

'How did you come by that?' the woman asks, of her this time.

'This?' Care rolls the carving between her fingers. 'It fell from Peter's pockets, when he – when they dumped him in the water.'

'Fell?' the woman says the word as if she doubts it. Reaches out her hand and takes it. 'Well, maybe.' She looks across at me, then stands, the carving in her palm.

'This is what I've sought,' she says to Care. 'My brother's amulet.'

Care shakes her head. 'That makes no sense. Why would Peter have it?'

'He was following you?' She waits for Care's nod of confirmation. 'For the boss?' Another nod. 'Then I suspect he was given this as a token of some sort. A means of identifying – who he sought.'

'The marker.' Care stresses the word. 'Peter said he was given a marker, to help him find someone – some partner I was supposed to have.'

'He would think that.' Augusta's voice drops to a near whisper. 'The man in charge. He would have taken it. I see that now.'

Again, she looks at me, and I blink up. The only confirmation I can provide.

'The boss.' Care spits out the word. She turns toward where the low building still smolders. 'One day . . .'

'You've done as you've promised. You've done the job,' says the woman, as if to cut her off. 'Not by the means you intended perhaps, but you did.'

The girl brushes the compliment off as if it were a fly. 'My job,' she says, the word is bitter. 'Yes, I've learned to do that. But is this what it was all about – AD and Peter? Why they died?'

'It's more than what it seems.' The woman shakes her head. 'It's an ancient piece. I gave it to your mentor, my brother, if not in blood. In recognition of a promise, of sorts. That he would keep on fighting. That he would right the wrongs.'

Care starts back in recognition of the words. So much more than cant.

Before she can speak, we are interrupted by a splash. Farther down the wharf men are staring at the water.

'Demented whore.' The voices reach us. 'Waste of scat.'

'Drug crazed?' Someone asks.

'Love crazed,' comes the answer. 'She went for Sarnsby 'cause he did her pimp. That scrawny creep. And it was boss's orders.'

Care steps forward, as if she would join the group. Stops at a safe distance and peers over the low wall. I do not know if she can see the pale hair spreading on the tide, or merely waits in reverence, wondering at another colleague gone.

I would join her, but just then feel a worn hand, cool as leather, on my back.

'You've fulfilled your promise.'

Augusta crouches once more beside me, her hand gentle on my fur. In the other, she holds the carving – the amulet – which once she gave to me.

'You've brought it back. I can use it, you know. Use its strength, but if I leave, and she continues on this path. If she takes on the boss . . .'

I close my eyes, remembering. A promise and a transformation. The power to keep fighting, beyond the grave. Beyond this form. I raise my snout and take in the air. It is good to be a cat. To sense the world in such detail. To experience the night. I am old, but I have gained much in my many lives. I will stay as I am, with her, and be ready.

'We're good then?' I open my green eyes to see Augusta nodding. Some part of this she has understood. I meet her gaze. 'We're good.'

She turns and disappears into the night as Care returns. She's tired, is the girl. Exhausted beyond reckoning. Her shoulders sag and without her coat, she shivers as she cranes around, searching for Augusta. But the woman has disappeared, and I reach up in her place, putting my forepaws on the girl's knee. She lifts me then and holds me close, burying her face in my rich fur.

'Excuse me?' Another voice, and Care looks up. A young woman, pale as water. Thin. 'Miss? Someone told me you could help me, maybe? My girl went missing, some days ago, and I confess, I'm scared.'

ACKNOWLEDGMENTS

Writing is lonely work, but it takes support and assistance to make a book. For that – as well as multiple readings, advice, encouragement, and patience – I am eternally indebted to Jon S. Garelick. I am grateful as well to Brett Milano, Karen Schlosberg, Sophie Garelick, Frank Garelick, Lisa Jones, John McDonough, my agent Colleen Mohyde, and my editor Kate Lyall Grant for all their assistance as well. All the rough spots are despite your best efforts, and I thank you. Purrs.